D1338107

The author, Charles Brister

THIS IS MY KINGDOM

Short Stories about Miners
at Work and at Play

by

CHARLES BRISTER

(Compiled and Edited by Ron Thompson)

© World Copyright

DUNDEE
DAVID WINTER & SON LTD.
15 SHORE TERRACE

For my 'neighbours' who made Hell tolerable, and for their womenfolk who, sad-eyed, daily watched their men clump away into the unknown. . . .

HOW IT ALL CAME ABOUT

By Ron Thompson

It seems to me that the significance of what is written between these covers lies partly, at least, in the nature of the writer, and for that reason I will attempt here to explain why this book of short stories is now before you.

It is my one regret that this could not have come from the author himself but, alas, Charles Brister is dead, and yet, while I mourn that fact, I am deeply conscious that his passing has conferred on me the high honour of being associated with his work in this way. When a dear friend dies what more can you ask for in the way of compensation?

But the question I must bring myself to answer for you now is simply this—Why should an Englishman from the lovely coastal town of Rottingdean in Sussex have finished up his working life down a pit in the Kingdom of Fife, and then spend his last years writing about that experience from his home on a dreary council estate in the town of Methil?

There was certainly no external reason why he should commit his destiny to this bleak spot on the east coast of Scotland. None at all. In fact, as a global traveller, first as a Merchant seaman and then as a Lieutenant-Commander in the Royal Navy during the last war, he had all the experience necessary of fashionable living in exotic places to recognise that whatever else Methil had to offer it certainly wasn't environmental charm or the opportunity of enjoying the fleshpots.

In the light of that, then, his choice of Methil as the place in which to put down his roots must seem totally and utterly incomprehensible. Decisions that stem from a compelling inner force of an almost-spiritual quality nearly always are, and rather that I should flounder for words of mine may I just repeat his own, offered once to me in explanation:

"When my ship first came to Methil in 1935 the first people I met coming out of the dockgates were a couple of young miners 'hunkered' at the roadside discussing life in general," he told me. *"As I stood and listened I saw in them a deep-seated strength of character and a tremendous determination of purpose. It was an impression that was repeated time and again during my short stay. These people made we want to be one of them and that feeling became so overwhelming that in the end I had no choice at all."*

In 1946 Brister redeemed that pledge by returning to Methil for good and, because it was the only job he could get, went down the pit as a trainee miner. He stayed underground for twelve years until a serious heart condition forced him to the surface and rendered him a semi-invalid for the rest of his life.

At that point he decided to devote the last of his energies to telling others what he had discovered himself as a collier in that vast Kingdom below the surface of the earth; in these subterranean vaults haunted by the unfriendly forces of Nature and far from the sight of the rest of us who go on our complaining ways under the protection of gentler influences.

What Brister attempted to do was to weave a social history of a little-understood people into a fabric of entertaining short stories based on actual experiences.

Whether he has succeeded is for others to decide. I can only tell you that as a person he was both compassionate and humble, and yet streaked with the faint arrogance of one who was convinced beyond any doubt that he was producing good work. Above all he considered himself to be a realist, and never more so than when he looked at life and the purpose of it all, and here now, in words which I have borrowed from Chapter Three of this book, the author puts the human existence into his own chilling perspective:

"For there is only the one life and it is so quickly spent; and we return to the void from which we came, and in a little small while we are as unknown as we were before we came into the world.

"Our children may spare us a thought when they are old and nostalgia is having its way with them. Then, they too die, and we, together with our lusts and our prides, our stupidities and our strivings

and our clutchings, are forgotten. For a few years more our only hope
of memory is the chance reference a grandchild may make; we have
become no more than the necessary adjunct to an adult remembering
of childhood.

"After that the final silence descends and we are no more."

Charles Brister was cast into that oblivion on the twentieth of
March 1971, unaware that his act of faith in a community would
find its way on to the bookshelves in this form. It was one of his
final wishes, however, that others should be told of the colliery folk
he loved so well. That is why this book has come about.

FOREWORD

I only want to be known as the Unknown Miner because I'm just an ordinary working man whose name would really mean very little to anyone outside Fife.

I've been asked to write this because I was possibly Charlie Brister's closest mate from the time he came to settle in Methil after the last war. We first met in a local hostel where we lived together for a number of years and, of course, we were down the same pit for many years—although I could never understand why he remained a miner so long.

He was an intellectual who, in many ways, was really out of his depth down the pit. But let me emphasise that he was a good miner and a dependable workmate in the best colliery tradition. It is my guess that, after being in the pits for a few years and deciding that this was the world he was going to write about, he had to stay a miner himself to gather as much material as he could for his stories; to keep in touch with the raw material as it were.

Do you know that he always carried a pad and pencil with him wherever he went, and at any odd moments you would see him taking hurried notes of something he had just seen or heard—yes, even down the pit he would scribble away. Nothing went past him. He was the most curious person I have ever met. That is why the stories in this book are so true to life. Nicky McFish and Bomber Brown and all the other characters are based on real people, and Charlie has brought them all back to me as if it were only yesterday.

Apart from his writing he was a great reader and lover of books—mostly the classics—and he kept giving me these books to read then asking me next day how I had enjoyed them. "Enjoy them?" I would say to him. "Why, I didn't even bloody well understand them!"

Yes, to have known Charlie Brister was an unforgettable experience. He really loved life, and when he was given the chance of a few more extra years by having a big heart operation he never hesitated for a second. Although he never made it I know he would never regret that decision.

He lived for his writing. What a pity that he couldn't have read his own book.

LIST OF ILLUSTRATIONS

DRAWINGS

PHOTOGRAPHS

Many people have supported me
in all sorts of ways in launching
Charles Brister's book, and to
the undermentioned I would
wish to say a very special
"thank you" . . . .

. . . . . For the artist's drawings,
including the illustration on the
front cover—D. C. Thomson &
Co. Ltd., Dundee, whose staff
on the *Scots Magazine* and the
People's Journal have been
particularly helpful; for the
photographs—The National
Coal Board, Scottish Region
(including those taken from
their collection by the late Rev.
F. W. Cobb, of Eastwood,
Notts); for their assistance and
unfailing encouragement—
Alex. Coupar, Dundee, and
William J. Smith, of the
publishers.

CHAPTER ONE

OLD WULL

THE most striking feature of the older Scot's collier is his calm sagacity in matters pertaining to his work; a combination of skill, experience and something else which I can only call "an awareness," an instinct, as it were, for threatening danger.

This subtle, inbred sense was most highly developed in an old collier whom I got to know very well and who was called Old Wull. I mention this because, by a quirk of circumstance, what first drew me to the man was an unaffected display of naked terror.

It happened in the cage, and as it is in that swift-plunging steel prison that the collier begins his day it will be no ill place for me to begin this story. We were being dropped into the depths, as usual, in batches of fifty, a profane, wild-eyed crowd, still half-asleep.

"Ah'll need tae move," gasped an anguished voice from out of the mass of flesh, tight packed in the whirling darkness.

"Move?" ejaculated another voice disgustedly. "You're aye wantin' tae be different."

". . . move," groaned the sufferer, ". . . need tae get ma hand up . . . fag's burnin' ma mooth. . . ."

"Spit it oot," someone advised and asked of us all, "Hoo glaikit can they get?"

There was a convulsive flurry of movement and another voice said sharply, "Ah'm bliddy sure he'll no spit it oot. He's jus ahint me!"

"Let the bastard burn!" came a derisive comment from the back of the cage and there was a burst of callous laughter.

But I hardly heard this and I had forgotten the unfortunate who was afire; for someone had struck the sparker of a lamp and in the quick, wayward flash I caught sight of the face of an older man at the far side of the press and if ever I saw stark, unabashed fear in a human face it was at that moment. I looked for that face when we had grounded in the brightly-lit pit-bottom, for I felt a little guilty at having surprised him in his secret daily purgatory, and having found him, remembered.

It was several months before I came across him for the second time and on that occasion it was his uncanny prescience of threatening danger, and extreme mobility in a confined space, that impressed me most.

One day I chanced to join a small group of colliers who had crawled off the low 'face' to enjoy their piece in the comparative comfort of the 'heading' which at that spot was six feet high. Most of them were crouched together and, as they warned me that shots were about to be fired, I sat down with them until it should be safe for me to proceed.

A few feet away, on the opposite side of our little tunnel, sat the man I had seen in the cage . . . Old Wull.

Suddenly, with the swiftness of a squirrel's leap, he threw himself across the heading, landing on hands and knees, his piece-box and water-bottle flying unheeded into the surrounding gloom.

There was an immediate suspension of conversation; the eyes of the other men rolled whitely, warily in their black faces. A great greeny-yellow puff-ball of decay, hanging from the rotting wood of a roof support, danced like a death-mask in the sudden vortex of air created by the movement of Wull's body. A young collier, feeling a sense of nakedness, furtively drew his feet beneath his buttocks; the sounds of chewing slowed and stopped and there was left only a palpable silence in which we could hear plainly the harsh rustle of our own breathing.

This ear-straining pause lasted for perhaps forty seconds, then, with a brief sibiliant sound as of tearing silk, a huge mass of rock crashed to the pavement at the very spot where Old Wull had been squatting.

There was a collective grunt of relief. The young collier (and I) stared with awful curiosity at Old Wull who was casting about for another perch; the older men, apart from robbing their own slender supplies to make up the lost food and pressing on Wull their water-bottles, made no reference to what, in my opinion, had been a remarkable illustration of that sixth-sense which is the right of those who are collier born. By and by I got to know Old Wull better and, on not a few occasions, owed my life to a sudden jerk of his iron-hard hand.

He was a small man, powerfully muscled above the waist and with the spidery, unused legs of the lifelong worker on the knees. His head and face were a perfect circle topped with a thick mop of lint-white hair; his skin—the dough-coloured skin of the worker in the dark—was pocked freely with blue scars where his old enemy had marked him, and his eyes were dim and almost colourless.

His features were singularly lacking in expression but this was almost certainly due to the poor eyes, for his was an alert mind, eternally curious about the world and other peoples. But no matter where we wandered to in our many verbal excursions always we came back to coal and the ways in which it might be 'wrocht.'

I remember once we were talking—a hushed little group in the darkness—of a man who had been killed several months before. That very morning men driving an aircourse up through what had been the 'waste' of the Section where the accident had occurred had come upon the top half of a set of false teeth. It was this gruesome find that had brought the subject, normally taboo underground, to our lips.

"A big nose o' coal come over an' knocked him against the conveyors," said a young stripper who had been there when it happened.

"Aye," Old Wull nodded his head in mystification. "But he wis bound tae get hurt sooner or later. He wis feart ye see; he didnae ken the natyure o' the coal. A man that's feart 'll aye get hurt. Ah couldna unnerstand him ava. It wis a brae coal tae work yince ye kent the natyure of it. . . ."

"It was some nose o' coal tae," the young stripper said. "It tuk' six o' us tae roll it affa him."

"It wis a noisy coal, ye see," Old Wull ignored the interruption.

"Aye creakin' an' spittin', an bits fleein' aff the face like bullets, but that wis just its way o' lettin' ye ken it was goin' tae tak' a seat so ye didna get catched. There wis an awfy weicht on that seam but it wis a braw coal tae work if ye didna get feart at it."

"He wisna a steady worker neether," the young stripper said. "He spent mair time in the coal cellar than in the coalpit."

11

"That's richt enough," Old Wull agreed gravely. "He didna work muckle. But it wisna that he wis lazy . . . just feart . . . an that wis his trouble . . . him no kennin' the natyure of the coal. . . ."

This incident showed plainly the belief of the older collier; that the coalface is a personality, unedifying, often malignant, but within certain, clearly defined limits, comprehensible, and he has little sympathy with those who try to work a particular seam in any way other than that which is dictated by natural conditions and local pressures.

" 'Cos," he said on another occasion, "it's no the same for you young fellas as it was when we were young. Today ye canna see nothin' for stour, an' ye canna hear nothin' for machines roarin'; an' s'posin' ye could hear, they hydraulic props dinna give a warnin' creak like the old wooden trees that we used. You young fellas that's on the modern power-loadin' faces are mebbe makkin' braw money—but the guid Laird alane kens what amount of dust you're swallowin'."

"Ah'll tell you this," he leaned forward and tapped my knee, "there's few o' them 'll see forty-five, for a' their cars and continental holidays."

He picked a piece of coal from the heap on which he was sitting and threw it idly to where two bright, beady eyes watched us. But the rat knew that no ill was intended and ignored the missile.

"Aye," Wull sighed. "It was different when I worked at the 'face' as a young fella. In they days each man had his ain 'place'; just you an' a laddie, an' he'd likely enough be your son or your nephew.

"There wis nae coal cutters to undercut the coal in they days. You lay on your side hour after hour and took the feet from the coal with the pick. Aye," his eyes twinkled. "Ah've seen you look at me whiles, Chairlie, 'cos Ah've tuk a brukken pick hame an' shafted it masel'. But we aye shafted our ain picks an' set them to our ain way of workin'.

"Then, when we'd takken the feet from the coal, the weicht sat down and broke it aff. The laddie 'd bring up a tub an' we'd fill it, an' then anither an anither. . . . When a' the coal wis awa, the roof had to be secured—it wis a' wood we used in they days—an' the stane that had come awa wi' the coal had to be packed at the sides of the road to stiffen up the props an' help 'em tae steady the roof.

12

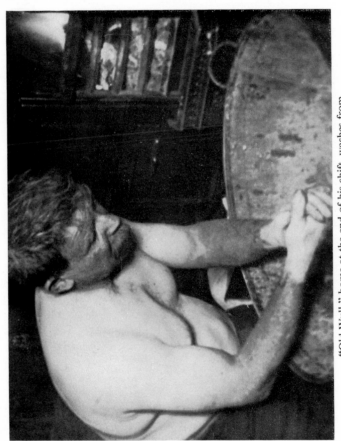

"Old Wull," home at the end of his shift, washes from the family bath in front of the fire

"If there wis time ye'd mebbe leave the laddie tae the packin' an' stairt again tae hawkin' at the coal so that the weicht would have a chance tae get workin' at it afore we cam back the next day 'cos that gave ye a braw stairt awa.

"A man's place wis his ain, ye see." He waved his hand gently, anxious that I should grasp fully the importance of what he was saying.

"It wis in our ain interests tae try an' get ahead so that if a day cam when ye mebbe felt no weel, ye could tak' it easy withoot lossin' wages or fallin' ahint with your work. There wis no goin' on the National Health for a coupla weeks then, if ye had a sair stomik. And with the place bein' your ain you aye took guid care tae see that the roof wis richt secured. If there wis nae material you didna squat on your hunkers, the way Ah've see some o' these young strippers dae, with the hale place on the move aroond their lugs, roarin' for the Material Laddie tae bring 'em a prop.

"You took a pride in your work when you had your ain place, an' if there wis nae material, you went an' got it.

"They go too fast today too, that's anither thing. When Ah wis young you'd see a collier stop now an' again an' jus lay the palm o' his hand against the face and 'feel the coal.' There's many a time when you'll no hear nothin', an' you can never *see* if a face of coal is goin' tae roll over on tap o' ye, but you could aye feel if it was goin' tae do somethin' wild . . . like a wee faint tremor went through your hand an' it gied ye time tae leap oota the way. You never see a collier dae that noo, they dinna have time. We went at our ain speed, but today they've tae go at the speed of the machine.

"Yince that Shearer stairts awa along the faceline they're a' fleein' like eedjits tae keep up with it an' if it staps for a second the Gaffer's bitin' lumps oota the Section telephone."

"Why, Wull," I said provokingly, "I do believe that you're wishin' you had the bad old days back again?"

"Na, na," he grinned. "Ah'm no as daft as that. We're far better aff noo than we were then, Ah'm no gainsayin' it. But we had happiness then too.

"You spoke jus noo of the bad old days, but they warena all bad, there were good days as weel. An' we were closer then tae yin anither than we ever are the day. Ye ken, there wis mair neighbourliness, an'

13

folk went mair aboot each ither, 'cos, if your neighbours didna help ye there wis nae ither buddy, but still, it wis a good thing an' it's a pity that it's fadin' out. When Ah wis young a colliery village wis a ticht little community where everybuddy kent the same sorrows and shared the same burdens.

"We wis hairder too, in they days. It wis only nat'rul, Ah s'pose, 'cos the weaker ones just didna survive tae grow up ava. We wis bare-assed a' the year roond, an' barefut from April tae September, us laddies, but Ah canna see that it ever did us any hairm.

"Ma faither wis aff work for lang periods due tae accidents an' troubles but we never went hungry. We mebbe didna get nae fancy foods but what we did get was stuff that put a linin' on your gizzard an' that's what a laddie needs, 'specially when he's bein' bred up for pitwork.

"Why, we got things then that folk dinna get the day. We'd go to the berries in the summer an' in the Autumn there wis the brammles; ma mither aye kept a press fu' o' her ain brammle jelly. And we had oor ain elderberry wine; ma faither made that.

"And we had a boat, o' cos'. Maist o' the colliers had a yawl at that time. They were braw boats too, aboot seventeen foot lang an' seven foot in the beam with a dippin' lugs'l. Why, we even used tae have a regetta every year at the Fair. We had fun tae, there used tae be mair capsizes than anything else at the regettas.

"It wis nat'rul, o' cos'. Fellas that's been dicin' with death in a black hole in the grund a' year think little o' takkin' a chance oot on the Forth aneath God's blue sky.

"It wis an ole boat oors; it had been ma grandfaither's, but it would aye get us a mile affshore an' back; me an' ma brithers bailin' an' the ole fella fushin'.

"When we got hame ma mither 'd be waitin' an' her face 'd shine like the sun when we filled the big sink with slapping codling. An' o' cos' there wis the seacoal. We used tae get threepence a bag an' we could fill an' deliver ten bags in a day. Our ain coalcellar had tae be filt first; ma faither would never allow our ain coalhoose tae fa' back—that aye had tae be kept filt.

"Aye, we managed. Ah'd be the last to suggest that we were better aff then, far from it, but we aye managed. Mebbe we were mair fort'nate than others, havin' the Forth at our door 'n the seacoal 'n that, but we aye managed, aye, but did we."

"You've surprised me, Wull," I said. "I took it for granted that the colliers considered themselves to be vastly better off today."

"Och, they are," he told me emphatically. "They are, 'specially in England, dinna misdoubt me. Even here in Scotland there's been an improvement. But Ah'll tell ye one thing that's no changed . . . no, an' never will." His voice had a new intensity and his eyes twinkled at me from under straggly white brows.

"Pits!" he said. "Pits! Ah've never seen a coalpit yet that wis fit for twa dugs tae ficht in an' nae fella that has a grain o' sense 'll ever go near one."

There spoke the true collier, who, no matter his secret pride in the skills garnered over a lifetime; his absorbing interest in the craft of coalgetting; the pleasure he derives from mastering great natural forces, hates with a deadly hatred that centre of his existence . . . the Pit!

I remember him once explaining to me, in his soft unhurried voice, how the weight, eternally thrusting down, sought to 'get vent' and would take quick advantage of any weak spot in the area that had been exposed by the removal of coal.

To illustrate his point, he half-raised an arm and rapped his knuckles on the grey, infinitely menacing roof that glistened with moisture only inches from our heads. He picked up a fragment of redd, and using a larger piece of stone for paper, scratched a diagram to demonstrate how, if we did not encourage the 'waste' roof to fall, then it would seek outlet at the 'face.' ". . . and that wouldna do," he concluded.

But I hardly heard him for I had suddenly realised that, crouched there in the darkness with his primitive pencil gripped between his twisted old fingers, he was a modern re-incarnation of those neolithic men who drew pictures on the underground cave walls of Cromagnon.

"And another thing," he said. "You neednae tak fricht and be gettin' ready to flee, Chairlie, every time the roof gies a bit rummle. Just you watch me; 'cos if it's likely to shut, Ah'll be off . . . and Ah'll tak' some catching. So just you stop worrying and watch me. As lang as Ah'm here . . . it's safe enough."

15

And this was no more than the simple truth. He could estimate to a couple of feet how, and in which way, the roof would fall; which props should be first drawn and the best way to set about their withdrawal.

His knowledge of the way the 'metals'* would behave was uncanny, and saved us a great deal of time and heavy labour. There is little satisfaction in withdrawing a prop from the 'waste' if one has subsequently to dig it out from under several tons of fallen rock. Thanks to Wull's inborn skill we were seldom faced with this problem.

Although, due to dangerous conditions, we had many hectic shifts, I cannot recall ever seeing him flustered or in any way put off 'his way o' daein'.' Whether we had a quiet night or a terrifying night he was the same unruffled old collier. Once, when many of the men were talking of 'puttin' the graith on the shackle an' gettin' up the Pit' he told them equably—

"This Pit's oor breid an' butter, lads, an' it has tae be wrocht. Good or bad, it has tae be wrocht. Any daft nowt can go away hame an' let the place shut ahint him, but it tak's a collier tae keep a place goin' an' coal coming oot when things are bad. . . ."

He had a tremendous authority and power over the other men, although he was quite unaware of this; it may be that the very secret of his power lay in the fact that it was completely unconscious.

His day-to-day contacts with those who were in positions of authority were marked rather by timidity than audicity as the following little scene will illustrate. At the time I was working on the coalcutter and, crawling along the 'face' towards the end of what had been a nerve-racking shift, I passed Wull and his neighbour. Both men were breathing heavily and rivulets of sweat coursed down the matt of dirt that coated their trembling, naked chests.

I heard Wull's 'neighbour,' also a veteran of the first war, say gaspingly in his droll way—

"Ye ken, Wull. We should get the Crox-de-Guerre for the perils we've faced this night. Aye, Wull—the Crox-de-Guerre!"

Wull picked up his heavy mash and braced himself anew. "Come

---

*'Metals' is the general term used by colliers to describe the rock strata surrounding the mineral he is extracting.

on," he said unemotionally. "Ah ken what we'll get if the last of they props is no' oot when the Gaffer comes roon!"

My last glimpse of Old Wull was on a Sunday forenoon in the local Miner's Institute and he was unaware of my presence. He was talking, quite unaffectedly, to another man, and I cannot close this episode with better words than those he used that Sunday.

". . . she wis a Pit-head lassie, o' cos', but when she'd turned fifty it was ower haird for her an' she got a job cleanin' in the schules. She wrocht there till she wis seventy-eicht. She's a hairdy ole woman, ma mither, an' a grafter a' her days. But she's eichty-nine noo an' she's done. Ah've tae do a'thing for her, 'n she greets when Ah've tae leave her to go tae ma wark, but the neighbours aye tak' a run in tae see the fire's richt an' mak' her a cup o' tea.

"Ah've gotta wark . . . her pension an' the dole 'll no keep us. An' anyway, Ah've aye warked 'cept for the fowerteen war when Ah wis in the sodgers. What would Ah dae lyin' aboot the house idle?

"Ah've been washin' the day, wi' it bein' the Sabbath. Ah aye likit tae keep ma things clean, even ma pit-claes. The moleskins 'n that dinna matter but Ah like ma underclaes tae be clean. So Ah've done a washin', 'n bathed 'n changed ma Mither, a' afore eleven o-clock o' the day . . . 'cos, Ah stairtit at five this mornin'. Ah've aye been accustomed tae the early risin' for the Pit.

"Ah left her sittin' up in bed as clean as a new pin, 'n weel happed up, 'n a cup o' tea, 'n her specs, 'n the Sunday papers at her hand. She canna read, o' cos', but she whiles looks at the pictyures, 'n a big fire goin'.

"But she stairtit tae greet 'cos Ah come oot, an' Ah telt her Ah wis awa doon tae the corner for a smoke at ma pipe . . . Never spit in the hoose," he shook his white head violently.

"Ah've smoked a pipe for forty-five year noo but Ah've never spit in the hoose. Ah wis twenty-five year marrit, 'n Ah had a guid wife, 'n she'd tell ye the same but she's deid. Never spit in the hoose. Always went tae the door tae spit, or doon tae the corner o' the street. . . .

"Aaah! but the ole leddy kent Ah wisnae jus' awa oot for a smoke . . . she kent where Ah wis awa tae—you canna kid the ole yins— she kent.

" 'You're awa doon tae that Club for drink,' she howls.

" 'Oh, for Pete's sake, Maw, Ah'm surely entitilt tae a pint o' beer efter warkin' in a stoury coal-pit a' week!' . . .'n mind, she's a' cleant, 'n the hoose is braw, 'n a big cheery fire goin'. But she's aye after me, nae matter what Ah dae. Ah'm sixty-nine year old but tae lissen tae her, Ah'm still jus' a bit laddie."

"Could you no put her intae a Hame ? " I heard the other man ask. "What aboot they Ole Folks'es Hames . . . they get awfy weel looked after in them."

"Na," Wull said simply, seriously. "Ah couldnae dae that. She's ma mither . . . it's ma duty tae look after her . . . Ah'm her son, ye see."

THE PIT

We do not live,
Who live within the realm
Of deep ensoilment.
Our spirits fly
Where vagrant, questing airs
Grace the sun-warmed beauty of the sky.

Locked are we
Away, and may not leave
The sordid womb
Of Earth.   We do not fear,
(for we are always there)
The ravishing importance of the tomb.

Hush !   We are lost,
Who strive within the curve
Of Earth's dark elbow.
We sing for such a little while
Each day, beneath the sky.   Then,
We must go below.

19

CHAPTER TWO

THE BOMBER AND THE WHIPPET

IT was piecetime and we were sitting at the side of the Heading. Heelplates McSobb and Beetle McSair the propdrawers and myself, second man on the coalcutter. My 'neighbour' Nicky McFish, the leading cutterman, was last in crawling off the bench of stone at the roadhead.

"What's this?" he demanded, focussing his light on a wooden prop lying in the centre of the road.

"Better fling it tae the side," suggested Heelplates through a mouthful of bread and jam. "Afore someone trips over it."

"What's wrang you never flung it tae the side?" bristled Nicky. "Wis you waitin' for me tae trip ?" He stepped carefully over the prop and sat down beside us. "That'll dae for the Bomber," he cackled. "He's due roon, just aboot the noo."

Bomber Brown, our Section deputy, was continually falling over things, but the prop was a big one and Brown wasn't blind. "Come off it, Nicky," I said. "Even the Bomber won't fall over that, it's sticking up like a sore thumb," and Heelplates grunted agreement.

"What'll you bet ?" Nicky rapped out his favourite expression. "That Ah canna mak' the Bomber fa' over that wooden tree."

"Twenty fags," said Heelplates and Beetle together with almost indecent haste. Nicky looked at me.

"You know I don't bet, Nicky," I told him. "But if you can make the Bomber fall over that prop, I'll treat you to a roll and egg in the Canteen at lousin' time."

"Ah'm no wantin' pisened," Nicky said badtemperedly. Like most colliers, he was an inveterate gambler and regarded the non-betting fraternity with a jaundiced suspicion.

"The Bomber's agin bettin' too, is he no?" asked Beetle.

"Aye," said Nicky. "But he wisnae aye like that. He used tae be

20

an awfy gambler the Bomber. There wis a time when he couldnae watch twa flees crawlin' up a windy 'thout haein' money on yin o' them. By jings, thon whippet cured him o' a' they notions."

I scented a story. "What whippet?" I asked gently.

"Well," said Nicky. "Ah cried it a whippet, but only for the sake o' conveenience. The good Lord alane kens whit it really wis. Ah've kent a few racin' dugs in ma time, but Ah never see yin like thon. It had a lang greetin' face on it, that wis as mournfu' lookin' as Bomber Broon's hissel', an' one ee. It wis the colour o' mud, an' it had nae tail tae speak o'. Ah think it bit its ain tail aff in yin o' its moods. By jings, it wis some dug thon, wi' legs as lang as broom-shanks, an' feet as big as the Bomber's.

"Well, as Ah said, the Bomber wis a great boy for the bettin' but he aye lost, an' he wis desp'rit for a dug o' his ain, 'cos he thocht that wis the way tae mak' money, but ye ken yersel's whit a minin' village is like. A' the dugs is kent, an' them that can run, canna be bocht. Well onyway, the Bomber goes through yonner fer the Gala, Coatbridge or someplace, an' when he comes back he has this dug. He kent nothin' aboot dugs, o' cos', so it wis me that got landed wi' the job o' advisin' him whit tae dae.

"By jings, Ah never see a dug like thon. It wis mair like a human bein', wi' the moods it used tae tak'. One day it 'd be pitifu' tae watch it runnin', it couldnae a'caught a cold, an', o' cos', the Bomber used tae loss the heid an' gie it a kick in the ribs tae try an' stir it up.

"Ah tell you this, four pun' o' gelignite hung on its tail wouldnae a moved thon thing when it didnae want tae go. Then anither day, it would tak' yin o' its notions, an' screitch alang like yin o' they Roosian rockets, an' Mick the Miller couldnae a catched it.

"The Bomber 'd be over the moon then, an' he'd buy it a half a pund o' black pudden. Man, Ah never see onythin' sae daft on black pudden as thon whippet o' the Bomber's.

"Well, the time comes when the Bomber decides that it's time that the whippet wis contributin' tae the hoosehold, so he enters it for the Saturday meetin' at Kirkcaldy. An' we tak's it in on the Wednesday, tae run it roon the track, so the stewards an' handicappers could get an' idee o' its time an' register it. Well, it musta been in yin o' its moods, 'cos they wis nae life in the thing ava.

"The Bomber gies it a couple kicks tae liven it up, but he'da been as well kickin' hissel.

"It lollops roon' the track like a dromedary wi' the hiccups, its tongue hangin' doon atween its legs, an' its hintend stickin' up like a hump. Ah tell you, a' the handicappers' stopwatches had run doon afore it got roon, an' they wis a' laffin'.

"On Saturday, o' cos', the cussed thing wis fu' o' beans, an' the Bomber's fair delighted.

" 'We'll mak a pile the day, Nicky,' he says.

"But Ah warned him whit he wis up against. If thon dug flew roon the track like we kent it could, then he'd mebbe get accused o' enterin' another dug under the fust yin's name, an' then he'd be in the soup.

" 'We canna let thon thing run at its fastest,' Ah tells him. 'We'll need tae tire it a bit afore we gets tae Kirkcaldy. The best thing we can do,' says I, 'is tae walk it in, 'stead o' goin' wi' the bus. It's near ten miles, that should just aboot do the trick. It's nae use us bettin' on the dug, if oor bets is goin' tae get disallowed 'cos the dug's disqualified due tae hanky-panky.'

"Well, o' cos', even the Bomber can see the sense o' that, so aff we goes. We went the lang way, by the Stannin' Stanes, an' through the woods.

"By jings, Ah'll tell you, ye never see nothin' like this in a' your days. Thon mungerel run aboot like a mad thing a' the road. It flew here an' dashed there, chasin' rabbits an' groose an' onythin' else that wis daft enough tae move across it sichts. It never halted frae the meenit we left hame. Ah tell you, it musta covered a thoosan' mile that afternoon, no ten.

"When we gets intae Kirkcaldy, we has eight rabbits in a sack, twa groose, a White Leghorn cockerel that thocht it could run, an' a big ginger cat. The Bomber wis keepin' the cat for the dug's dinner.

" 'Well,' says the Bomber, 'If that beast isnae tired after that carryon, Ah'll gie up.' We'd put oor bets on, an' we wis stannin' at the finishin' post. Ah has a bit look at the dug, an' he doesnae look tired tae me, its one ee wis rollin' roon its head wi' devilment. Ah tell you, Ah didnae trust thon beast ava. Ah could see us feenishin' up in the jail over the heid o' it. Ah mak's up me mind tae clear oot,

22

there an' then, afore the trouble stairts, but the Bomber gies me the sack tae hold an' tak's the dug over tae the stairtin' boxes.

"Ooooh, whit a calamity! Yon cussed thing wis roon the track an' sniffin' at ma legs afore the ither dugs wis oota their boxes. If there hadnae been sae mony folk watchin', ah'd a' gien it ma boot tae sniff, Ah'll tell you. It woulda got you hung, thon creeture.

"Well, o' cos', it wis as Ah'd expected. The track stewards compares the times an' sends for the Polis. An' a' the Polis could dae when they arrived wis tae keep starin' suspeeciously at me, stannin' there like a bliddy eedjit haudin' ontae the sack."

"What happened?" asked the Beetle innocently.

"What d'ye think happened," Nicky snapped testily. "The Bomber got fined twa pun for substitutin' dugs wi' intent tae defraud. An' Ah got fined a fiver for poachin', an' had tae gie a pund tae the ole wife that owned the ginger cat. You shoulda heard her. By jings, Ah'll bet thon dug's ribs wis sair when we got hame. It musta wunnered hoo two humans could hae sae mony feet. An tell you, we wis near walkin' on oor hauns, no tae miss a chance o' a kick at it. . . ."

"Look out," hissed the Beetle as the Bomber crawled heavily over the bench and stood before us. "Watch that prop!" Heelplates and I cried together. The Bomber was not accustomed to such concern, and he looked at us suspiciously. "Lift that prop oota there," he said officiously to Nicky.

"D'ye ken, Ah'm s'posed tae be gettin' ma piece," Nicky complained.

"Ah ken you're s'posed tae get twenty meenits for your piece," the Bomber growled, "An' you've been sittin' here for an hoor, that Ah ken of. You've surely got awfy braw pieces when you linger sae lang over em."

"Here," said Nicky, holding out a grubby hand. "You wantin' a slice. Cold, fried black pudden."

The Bomber's face turned white, he flung out an arm in horror and retreated hastily from the proffered piece. His feet caught in the prop, and the next moment he was flying headlong through the darkness, his anguished howls echoing noisily from the roof arches.

"That's forty fags," said Nicky to Heelplates and the Beetle. "Ah'll get 'em on Friday," he turned to me. "See an' mind in the

23

canteen the morn. Ah've won that roll-an'-egg, fair an' square, an' Ah'll eat it if it kills me."

"Hoo did the Bomber get on wi' his whippet ?" asked Heelplates, his face sad at the thought of the twenty fags.

"Well, at fust, o' cos', he wisna goin' tae run it again, he'd got such a fright. But a' the lads wis aye on at him tae run it. Well, o' cos', there could be nae further nonsense about the dug, 'cos it wis well kent noo. The hale place wis talkin' aboot whit had happened. An' they gets the Bomber persuaded tae run it. Though he explained tae 'em that it wis a moody cuss, an' if it wis in yin o' its aff moods on the day o' the race he couldnae be blamed. Well, that wis fair enough, an' the Bomber shoves it in for the next meetin', an' a' the colliers in the village has their shirts on it, in spite o' it bein' handicapped oota existence. But that wis only nat'rul, noo the dug's speed wis kent.

"Well, the village is a' waitin' for the great day to come. An' the rest o' the colliers is aye hangin' aboot the Bomber's door askin' hoo the dug wis keepin', an' a' that. An' when it comes the day o' the race, the hale place flocks intae Kirkcaldy wi' the Bomber an' his whippet.

"By jings! Ah'll gie thon beast credit for one thing. It mebbe wisnae a very bonnie beast, but when it wis in the mood it could go, an' it wis in the mood that day. Cos', the Bomber had stopped giein' it the boot, an' wis giein' it black pudden, wi' it bein' a famous dug an' that, an' pappin' it wi' his haun', an' acting affectionate tae keep it in a good mood. Well, as Ah wis sayin', it mebbe wisnae whit you'd ca' a lovable sorta dug, but by the hokey, it could toddle, Ah'll tell you. Handicaps or nae handicaps.

"Thon affair wisna a race, it wis a pushover. Thon mungerel come oota the box like a bullet an' wis roon the fust turn afore the rest wis stairtit. There wis only one o' them could run onyway, a dug ca'd Hector the Second, an' by jings, it wis well named when you see the Bomber's mungerel goin' roon the track.

"They nearly burnt oot the motor tryin' tae keep the hare in front o' it. An', o' cos', a' the colliers is flngin' their bonnets in the air an' lookin' at the bookies, an' the bookies pullin' their bonnets doon ower their ears an' lookin' at the nearest gate. Whit a day!

"Me an' the Bomber is stannin' by the rails a few yards in front

24

o' the finishin' line. It wis an awfy windy day an' Ah took him there so as tae hae the wind ahint us. Ah tell you when thon mungerel reaches us, it wis goin' sae fast it wis smokin'. Ah think that wis the nearest the Bomber ever come tae haein' a smile on his pus.

"Here, whenever the dug gets abreast o' us does it no slap on the brakes. Youda' thocht it run intae a wall. The sparks wis fleein' frae its hintend wi' the effort o' stoppin'. Then it comes lollopin' ower tae us wi' a daft sorta look in its ee. It jumps up wi' its big feet on the rails an' gies the Bomber a big slobbery kiss in the middle o' his pus an' stairts sniffin' roon his pockets, while Hector the Second gallops on tae win.

"Ooooh! Whit a carryon. The colliers wis goin' tae lynch the Bomber, if the Polis hadnae got him awa. Talk aboot brucken hairts. Ah tell you, it wis pitifu' tae watch. Some o' them had pawned their best suits tae get money tae put on the Bomber's whippet. Aye, it wis a shame, some o' them wis near greetin'."

"You, too?" asked Heelplates maliciously.

"Oh, for Pete's sake," Nicky grinned. "Ma money wis on Hector. Ah'da been stupid tae bet the Bomber's dug, when it was me that put the black pudden in the Bomber's pocket at the stairt o' the race?"

> *"The collier is the last true explorer. Each day the snake-like 'face', one hundred to three hundred yards long, from which the coal is won, moves $4\frac{1}{2}$ feet deeper into the unknown and the collier goes where man has never gone before."*

CHAPTER THREE

LIKE A ROCK

I JUMPED off the bus at the traffic lights to save a ten-yard walk and, as I rounded the corner, Marcus Ogilvy, blinking comically in the bright sunlight of early July, came out of the pub and dropped into step beside me.

Though not drunk, he had drink taken, as the saying is, and his fleshy face was red, and his eyes protuberant and bloodshot. As a young man he had been hurt underground and he walked always with a slight limp and with his right hand pressed against his lower back as though to push himself along at a faster rate. But he had little wind, he gasped as we walked along and I found my step slowing to accommodate his laboured gait.

Although we worked near each other—on the same 'face' in the same section of the pit—we had had, apart from a word in the passing, small intercourse. At the time, roof conditions were good; and it is only when closures threaten that miners move away from their own small portion of the underground. We might find outselves together at the shift's end waiting for the cage; or I would see Marky's broad shoulders, pudding face and white-rolling eyes lipping over the edge of a man-haulage bogie as it rattled through the galleries of eternally dripping water.

I heard—through pit gossip—that he was often absent on Friday nightshift, "as he went away for week-ends," and I wondered idly where he found to go, for he was at least forty-five years of age and no oil painting; and as I have already said, he was no boozer.

But, although I wondered, the answer never came my way, and I was not so interested as to seek it. My idle curiosity remained idle curiosity. It is always better so; the collier does not concern himself with the private affairs of his fellows except in cases of need; or when directly invited to do so.

We, Marky and I, had worked the same three-hundred yard 'face' for eighteen months; had shared the same dangers and been part of the same larger group, and yet I realised, walking along the road with him that summer's day, that I knew little about the man by my side—did not even know where he lived.

Perhaps it was out of this thought that I said, "Where are you off to, Marky? I go straight on at the crossroads—on up the hill by the old farm road: I live just over the head of the Brae."

He said, "I turn right at the crossroads," and then asked, "Where have you been—for a walk?"

"No," I told him disgustedly. "Went away to Balcaskie to try and get some rhubarb crowns: heard that Danny Maguire had some to spare: it was true enough, but I was too late: they'd all been given away, so I had my journey for nothing. We've only recently moved into this house," I explained, "and there's a good big garden. I like a patch of rhubarb in a garden. I'm fond of a plate of rhubarb—cleans the blood."

"Come round with me," he said, "it's no more than a hundred yards off your road. I'll give you plenty of rhubarb: much as you can carry away. Not crowns," he was quick to emphasise, "I never part with my rhubarb crowns. I'm supposed to have the best in the district but I'll give you as big a bundle of stalks as you can carry away, 'n you'll get more if you care to come back. I've little use for them now: that's what they're needing, in fact—used up."

I said tentatively, "Neighbours not take them?"

"They dinna get the chance," he snapped; and I realised that I had touched on a sore subject. He said sullenly, "I bide clear of my neighbours: they've never had no time for me, and I've no time for them—pair of old widdy wimmin, one on each side. This way," he said, as we reached the crossroads, and, with me at his heels, turned right along a quiet street dappled with the shade of Poplar trees. I looked back at the fall of the Brae behind us; at the beach below and the shining reaches of the sea. "You've a grand view from here," I said.

"Aye," he nodded agreement. "Even from the downstairs windys, I can see right out over the Forth to the other side. At the holidays, the visitors all rave about the view. It was the view that first drew Mabel's eye—her and her mother's."

29

"Mabel?" I said. "Is that your wife?"

"No," he retorted with a quick shake of his thick neck, and I forebore to question further.

"Come in," he said when we reached his house. "Come in, Airch, you've never seen my place"; and there was a pathetic note of pride in the harsh voice. "Come on in." As though sensing my reluctance, he gripped my arm eagerly in his great hand and pushed open the gate and shoved me before him. "I've some lager in the frig," he said, and it was a plea.

I had expected to have to admire a garden, but I wasn't too keen to enter the house; but the thought of a glass of cool lager tempted me on that hot day, and I let him lead me past a trim, exactly symetrical lawn, and around the side of what is called a 'traditional' council house. He drew me past the front windows and along the side between a red brick wall and a neatly trimmed, high, privet hedge.

"Always go round the back," he explained. "What the neighbours don't see won hurt 'em. That's why I keep the hedges high—same reason: pair of nosy old bitches. Neither has a man body of her own and they didna believe in letting another woman have peace to enjoy hers. . . ."

And I, conscious of the grip on my arm and caught up, without quite knowing how, in this conspiratorial behaviour, nodded knowingly, and followed softly on.

Marky opened the door with a key he took from his pocket and from the moment I entered that kitchen I was acutely aware of the empty—the hollow, unlived in—atmosphere of the place: there was a stillness, a soullessness that somehow accorded with the perfect, almost painful neatness of everything in that poor lonely house.

The sunlight streamed through the windows, and, on the window-sill, a big khaki-coloured cat opened big drowsy eyes, twitched a whisker and went once more to sleep.

The need for a key told me—as much as did the oppressive air—that there was no one in the house but ourselves; and my thought of the key revealed another strangeness; for, even if the house was empty, it should not have been needed. In a Scottish mining village, doors are never locked. Marky bent to the refrigerator and I, conscious of the cold eyes of the other houses staring down upon us, looked around me. The furnishings were expensive and seemed but little used; and, in spite of the heat of the day, that kitchen had a frigid air of almost clinical cleanness. There was not a single fly— not one.

Marky straightened up with cans of lager and took two glasses from a cabinet.

"Cheers," he said, and I said in answer, "All the best," but my voice was hushed and I felt as though the very walls were whispering. Whispering——: "We are painted and garnished and bright, but we are lonely and unloved. We shine only for each other to see, for we are not a home but a bribe. We should have been the end; but we were only the means; now we are no more than the solace of a great stubbornness."

Marky bent once more to the frig, his glass in his hand, and I said, more to break the spell than for any other reason, "Watch you don't spill that beer or your wife 'll be after you: she had the place like a new pin."

He stared at me with his goggling eyes. He was on his knees with his head twisted back over his shoulder and his neck seemed to swell and bloat so that the skin grew tight and the short ginger hairs stood out like bristles: a ray of sunshine reached around the curtain and brassed his flesh like studded leather.

He said thickly, "My wife bides in Glasgow: we've been parted for twenty years."

"Oh," I stammered. "I'm sorry. I. . . ."

"Nothing to be sorry about," he grunted. "It's well enough known about here."

"I hadn't heard," I said, "but then we only flitted here three years ago; we're still practically strangers in the district. . . ."

He growled, as though I had not spoken. "She's waiting for a divorce: been waiting a good few years now; and she'll wait a good few more. I'll never give her a divorce: not after breaking up my home."

"What do you think of the place?" he asked, and went on, "Do I no keep a braw house, Airch? I'll tell you this, Airch, I can wash and mend and clean as good as any woman. Just the big stuff, blankets and that I send to the laundry; and once a month Mabel and her mother come through and give the place a good going over;

31

but day to day, I keep clean myself." He looked slowly about him, hands on hips, with an air of great complacency.

I said fervently, "I wish mine was as tidy, but with young children about the place . . . ach, but you'll know what it's like."

His eyes had a faraway look and he gave no sign, but he must have heard me for he said, after a second or two, "Took my bairns with her when she went, the bitch; my two laddies, Melville and Colin, and the bairn, wee Margaret. The bairn was only a year old; Colin wasna much more than two and Melville just a year older than Colin. Took 'em with her when she cleared out: she'd a hard neck doing that: my own bits of bairns. Sit down, Airch," he told me anxiously. "Sit down and content yourself. Here, I'll get another can of lager, and there's whisky in the house: you'll have a nip."

I wished myself well away, but for the sake of conversation, I said, "Surely you have the right to see them." But he had risen and gone into the other room. When he returned he brought two glasses of whisky.

"Plenty of this," he said; "the New Year bottle's three-quarter full yet. . . ."

I felt the true sadness then, and knew that I was stuck until he had told out his tale: there was more meaning in his last words than in anything else he had said. Imagine a Hogmanay whisky bottle still three-quarters full in July.

"Aye," he continued in that same harsh voice. "I'd the right to see them all right, don't you worry about that. She was the guilty party; she was in desertion, you see," and he hunched his shoulders about the cold comfort of the fact. "I went to a solicitor, but he never needed to fight the case: she brought them back on her own just two months after she'd gone away—was probably hoping I'd take her in as well. What a hope! No, no! When a woman blots her copybook with me—it's blotted for keeps. And yet. . . ."

He studied the glass in his hand with round, protuberant eyes . . . "I've often wondered if it wasn't a fly move on her part; but I don't think so . . . she hasn't enough a brains to plan out a fly move as deep as that. . . ."

"What do you mean?" I asked him.

"Well," he said, "the bairns bide with her now you see; she brought 'em back, but now she's got 'em. But they're grewn," he snapped with sudden violence. "They're grewn—they're no longer weans and she never had 'em when they were wee. She's mebbe got 'em now; but she never had em' when they were wee. Same's the house: she's mebbe got a house now, but it's no this one. She loved this house, and the garden, and the view out over the water.

"Why, I've caught her often, leaning over the sink, up to the elbows in soapsuds and a curly bit hair blowing across her face in the draught from the open windy, and she'd be staring away out across the sea, her eyes full of dreams: even in the dead of winter—in the quite cold days—I've seen her leave the fire and the warmth of the sitting-room here," he waved a hand expressively in a slow, all-embracing gesture, "and go through to the back; and I'd go out and find her standing beneath the stars, staring down at the shine of the water: calm and still she'd be, as if she was bathing in the milk of the moonlight.

"Even in the full of the south-easters she'd go out there to the scullery and listen to the high wail of the wind, and she'd watch the seas coming in over the harbour wall, big and green and full of wickedness; and the spray lashing all ways and the pier lights yellow in the cloud wrack.

"Aye, she loved it here. The sea and salt breath of the wind, and the garden with the dahlias that the neighbours had given her, growing from the wall right down to the house path in every shade and colour you could think of. It's good grund that, at the back of the house: that's how she could grow such braw dahlias. Even after I put the rhubarb in it was the same. We aye had the first rhubarb in the village and it was never forced—and thick!—wait 'll you see it, Airch." He gripped my knee, pressing the flesh with his thumb and fingertips, and his eyes shone with pride. "Wait 'll you see it . . . thick . . . you've never seen rhubarb with stalks as thick as mine . . ."

Then the passion and the pride went out of him a little and he relaxed his grip of my leg; and the pleasure went out of him and he sank back in his chair as though he had somehow shrunk.

There was a pause, and he said slowly, "Aye, she has a house now. But she'll no have a view like this from the back windy of a Glasgow tenement; and I'll bet this is still where she'd rather be in spite of all the trouble atween us. Aye, she'll have her memories of this house—it was her first decent home—and she'll have her thoughts and longings like any other woman. . . ."

I asked hesitantly, "What was the trouble?"

But there was no answer, and, as he was sitting back in his chair he was in the shade of a heavy window curtain so I could not see his face. I ran my lower lip around the rim of the glass and waited. I thought he had forgotten about me, but he spoke at last from out of his heavy breathing.

"Ach," he said slowly. "It was so long ago. . . . We never really got on; not from after the Old Fella got kilt, not from the start, I suppose; but the Old Fella covered up the first years. It shook her when he was buried underground. Up till then I don't think she'd really understood what a coalpit was . . . you know, the danger an' that. She never became reconciled to the fact that his body couldn't be recovered and given a proper funeral.

"She even wanted me to get another job: me! Can you imagine it? How the hell could I do another job: a collier's muscles are set; his very banes are developed in a certain way so he can do the work he was bred for. I'm talking about fellas like us," he hastened to explain, "that are collier born: no like those Bevin Boys that came to the pits after the war—not that many of them stayed. Oh, they've been trained to do a job underground: we all know that. I've worked aside them, but they're not what you and me would call colliers.

"That was my mistake, Airch. I married out of my class, that was the real trouble; if my wife had been off collier folk we'd never have had no bother. But she was full of fancy notions and fancy notions are no use ava in a mining community—no use ava.

"She'd never known want, you see: that was her misfortune; she'd never really known want and because of that her priorities were all wrong. Well, I bet she's got her priorities straightened out now," he said in a voice that tried to be exultant but merely succeeded in being pitiful. "Aye, I bet she has," he repeated. "There's nothing like a few years on the breadline for straightening out priorities," and I saw the bristly, carrot-coloured head nod, in solemn confirmation of the words.

By now the whisky was a slow warmth within me. Mellowed, I said, "Tell me about it," and pulled out a packet of cigarettes.

Above: A typical back-to-back miners' row with the identical
houses drawn up in strict regimental order

Below: Today many miners live on modern council estates,
away from the shadow of the bing

He watched the smoke dwindle and die before carefully placing his spent match in the pedestal ashtray he had placed between us.

"She was a city lassie," he began, "knew nothing about collier life. She was in service in the city: that's how I met her. I went with some other fellas to see a football game and afterwards we went to one of the big dance-halls and I asked her up for a dance—she was sitting all alone. That's how I met her.

"Her folk were both dead: that's why she was in service. Not because she liked it, but because she needed both a job and a home and that was the one way to get both. Not that there was much else for a lassie in those days—it's different now. She hated it, too; you know, the subservience, and not having her own home and her independence. She wanted her own home and a garden and flowers, but all she saw was the smoky back court of a city basement and she hated it.

"I think it must have reminded her of the orphanage where she had been brought up. Aye, she hated it. A gloomy old house where nothing was hers. They'd forget to pay her wages, and she'd be frightened to remind them for fear of being flung out on the street; and they'd give her their cast-off clothes and she was supposed to be grateful.

"And all the young men of the family seemed to think they had a right to torment her. She was just a wee bit thing, you see, and when they were home from college—the sons and nephews and their pals—she used to be in terror. They'd hang about in dark corners to scare her, and she'd be that frightened she'd switch on every light she passed. Then the old wife—her mistress—would give her a round of the guns for wasting electricity; and she knew it would be hopeless trying to explain because the old woman would have been horrified at the very suggestion that her precious laddies would play games with a servant girl."

Marky said slowly and with a tremendous air of concentration, "I think that's half why I married her. . . ." He paused as if trying to clarify the idea in his own mind . . . "you see, you felt she needed to be protected with her being that wee and delicate and feared. I bet she never stopped trembling all her waking hours in that house: maybe that was why she liked flowers . . . she was a bit like a flower herself.

35

"My father was still alive at that time, of course, and we lived in one of the old colliery houses down by the foreshore where the old pit used to be. You'll no mind of those houses; they were just back-to-back hovels built by the coalmasters about the middle of the last century, but the most of them had fell down and the Council had long since condemned the rest.

"The Old Lady had died the winter afore the time I'm talking about, and me and the Old Fella were pigging away thegither: it wasna very handy, as you can imagine, because we were both working in the pit.

"And that was the way of it. I married her and she settled in with us well enough. She was a good wee cook, mind, and a braw housekeeper. The house was just a crumbling ruin, surrounded by other ruins that had crumbled a bit faster and been deserted. There were no facilities at all. She even had to walk fifty yards through the tangle of fallen stones to fill a kettle of water, and in a hard winter the standpipe 'd likely as not be frozen. Me and the Old Fella were nightshift, too, so she was left alone every night in that miserable little hovel with ruination all around and the sea sighing and moaning only a stone's throw from the door. It was eery, mind, and I never thought she'd stick it after the city, and the bright lights. But she loved it: she was fair away with herself, you see, with her having her own home and she kept that old dump spotless.

"The Old Fella took a fancy to her, and she was for ever getting him to paint a windysill, or patch up a hole in the floor or replace a slate—he'd have done anything for her. She even had flowers growing in wee pots all over the place, and that's all it was—her having a place of her own after being kicked around other folks' houses all her days.

"Well, naturally it wasna long before she was expecting. As I said, she was a delicate wee thing; and she'd awfy leddy-like notions —you know, sota innocent. I laugh yet when I mind how she found out she'd fallen the first time—with Melville.

"She'd been out of sorts for a few weeks but she wasn't one to complain. In the end, however, the Old Fella made her go to the doctor. It was old Hugh MacDiarmid that was doctor here then; and a right hard nut he was, if ever there was one, though he was good to the wife. He knew his work, too. Thon fella knew more about us colliers' insides than the God who made us. But, anyway, off she goes to see old Shuggy MacDiarmid and tells him that she was keeping no well.

" ' I believe that, Mistress Ogilvy,' says Shuggy; 'and I can tell you now without going any further that your no-wellness is going to tak' feet.' "

"She just stood and stared at him, openmouthed.

" 'Do ye no understand me, ma lassie,' he roars. 'Your no-wellness is going to tak' feet and walk. You're expectin', ma lassie: did ye no ken? There, there, dinna greet, ma lassie,' and he starts to pat her on the shoulder, 'you're a proud woman this bonny day. Now just you go away hame and tell your man and he'll be as proud as your sel'. Away you go now, and I'll give a bit look in when I'm passing and see that you're keeping all right. . . .'

"He's dead, now, old Shuggy; but we all mind of him, us colliers that were reared about here. He was a good doctor and whiles more than a doctor. He kicked up hell with the Council to try and get us out of that house on the Shore afore the bairn was born; but a second—Colin—had been born, and the third was five months on the way and the Old Fella had been buried in a roof fall down in the old Seven West Section and the wife was half mad with grief afore we got allocated this house.

"By jings, but she was in her glory here—the wife. You never saw such a change come over a woman because up to then she'd been sorta ill-natured all the time she was carrying Margaret and I put it down to the Old Fella being kilt; but whenever we moved in here it was as if she'd landed in heaven.

"The folk on each side started her away with flowers and cuttings, once they discovered she was fond of such things, and if she saw something she liked in a garden—you know, if we were out walking—she'd not rest until she'd begged a bit root or a seed. Dahlias especially: she was daft about dahlias. And see and mind—everything had to be kept just perfect in the garden.

"Lotta muck!' He snorted the words with such vehemence it was like an explosion.

"I'd sooner have seen it down to a planting of tatties; but you've to buy seed for that, and we'd little money to spare what with the bairns and furnishing the place so I just let her alone till I could get

37

some good rhubarb crowns. I knew what 'd happen to her dahlias then. I knew there'd be trouble, too; but a man has to be master in his own house; especially a miner, because at work he can never be nothing but a slave: like a sailor and the sea."

I knew what he meant. A collier, like a seaman, works with natural forces that he can never entirely control.

Marky shook his head in perplexity. "She worshipped that garden, you know," he said. "The Old Fellas's dog was still living then—it was poisoned a wee while afterwards, by one of those old widdy witches next door, I think, though the wife would never believe it— and it thought the world of the wife . . . followed her every place.

"Would you believe what I'm going to tell you"—he paused for effect—"she even had that old mungerel traint to walk only on the paths!

"As for cats—she just needed to hear a cat and she was out in a flash with a stone in each hand and trying to look three ways at once. I've heard about women taking daft turns, but never afore about a garden: it was ridiculous the way she worshipped it.

"I mind once, in Autumn, coming in off the nightshift afore day-light, I hauled up some of her plants just to see what she'd do. Holy smoke, when she got up and looked out of the windy she was wanting away for the polis there and then and I had to tell her it was me that had done it for a joke. That was the first of me discovering that she had a temper. She went an awful length. In the end I lost the head and drew my hand across her chops.

"White! I've never seen a woman's face go as white as that afore; and it was nigh a month afore she spoke to me again. That's what happens, you see, when you marry out of your class. A collier lassie would have been neether up nor down about getting a thump across the jaw. A woman that's been brought up among us knows that when a fella works in a coalpit he's got to take it out of someone and she's prepared to accept a bit belting now and again just so her man can get things out of his system. But my wife couldna see that.

"It was the same with the garden: a lotta flowers and lawns where she should have been growing food. You could get a packet of swede seeds for tuppence then, but it was no use trying to tell her; she just couldn't see the force of it. If she'd had to rely on the soup kitchens for a meal same as we had in nineteen and twenty-six when we were laddies—but there, she'd never known real hunger.

"Why, when I was a laddie I never knew what it was to feel fed, and my father never lost a shift 'cept during the big strike. He could graft, too, the Old Fella, by cripes but he could work; but he still couldna feed his bairns.

"My wife had never known nothing like that: even if she only got the leavings from rich folks' tables, she was still a thousand times better fed than the family of a working collier. But I never argued about it. I just let her alone until I was ready—her and her dahlias. And see and mind, there's a few more that are going to have to learn the same lesson that she learnt. Aye, there's a lot of them growing roses right now that are in for a rude shock, nationalisation or no nationalisation.

"It'll no be long afore they'll be wishing they had a pot of rhubarb on the stove. Roses are braw for a bride; but they make cussed thin soup.

"That's the advantage of rhubarb for a collier compared to tatties and that: there's just the one planting. A fella that's working at the coalface is no able for a lotta digging when he's up aben. And it's nourishing, mind, by God but it's nourishing. I've seen me boil up a pot of rhubarb just to drink a glass of the juice. I've heard fellas, talking down the pit, say that there's stuff in rhubarb juice, you know, chemicals and that, and things that are no good for you, like acids. They're just havering. My bairns was all reared on rhubarb and you want to see them. I'm big, but you just want to see my laddies: giants, that's what they are—young giants; and Margaret— that's the bairn, though she's a young woman now—my but she's a bonny lassie is my wee Meg. . . ." His voice softened at the name, and faded as nostalgia took hold of him.

I said, but cautiously, "They live with their mother?"

"Aye," he told me, and the word was like a sigh. He went on in a strained, uncertain tone, as though he was feeling for words that eluded him. "Aye," he said. "They bide with her now. Oh, I'll give her that: she always sought after her bairns.

"When she first brought them back she admitted it was only because she couldn't give them a proper home, nor care, with her having to work, and she begged me to let her come through regular

39

and see them. How could I agree to a thing like that ? It would have just meant the bairns getting upset every time she could afford the fare from Glasgow. Na, na, she'd chosen to go away: the best thing she could do was to bide away; and that's what I told her.

"Ah! But she turned up the first Christmas after she'd left: had brought presents for the bairns with her way of it; and mind, she had the hard neck to come right up to the door with them. I wasna long in hunting her away, I can tell you—the bairns were all in bed, anyway. It must have been nearly eleven o'clock on Christmas Eve, and this 'd be her catching the first train after she finished work.

"The first thing I saw next morning was her: she was waiting down the road a bit, under the trees. It was bitter cold with a dreep of sleety rain through the wind, and she was all huddled up in an old coat. Of course, I kept the bairns inside on a cold day like that, and away from the windows. I couldn't afford to mebbe have them running out and catching a chill. Then when it was just about dark, she disappeared, and I took it that she'd had enough and was away back to Glasgow. Later in the evening, thinking that the coast was clear, I went down the street for a pint. I should have known better. She was a fly customer. She'd been hiding, and the minute I rounded the corner she was in here with the weans: playing games with them on my new carpet in front of the fire, and weeping over them: she had wee Meg up to High Doh. . . ."

"What did you do?" I asked.

He sniffed. "Oh, she'd skipped by the time I got back; but by then the damage was done. The bairns were all in tears and the Christmas ruined, and I was up twice through the night with wee Meg greeting for her Mammy—some Mammy. At the finish I had to take the wee soul into bed aside me to get her quietened. Can you imagine a woman doing a thing like that? She musta known it would upset the bairns to see her again. I'd had enough bother with them, as it was, when she first went away; but I was nightshift so I was in the house all day, and a lassie—she was a schoolgirl and the daughter of a chap that worked beside me—used to bide in the house all night, and I paid her for it. Then, after all the bother at the start when we were just getting a bit settled down, that daft eedjit had to turn up like that and upset them all again.

40

"I had all my worries, I can tell you, but I'd have put my bairns in a Home afore I'd 've let her come back, so if that's what was in her mind, she was backing the wrong horse. I'd never 've given her house-room again after what she did to me. . . ."

Tentatively, I asked, "What did she do?"

He said abruptly, aggressively, "She cleared out. She cleared out and left me just because I dug up her flowers to plant rhubarb that we could eat. Oh, h . . ." He paused, and then said slowly, "It didna just happen all at once. She kicked up a fuss about the garden, of course, and I had to give her a hammering. She went in the huff then, for a couple of weeks, but eventually she came out of it and started to talk again as if nothing had happened. Ah, but she was dealing with the wrong man: when they go in the huff with me . . . they can bide in the huff. I was easy what she did; and that's how it was.

"A couple of months musta gone by and I never spoke a word to her. She tried several times to win me over but she was wasting her time as far as I was concerned. She was going to find out that I could be as stubborn as her when I wanted to. On top of that, I didn't trust her. I was pretty sure that when I was out she was leaning over the fence and letting those two old devils on each side sympathise with her. It was all right for them; one was the widdy of the harbourmaster, and the other had a son down in England with a good job who sent home money every week. They could mebbe afford to grow dahlias—we couldn't.

"So there it was: she tried all ways to get me to talk, but she could make nothing of it. You know, Airch, I've no time for people that go in the huff over nothing and I made up my mind to teach her a lesson. It used to madden her, mind; me coming in from my work and talking to the laddies and the bairn and never a word for her. Oh, but it used to make her mad.

"I've seen her standing there at the windy listening to me and the bairns playing and laughing together as if she wasn't there, and she'd scrunch up that wee face of hers and twist her hands till she nearly hauled the fingers off the knuckles.

"In the end she fell back on the old trick that's aye a woman's last resort; you know, in bed, cuddling up and that. She was wasting her time: once my mind's made up, Airch, I'm like a rock. Rock,

41

Airch, just rock. And she had to be taught that she couldna make a fool of me and get away with it. A wee slap across the face for something she'd started anyway, and running outside screeching as if she'd been murdered; and all for them two old witches to hear. She had to be shown where she got off, and I was just the boy to show her.

"After another month she must have realised that she was really up against it this time and she tried to force my hand.

" 'I'd be just as well sleeping with Margaret,' she said one Saturday evening; 'that'll let you have this room to yourself. . . .'

"What a lassie's trick! Honest, Airch, women think men canna do without them. She thought sleeping alone would bring me to heel— what a drop she got. I never even answered her. So that was it: she started sleeping with wee Meg, and after that we'd 've been as well biding in diff'runt houses for all the contact we had.

"Then, one Saturday, a couple of weeks later, I went away to Aberdeen with the local team, and when I got back—it must have been one in the morning—she'd gone: her and the weans; and the house was empty. I suppose she thought that by stealing my bits of bairns away she'd make me toe the line . . . well she was wrong Same as she's been wrong about the divorce. I bet she thought when Mebel started coming here that it 'd provide her with grounds for a divorce: well, she's wrong again. I'd see her fried first."

The chair creaked as the heavy body moved. I saw him put the glass gently on the fireplace tiles. It was strange how the one corner where he sat should be so shadowed when the rest of the room was filled with bright sunlight; it must have been the way the sun shone through the trees outwith the house, and the way the heavy curtains were hung.

"Who is she? Mabel, I mean." I had to ask the question.

He said, and his voice changed and became almost diffident, "She's a girl that came here for her holidays: her and her mother, and we sorta palled up the gither. I said girl, but she'll be all of thirty-one or two. A fine looking woman she is. You should see the body she has on her: just watching her walk across the room makes you take notions. She's a Cath'lic with jet black hair."

42

Men emerge from the cage into the soft afternoon sunshine while others savour the last precious moments of daylight before their downward journey into the darkness

He made a strange sound in his throat that was meant to be a cough, but it was too thin and effeminate to be a collier's cough, and said dreamily—

"It was a couple of year back: just a few months afore the bairn went through to Glasgow to bide. . . ."

"Margaret?" I said in surprise, "your daughter?"

"Aye," he grunted. "They're all through with their mother now. Melville went as soon as he was eighteen. At the time he was training as a draughtsman and he was supposed to have been sent through to one of the big shipyards on the Clyde; but he never came back. I went after him but the polis said there was nothing I could do. So long as he was turned eighteen, he could bide where he pleased.

"Colin left sooner. He went into the sodgers at fifteen as a boy entrant—he never had the brains of Melville, Colin didna, and anything's better than the pits—and when his first leave arrived and he never came home I knew where he'd landed.

"The bairn stuck to me, though: aye, that she did. Fair away with herself she was; you know, looking after the house, here, and me going out to the pit every night. She loved being the housekeeper—even when she was dressed I've seen her put a pinny on to go out to the baker's van so the neighbours would ken she was doing the house. Aye, we got on grand, the bairn and me. And see and mind, she's a braw wee housewife—my wee Meg: the laddie that gets her 'll get a wife in a million. . . ."

"But she has left, too." I asked the question softly, easing it out in a half-whisper.

"Aye," he said. "It was after I went through to Glasgow the first time to see Mabel—just a week-end at the New Year; but when I came back on the Monday, Meg was away. But she writes to me."

His voice now, in spite of its pathetically defiant note, was a desperate plea for understanding—"Aye writes to her Dadda and tells me what's happening with the laddies and what she's been doing herself. She gotten on to be a typist now and she's a braw job in some big office. She said something in the first letter about her Mammy telling her to write to me, but I'm no believing that: my wee Meg would never need to be telt to write to her Dadda—she aye clung to me. . . ."

43

He fell silent then, and his beefy face, striped with light and shadow, was like a Chinese lantern seen through a slatted screen. One huge hand lay against the leg of his trousers and the collier-white flesh shone leprously against the dark background of the cloth.

Looking at that great paw, I could not help but think of all the wealth it had produced: the black gold hacked and hewn out of the deep dark twisted guts of the wet-gleaming rock. I thought of what he had told me of his life, and I felt as though a great wave of hopelessness had washed over me leaving me utterly sad and forlorn.

There is so much of what one might call unavoidable misery, and so little joy in life, that it is cruelty to ourselves to lose a single smile. I stared at that big blue-scarred hand, hanging so limply now, and I thought of the sorrow his stubbornness had brought . . . and for what ? She has garnered a few sticks and made another home as the human animal always will; and she has gathered her children about her, while he, like a dumb ox, is left to wallow in the dark stall of his senseless vanity. Such a pity: such a great pity.

For there is only the one life and it is so quickly spent; and we return to the void from which we came, and in a little small while we are as unknown as we were before we came into the world.

Our children may spare us a thought when they are old and nostalgia is having its way with them. Then, they too die, and we, together with our lusts and our prides, our stupidities and our strivings and clutchings, are forgotten. For a few years more our only hope of memory is the chance reference a grandchild may make; we have become no more than the necessary adjunct to an adult remembering of childhood.

After that the final silence descends and we are no more.

I felt suddenly, sitting opposite this resentful man—this guilty man who yet raged at fate and whose very guilt was useless for he could not comprehend it and was aware only of a sense of injured innocence—that the whole sorry business had been revealed to me in one precise vision of infinite clarity, so that I saw, as from on high, the whole of the tragedy that is Man—and the Life of Man; and, so powerful was this sensation that, torn between foreboding and compassion, and an urge to announce the revelation, I half rose in my chair.

My sudden jerk of movement stirred Marcus and he sighed and I sat quietly down again and waited his words.

"It was three years back, at the tail of the winter," he resumed his story. "You mind that old Heading down the East Crosscut. . . ."

I nodded.

"I got my leg bruck down there," he said, "the coal come over on top of me and I was off my work for six months. I've always been a saving fella when I had a bit to save, and I had a wee thing put by; but that was a long spell to be out to grass, and after four months I was about skint. Well, you know what it's like about here at the holiday time: most of the folk that have a room to spare take in visitors. So, I put an advert in the paper, too; and that's who came— Mabel and her mother, an old widdy. They came from Glasgow for a fortnight, but they liked it that much—the house and the view of the sea and that—they stayed for a month: least, the Old Lady did: Mabel had to go back to her work, but she came through at the week-ends.

"I got on awful well with them. The old wife took over the running of the house from Meg and you could see the difference right away. The bairn had been doing well for a young lassie, but you could hardly expect her to be as tidy as a grewn woman; and Mabel used to muck in, too, at the week-ends.

"I missed them after they went back. I'd never seen the place so clean. They asked me through to spend the New Year with them, and since the bairn left, I've got in the habit of going through most week-ends, or, if it's the summer, they come through here. She works in a big store, Mabel, in the clothing department. Here . . .!"

He lumbered to his feet and grabbed at my arm. "Come upstairs with me," he said excitedly, "and I'll let you see something."

I climbed behind him up well-carpeted stairs to a sunbright, spotless bedroom, and he proudly pulled out drawer after drawer and displayed the contents.

"By jings, you've got some clothes there, Markie," I breathed at his shoulder. Shirts, pullovers, socks, underwear; shirts especially. "You've enough there for an army; they're all split new, too; when do you ever wear them?"

"Ach," he said, and slammed the last drawer shut with a sudden air of despondence. "I was never a great one for dressing up, and I'm seldom out 'cept going back and for'ard to the pit; and any old rags do for that."

I said, in an attempt to cheer him, "I wish I had a wardrobe like that: there's enough there to see you to the grave."

He nodded his head with a sort of bovine gravity. "Aye," he said thickly. "She's good to me, is Mabel. She's good to me. See this room." He waved his arm about him. "This is her room when she's here." He moved to the window and stood there, staring with his big eyes at the trees along the pavement verge, and at the leaves, fanning gently in the clear bright air.

He said, without looking round, "Aye, this is Mabel's room: it was her put up these fancy curtains and that quilt on the bed. Aye, and I've been through hell on that same bed. Would you believe that, Airch. I've been through torment on that bed. I don't just rightly know how it all came about. I think she called me up here to help her with something in the afternoon, one day, and her Old Lady was away out shopping—but we finished up on that bed there. I dunno how it all came about because Mabel's a respectable girl. But there it was and it was a near thing, I can tell you that, Airch, a near thing. I was about off my head that day, Airch, and Mabel wasna in much better state. I wouldn't like to go through the same again, Airch, no, that I wouldn't. I'll never be nearer making a fool of myself . . . and Mabel—she told me afterwards that she nearly let me have my way, but she thought of the Sacred Heart of Jesus, and it saved her." He looked at me with his big round shining eyes, and I was forced to look away.

"Can you imagine," he asked me, "what that poor creature must have suffered that day?" He shook his head in respectful wonderment and led me downstairs again with the short tripping steps that are so much a feature of heavily-built men.

I said to the back of his bristly head, "But surely, Marky, if you are as desperate as all that for each other—and from what you've told me, it would suit her mother to live here—why don't you . . .?"

He shook his head reprovingly. "She's a Cath'lic," he reminded me. "I'd need to get a divorce and everything. . . ."

Opening the back door he waved me out first and we stood together in the bright sunshine. Out there in the air I realised the true oppression of the house. I felt as if I had been released from prison.

"And she's her mother to think of," he continued. "It'd break her Old Lady's heart if Mabel did anything wrong and her no married. I wouldn't like to upset her because she's a good old body, is Mabel's mother: she's looked well after my interests. It's her that gets me all the news about the wife and the bairns. She has friends that live near where the wife bides, you see. It's a useful thing to have a spy in the enemy's camp. It was her that found out about the fancy-man; if it hadn't been for that I might have fallen for the wife's fly move."

I stared at the thick neck, pitted from youthful acne; at the cropped head of sandy hair; at the great shoulders and powerful back.

"Fancy-man," I said: "what do you mean?"

He did not answer immediately but bent down and began to wrench off rhubarb stalks. As soon as he had a handful, he half-turned and held them up to me. When he did answer my question, he spoke without looking up.

"A wee while back," he muttered, "the wife wrote me asking for a divorce. It was a plausible, sympathising sorta letter and, as it came just after Mabel and me had had that rough and tumble on the bed, I was half inclined to give in and let her have her way. Ah! But would you believe it; this is the fly bitch taken up with a fancy-man and wanting to get married to him. It was Mabel's mother that found it out: if she hadn't told me what was going on I'd have made a right monkey of myself. A divorce; so that she can marry him— whoever he is—and settle down with my bairns and live happy ever after: not on your Nellie! But it's a good job Mabel's Old Lady had her spies out or I might have fallen for the trick. . . ."

"But surely. . . ." I began, and then stopped as the heavy head wagged refusal over the rhubarb leaves.

"Never," he growled, and the word seemed to strike the earth and rebound upwards through the red stems and the flat, thick-veined leaves. "Never," he growled again with even greater vehemence. "Never! I'll see her roasted afore I'll give her a divorce. She made her bed—well, she can lie on it: if she canna get sleeping that's just too bad; but I'll never give her a divorce."

47

"That'll do, Marky," I said. "That'll do fine: that's as much as I can carry."

He looked round at the great armfuls I held, his expression bemused, as though he could hardly believe he had pulled so much. He stood up and ran a probing finger round his neck between the jersey collar and the skin. He was panting after the exertion, and he spoke in short gasps.

"There's plenty—you'll get more anytime you're needing it—just look in anytime—there's not much gets used now—and I'd burn it afore I'd give any to those two old witches next door. Each year, at the back-end—when it's jam-making time—I pull what's left and dig it in just to spite 'em."

I turned away with my load, and he followed me to the front and held open the gate for me to go through; then he laid his hands on the top spar and rested his weight on his wrists.

"You know," he said thoughtfully, "I've often wondered what would happen if we could get to find out, while we were still laddies, what sort of life lay afore us . . . I've often wondered. . . ."

"Well," I said firmly, "I must away: thanks a lot."

He jerked his head and muttered, "You're welcome."

Glad to escape, I marched off, but after a few yards he called to me.

"That's the tree: mind I was telling you about her standing chittering all one night under a tree. That's it, the one you're just passing. . . ."

I fought successfully the impulse to look back; but his shout took me astray and the armful of stalks I carried brushed against the bark with a sound like tearing silk, so that it seemed as though the very tree had sighed for pity's sake.

Walking homewards I thought about Marky, and wondered at a pride so fiercely, blindly stupid that it could destroy a man's innate humanity: destroy it so completely that nothing was left but the semblance of a brute beast which, while kicking savagely in the swamp that sucks it down, still pauses to rub its hot, tortured hide against the walls of its tomb, luxuriating in the sweet coolth of the deadly mud. I thought of all the things I would have said to Marky had I not known it would be fruitless, and I said them now, to the empty street.

"Do you think it will matter," I demanded of the pavements, "that you have refused to surrender a position that you took up twenty years ago in a fit of anger; do you think it will count for anything that you held out; do you think it will make a single jot of difference to the world and the countless millions who are unhappy through no fault of their own, that you, who might have lived happily, chose instead to be miserable ?

"You have lost your children and your wife; you are without a home—for that place I have just left is only a house. Even today, when you could still, perhaps, pluck a little pleasure from the tree of existence, and allow others to do the same, you will not unbend and admit that you are lonely. If all this anguish was to achieve some immortal end, I still could not endure it; but it will not be remembered tomorrow. Oh, what a waste: what a cruel, sinful waste!

"For an infinitesimal second of our endless journey through the darkness, we are permitted that tiny light which we call life. And you, Marky, must obscure your little gleam with a hood of needless sorrow."

A couple of months later, on a Thursday, just after midnight, Marky was killed. The whole length of the face 'took a seat' as the collier says, and we had to run for it. Everyone got clear except Marky and the two men who were with him. The bodies were never recovered for the lower end had shut tight.

Coming home from the football match on Saturday, a week or two later, I passed the end of the street where Marky had lived. I remembered the rhubarb. And I remembered too, for the leaves of the trees were sealskin-streaked and brittle in the winds' fingers, that it was jam-making time.

That evening after dark I walked round to the empty house with a spade and a sack.

"*In a world of canteens, tea-trolleys to the work-bench and sporting commentaries relayed to the shop floor, the collier still squats amid the livid puffballs of decay with his 'piece' and his flask; his seat a rock and all around him the damp odours of the underworld.*"

CHAPTER FOUR

TRILOGY . . . . . ESCAPE

Part 1—The Man Who Ate Grass

FOR several months during the final stages of my 'face' training
I was constant nightshift, working on a coalcutting machine as
second man to Nicholas McFish—Nicky as we called the wiry, small
man with the quick wit and the slow tones of the West of Scotland.
With his droll face and puckish eyes, he was like a laughing gnome
of the underworld.

There were but four of us in the section at night. Myself and
Nicky, and working in front of us, the two propdrawers—Old Angus
Cuddie, the leading man, and his neighbour, a youth called McCodd.

As the waste roof supports were drawn or knocked out the roof
collapsed at our sides with a shattering, dust-clouded roar. As each
drift fell we huddled against the unfriendly face which offered a
spurious shelter, and the two propdrawers made wild leaps in search
of a dubious safety.

It is an unwritten law of the pits that cuttermen do not cut past
steeldrawers. For besides the terrific increase of roof pressures which
follow the cutting process, the noise set up in that confined space by
the whirling picks as they tear blindly at the hard black wall is
deafening, and like all colliers the propdrawers rely on hearing more
than any other sense. Each roof creak, each strained whisper from a
cracking prop; every sound bears its own vital message to the grim-
faced, crouching collier.

If, as sometimes happened, we drew too near the straining men,
Cuddie would turn his round, moon-like face towards us and roar,
"Switch that muckin' brass band aff, willya, an gie'us a chance tae
hear what's happening. We're goin' tae get buried yet over the head
a' yu two bastards."

And Nicky would reply, "Ah shut yure pus, yu greetin' faced ole blether." But he would switch off the power and we would huddle companionably against the long, low machine. And squatting there Nicky would suck at the piece of coal in his mouth and talk. For to Nicky, talking was the very breath of life. Hunched there in the darkness with bright, bird-like eyes ever wandering watchfully from roof to face to waste and back again, Nicky would tell me stories.

His droll lips would pour out words that I hardly knew whether to believe or not and his pawky, cynical smile would deride man and his world; his futile hopes and dreams and sorrows in this life, which is such a brief and feeble glimmer before the everlasting darkness and decay that awaits us all.

"Och," he signed once, as we crouched waiting. "Ah whisht Ah wis back in the army again. Nae worries, nae responsibilities. Food, claes, money, all provided. Nothin' tae dae but walk aboot in ma nice new battledress, sayin', 'Yes Sir' or 'No Sir' as the situation required. Gie me war, onytime. Yu can hae yure muckin' peace."

"You might have been killed in Burma," I reminded him. "Aye," he agreed, "an' Ah micht get killed doon here. In fact Ah've a better chance o' gettin' killed doon here than Ah ever had in the Army. Na, Na, it wis a braw life, an' every Friday yu just walked up tae the pay table an' held oot yure hand."

"Yes," I said, "but you didn't get much of a wage in it."

"No," he conceded, "but they're wis nae corns an' blisters on the hand Ah wis haudin' oot either. An' Ah felt like a human being tae, no a bliddy black ape."

I said thoughtfully, "I've never met a miner yet who didn't hate the pit."

"An' yu never will," drawled Nicky. "In every collier's heart there's a department labelled 'Hoo tae escape frae the pits.' It's like them filing cabinets they have in offices. Ye ken, like yu see on the T.V. Well, as the miner goes through life, them that survive long enough tae go onywhere that is, he's fer ever dreaming aboot gettin' awa. He hears aboot jobs he could mebbe dae. He prays fer war tae break oot an' studies the political scene, so as tae be ready tae jump intae khaki quick afore the bliddy Government can stop him wi' a Direction of Labour Act. Ah tell yu, by the time the average collier is forty he's gathered a hale office fu' o' information on hoo tae get oota the pits."

"There's a lot of talk just now," I said, "of the increasing use of oil and the approach of Atomic Energy. They may close all pits and the Miners Union doesn't seem to like the idea."

"That's the Union," Nicky snapped. "Never mind the Union, it's the collier Ah'm talkin' aboot, an' as far as we're concerned they can shut the muckin' lot the morn. In fact Ah'll stay oota ma bed an' help em' tae fill in the shaft o' this one. Na, na, the working collier'll no worry aboot pits bein' shut. As far as we're concerned, it's the sooner the better."

"And how are we going to live?" I enquired, not without malice. "You won't get fat on the dole."

"Ah've a better chance o' fattening up on the dole than Ah have doon here. Don't worry, we'll live a'richt—we never died in winter yet. An' since the Yanks bought the British Empire off the Labour Party things are better still. Our new owners tak' an' awfy interest in what's goin' on over here y' ken. They'll no let us starve, don't you worry. When a man's bairns get hungry the first thing he does is tae join the Communist Party. Can you see the Yanks sittin' quietly by an' watchin' seven hundred thousand miners, the most militant section of the British workin' class, move intae the ranks o' the reds? Aye, that'll be richt," he laughed sardonically.

"Ah tell yu, the dollars'd just flow in. We'd prob'ly hae tae open the shaft again tae store the food parcels for British miners that'd be comin' over in shiploads. Shut the pits, aye, the bliddy lot, an' as soon as they like. The Yanks'll keep us. Oota fear a' what we micht dae."

"But," I insisted, "In spite of what you say about colliers hating the pits, and I agree, it's true, most of them are still in the pits."

Nicky sighed. "Aye," he said softly. "But ye must mind that tae be a collier is no just tae hae a certain job, but to follow a way o' life. An' once a man gets settled intae a way o' life it's hard fer him tae change it. 'Specially once he's married an' got bairns. But let a war, or an economic crisis like the big strikes in the twenties, force men oota the pits and they never come back. Look at the advertising the Coal Board has done since the war tae try an' get men. Heavens, they musta spent millions. Aye, men mebbe stay in the pits but even

53

a collier can hae his dreams. Man, Ah tell yu, there's been some queer dodges thought up tae escape from this." He indicated our tomb-like surroundings with an all-embracing wave of a thin, blue-scarred hand.

"Why," he said, "there wis one fella learnt tae eat grass."

"What?" I cried, but the puckish wee face was straight and solemn.

"Ah'm tellin' ye," Nicky's voice was emphatic. "He learnt tae eat grass."

"But how . . .?"

"It took a while, o' cos." Nicky shifted the piece of coal in his mouth and spat. "It happened a few years ago," he went on. "Nineteen forty-eight, Ah think it wis. The pit wis nationalised onyway, not that that made ony muckin' difference, so it musta been after nineteen forty-six. That's what started this bloke off. He'd come back tae the pits after the war under the delusion that things would be changed.

"It wasnae long afore he fund oot that the Government had nae intention o' changing onything. It near broke his bliddy hairt. He was a bachelor but he wis fifty year old an' that's a bit late tae change one's whole way of life, but he wis determined tae get oota the pits. He had a wee, twa-room hoose doon by the beach that wis his ain prop'ty, so he'd nae rent tae pay. All he had tae worry aboot wis grub. We wis warkin' in the same section at the time an' he useter tell me a' his plans.

"Well, at first o' cos, he got nowhere. But one nicht he brings oot an article he'd cut from a paper. This was by some Professor, an' this Professor wrote that eventually the scientists would do away wi' coos an' such-like. Apparently coos tak' a' life-giving food frae the grass and convert it, an' then we eat the beef an' milk an' cheese. Well, someday there wis goin' tae be nae coos because it wis such a slow an' wasteful system. Instead, we would get our food direct frae the grass. In fact this Professor said there wis nae reason why a human being couldn't live on grass noo. It was just a matter of giving the human stomach time to assimilate the new diet.

"Well, this fella Ah'm tellin' ye aboot wis a richt determined bastard. Gie him time an' he'd pluck a rubber duck.

54

" 'Nicky,' he says, 'Ah'm goin' tae try that. Ah'll gie masel'
three months fer ma stomach tae get used tae it.'

" 'Away,' Ah says, 'Yu daft goat, yu'll dee o' starvation.' Ah——
but there wis nae shiftin him. He goes on to a grass diet. It's a
bliddy good job it wis the spring o' the year, Ah'll tell yu. Every
morning when we come up the pit he'd go roon' the roads wi' a
sack, plucking grass from the verges."

With the physical dexterity of the true collier, Nicky went from
hunkers to knees in one graceful movement. Kneeling, he urinated
against the conveyors and dropped effortlessly back on to his
haunches.

"Well," I demanded, "did it work?"

"Aye," Nicky nodded, "it worked, an' Ah'll tell yu this, there
was no-one mair surprised than me. But oh, he wis a dogged one
this. An' what he suffered at first! Man, yu've nae idea what that
fella went through. At the end o' the first month he wis doon tae
seven stanes an' useless fer face wark. Christ, he could hardly lift a

pick. So he got a light job watching a pump. Then, at the end o' another two months he puts in his notice. He wis a pair lookin' creeture, Ah can tell yu. Naethin' but skin an' bane. Ah've seen mair fat on a butcher's knife. But by Christ, he'd managed it. He wis living on naethin' but grass an' could leave the pits fer good.

"Ah used tae see him noo an' again during the summer. He'd be roaming the road verges wi' his sack. An' Ah'm tellin' yu, he wis as fit as a fiddle. Broon face, an' eyes as bright as dollars on a nigger's backside. Nae use fer wark, o' cos; he'd nae strength, but he didnae need strength; he wis finished wi' wark.

"He telt me he wis doin' fine, an' when Ah crawled doon this bliddy, black hole every nicht Ah used tae envy him, Ah can tell yu.

"But he slipped up in one thing—he forgot the winter. O' cos, he couldnae eat a' the grass he collected, an' he did dry an' store some of it. But the grass yu get at roadsides is only muck an' it doesnae mak' a good quality hay. In the Autumn, when he realised what was in front o' him, he had tae stop an' consider. An' what dae Ah see, one night in October, but him stannin' in the pit bottom. O' cos, Ah wanted tae know what wis wrang, an' he telt me his plan.

"It seems he wasnae gettin' enough nourishment from the muck he'd saved. But a' summer when he wis roamin' aboot collectin' grass he'd kept passin' a wee field o' pasture. Aboot five acres, he said, an' the best o' feedin', either as green food or as hay fer winter. He realised that if he could just get aholt o' that field he wis set up fer life. The richness o' the verdure had made his mooth watter wi' envy a' summer. So he approached the farmer and the old boy wis willin' tae sell . . . at forty pun' an acre.

"Well, an Ah telt yu, he wis a determined cus this. He'd a' g[1]o shite oota a wooden hoss. An' this is him back at the pit tae earn the dough fer his field. Oh Hell!, it wis pitifu' tae watch him tryin' tae dae a shift's wark. Ma neighbour had been hurt an' wis aff, an' so the old crank wis sent wi' me.

"Ah tell yu, the fust couple o' weeks Ah had tae carry him. He wis willin' enough mind, but he just didnae hae the strength. An' at snacktime . . . Man, it woulda' bruk yure hairt tae see him. Sittin' there in the dark munchin' a wisp o' straw, an' the rest o' us wallopin' intae bread an' cheese or jam.

"Well, o' course, it couldnae go on like that. Ye ken yersel' what face wark's like. Yu need the best o' grub an' plenty o' it if only tae replace the sweat yu lose.

"Ah made up my mind tae hae a word wi' him. After a', Ah'm no able fer twa men's wark. But the very next morning, when Ah comes oota the baths, who's goin' intae the canteen ahead o' me but his nibs.

" 'It's nae use, Nicky,' he tells me when we wis sittin' doon. 'Ah'll need tae eat human food again till Ah've warked fer that money. It'll no be long,' he says. 'Six months'll do it if there's nae accidents.' "

Swinging his head round Nicky studied the sweating prop-drawers, straining in the waste a few yards ahead of where we sat.

"Hope they're no goin' tae be a' nicht," he muttered almost to himself. "Or we'll hae tae flee like maniacs tae get finished, an' fleein' in a coal pit's ower bliddy dangerous."

"Ah—man," he went on. "It woulda made yu weep, watching this pair bastard. He suffered mair gettin' back tae human food than he had goin' on tae grass. Ah tell yu, he muckin' near killed hissel'. Just to show yu. Yu ken that canteen parrige?—it's that thin that after a bowl o' thon yu've tae run up the road wi' a cork fer fear yu dinna get hame in time. Well—THAT STUFF—wis too heavy fer him! Man, it woulda bruk yure heart what he went through. Ah wouldna a' believed a man coulda' survived sufferin' like thon."

"But he did," I exclaimed.

"Aye," Nicky drawled. "Aye, he stuck it oot. Ah tell yu, he wis a determined ole bastard this. He coulda' learnt a cat tae swim, him. It took twelve months though, no six. He wis never awa frae the doctor's an' the chemist's. His bliddy stomach wis ruined. It musta' cost him a fortune fer pills. They even wanted tae operate, but he wouldna' let em'. He stuck it oot an' earned the money an' bought his field as he'd planned."

"And then . . .?" I asked curiously.

"An' then," Nicky said sadly, "he had tae start learning tae live on grass again. Oooh . . . fer Christ's sake . . .!"

I followed the beam of Nicky's light to where Cuddy and his neighbour crouched against the face.

"What're yu sittin' there for," Nicky roared. "Are we goin' tae get on wi' oor wark or no? We're wantin' finished tae, yu ken."

"One o' these nichts," Cuddy howled, "Ah'll toss yu an' your bliddy coalcutter intae that waste afore Ah draw it." Then grudgingly, "Aye—yu can come on a bit noo."

"It'd tak' a man tae toss me in the waste," grinned Nicky as he turned to the controls. "No a crimson-arsed, ole ape like yu."

Before the hellish clatter of the machine could start I touched his arm. "Wait," I said urgently. "What happened to that chap? Did he manage to get back on a grass diet again?"

"Na," Nicky said provokingly. "That's him on the propdrawing. That coo-faced ole bastard up there, that's him." He hauled up the clutch, and his eyes, framed in the light of my caplamp, were laughing mischievously.

* * * * * * * *

Part 2—William the Workless

WILLIAM'S arrival at the Hostel had all the aspects of a visitation from a hitherto unknown world.

His clothes, if not of Saville Row, looked as though they were, which is, after all, what matters. The curls in his hair had not been placed there by Nature, but that, after all, is not what matters.

He appeared to have shoes, socks, shirts and handkerchiefs to match the various shades of his many suits. To the Hostel residents who possessed, as a rule, one shirt and pair of shoes apiece, one pair of socks between three persons and no handkerchiefs at all, William was a blatant example of unbridled luxury that took their collective breath away.

William's arrival shocked the Hostel to its prefabricated, ferro-concrete block foundations. The effect produced by William became apparent everywhere. If a new advent was not proclaimed it was certainly accepted, and residents and staff reacted in a variety of ways, each according to his own particular idea of sartorial salvation.

A great many sacrificial fires were lit on the altar of borrowed tobacco. Huge quantities of rum were consumed—on tick, of course—as an aid to cogitation.

Miss Bootle, the housekeeper, with the approval of Miss Black-thorne, the Manageress, changed the ancient, greenshaded black-out curtains, substituting for these sombre old friends atrocious peculiarities in what was termed folkweave.

The roller towel at the sink in the Dining Hall, where the residents forgot to wash their dishes but always remembered to wipe their grubby hands, was now changed daily.

Lucia, the glamorous typist, who for months had sulked at the corner desk, now demanded her turn at the Reception Window. A housemaid in 'A' block had a perm, a housemaid in 'C' block could not afford a perm and contemplated suicide, but compromised by having her teeth out—all three of them.

An assistant cook returned her engagement ring to a Polish Prince who was now deputy-junior-assistant-ratcatcher at the Motley Pit.

A resident in 'B' block bought, not without misgivings, a pair of socks. Three days later another ambitious, but impecunious, resident stole them from the drying room.

Several residents, in a final onslaught of despair, tried work. It was reported later that one of them reached the previously, unheard-of-total of four shifts in one week.

McKenna enrolled seven new members of the envious, suffering proletariat in the Hostel Communist Party. A rise in pay for miners could not have created a greater stir.

Not content with the spiritual chaos, of which he was the un-conscious cause, William further provoked Hostel speculation by being, and remaining, a mystery.

Each morning at 9.29 a.m., attired as for a diplomatic function in 'Free Europe,' he strolled into the Dining Hall with a careless elegance that stunned his envious watchers. Serving of breakfasts ceased promptly at 9.30 a.m. He ate alone, displaying no wish to join any of the noisy groups of late breakfasters. For lunch he appeared at 12.59, thus avoiding the backshift whose meal finished at one, and finishing before the arrival of a sweaty, vociferous day-shift at two.

For the rest of the time he was, to a large extent, invisible. Occa-sionally he was seen entering or leaving the Hostel, attired as always in the height of fashion and with the benign air of a man of ample leisure.

As he appeared to toil not nor spin, his presence at the Hostel was questioned officially by a suspicious McKenna, Communist secretary of the Residents' Committee. For the Hostel was for N.C.B. employees only. But McKenna was informed coldly by Miss Blackthorne that William was a miner, and what was more, had the documents to prove it.

Retiring discomfited from the Manager's office he sought for ways to trap the artless William, for McKenna's soul was steeped in the endless ramifications of a bitter class war. He found it hard to reconcile an aristocratic air and bourgeoise habiliments to what he saw as the socially-correct status of an underground manual worker. He neglected no opportunity to observe the apparently aimless wanderings of the well-dressed stranger. McKenna had all the dogged persistence of the Marxist-trained, and gradually the following facts emerged.

Every second Friday William was observed entering or leaving the Manager's office at one of the local pits—there were eight in the district. Every second Friday William was seen at one of them, having had, or waiting to have, an interview with the Manager of that particular colliery.

Every second Monday William was to be seen in pit clothes. Again, every second Monday, he was at a different pit. McKenna was dubious but there could be no doubt of it.

Stan, the Hostel's chief male gossip, reported him at the Motley. Mick Maguire had seen him at the Lady Eleanor. Ladislas Staniswyk found him at the check-box of the Magdalene. McKenna, sifting the evidence, was convinced of its truth, for William in pit clothes was, if possible, more impressive than William in the garments of civilization.

His brass carbide lamp shone like a golden eagle from the front of a new, black, shiny, safety helmet. His glossy moleskin trousers actually had a crease. The buckles of his kneepads reflected the light with a myriad twinkles. The steel-shod toes of his pit boots appeared to be chromium-plated, and polished at that. He carried a pick, mash and shovel, and these, too, were new and unused. There could be no doubting the evidence. William, the cynosure of all eyes, strolled like a subterranean Apollo through the dusty, heat-oppressed obscurity of the pit head baths.

No one, however, had seen William down a pit—nor for that matter in the cage, which is the first, heart-shattering step in the miner's daily Odyssey. The furthest that William seemed to get was the check-box, and here, every second Monday, his pilgrimage appeared to end, and he returned disconsolate, but unsoiled, to the baths.

As the mystery deepened, so waxed greater the curiosity of the Hostel in general and McKenna in particular.

"He's no miner," swore McKenna doggedly.

"Kathie in the office telt me he is," said Stan. "He had the form from the Labour Relations Officer and he couldn't get that if he wasn't." Syntax, it will be noted, was not Stan's strong point, though he could claim a careless familiarity with the first syllable, spent with a 'i'.

"I think he's a Coal Board Official," put in George the Highlander.

"But he don't never go down a pit." It was Tommy the Norwegian.

"That's why I think it," and George grinned with the sweet simplicity of a logical mind.

"Aye," said McKenna doubtfully. "But in that case, whaurs his car? Nah, nah! if he was a Coal Board Offeecial he'd hae a big car at the taxpayers expense."

"There's one thing certain," said Louis the French Pole, "if he continues to do nothing with such obvious ability a car cannot be withheld much longer."

"He don't stay here if he's a Coal Board man." Alphonse's white teeth flashed in his black negro face. "Dey keep him in big hotel. Two-tree pound a day place."

Martin said quietly, "I don't think he is a Coal Board Official." They listened with interest, for Martin, who came from Edinburgh, was a pacifist and was doing his National Service in the pits. This, in the opinion of the mining community, was the action of an idiot and it had ensured Martin the reputation of a lunatic. They regarded him with the awe that all primitive peoples give to the insane.

Even among people other than miners he would have been considered, to say the least of it, peculiar, for he read the Bible with evident enjoyment and had once stated in public that the New Testament was not an official handbook for the conduct of Rangers-Celtic games.

"I spoke to him the other day," Martin went on. "He is quite intelligent. Without waiting to see the effect of this ironic bombshell, Martin, sinking back in his chair, returned to Damascus and the Street called Straight.

McKenna glanced at him with faint respect. "I'm goin' to find out," he grunted. "I'm goin' to find out, and if he aint a miner he's goin', an' quick too." There was a murmur of assent from the group.

"Filled your coupon in yet, George?" Stan returned with relief to more important matters. McKenna scrambled to his feet and hurried away. "What's wrong wi' him?," asked Stan of the assembly. Martin looked up. "You can hardly expect a Communist to enjoy a discussion of football pools," he told them primly.

"Why not?"

"McKenna's filled with missionary ardour. His life is devoted to saving the proletariat."

"What's that got to do with the coupons?," asked Stan aggressively.

Martin looked at the Dundonian in mild consideration. He went on. "You must remember, Stan, that the burning desire of every member of the proletariat is to leave that magic circle with the utmost despatch." He smoothed down the page of his Bible. "Given fifty years of football pools there won't be any proletariat." He chuckled. "McKenna finds it difficult to contemplate that awful prospect with equanimity," he added.

There was a puzzled silence. Martin saw, not without a faint sadness, that his remarks had been wasted. "Never mind," he said with sudden hopelessness and went back to his reading.

In the end it was Stan who plumbed the mystery. It was nearly fourteen weeks since William's arrival. They had become almost accustomed to his nonchalant passage through the variegated life of the Hostel.

On the day in question Stan was leaning inelegantly on the counter of the Hostel shop. He was interested, not in the wares exposed for sale, but in the shapely legs of the shop's custodian. It was Saturday morning. He had money, and not a care in the world. For the rest of the week he would have no money, and all the cares in the world. Stan was happily following the oldest occupation in history— waiting for the pubs to open.

William sauntered through the main entrance. He gave Elsie a polite good-morning, nodded graciously to Stan and entered the red public telephone box next door to the shop.

Elsie leaned swiftly across the counter. "He's booked out," she whispered. Stan looked into her wide, brown eyes. "Is that right?," he asked, matching his tone to hers.

"Yes," she said softly, and nodded towards the reception office. "Lucia told me. He paid his bill this morning up to Monday afternoon."

Stan whistled under his breath. Burdened with information, he started to move away. William's voice came clearly, seductively through the defective, half-open door of the booth.

"Hello," he said. "Is that Blackdepth's Colliery? It is, good! May I speak to the Manager?"

There was a pause, and then again—"Good-morning. I have some information I think may be of use to you. My name?—it would mean nothing to you. In any case when you hear what I have to say I am sure you will agree it is better that I remain incognito."

William's voice was the cool, cultured aridity of upper class probity, in which blossomed the edged flower of a faint authority. It was a voice calculated to impress.

"I understand," William went on, "that yesterday employment was sought at your colliery by a person calling himself"—there was a rustle of paper as though he were referring to a document— "W. G. Watkins."

There was a brief crackle of faint syllables. Stan's ears were standing up like an Alsatian's. "You will understand," said William, "that I give you this information from a sense of civic responsibility, certainly not from any animosity towards the individual concerned." There was a suggestive silence. "This man," the sauve, polished voice went on, "is a fanatical communist agitator. He came to this district from the Lothians. I can tell you, in confidence, he was hounded out of that area. If you employ him, a matter that you must

63

decide for yourself, I think I can guarantee that your pit will be a hot-bed of industrial unrest—within a month—probably, completely idle. . . . In any case, half-paralysed with strikes and disputes."

William was silent. There was a crackling vagueness of distant expletives. Stan was transfixed with horror. He was a Communist, Stan. Politics were a lost world to his football, sex-drugged mind. But he had been long enough in the pits to acquire to the full the blind, unthinking, tragically-beautiful loyalty of the miner.

He turned to Elsie. Her eyes met his in an understanding glance. "You heard," he said bitterly.

"Yes," she told him evenly. "I heard." Elsie was a miner's daughter. Stan hurried away to the billiard room.

William left the telephone box with the satisfied smile of a job well done. He stopped to exchange a few words with a strangely-distant Elsie. There was a sudden hubbub of noise from the direction of the Games Room. A group of men pushed through the doors of the lounge and advanced threatingly on William. A group consisting of seven nationalities, four colours and twelve men.

"Hey," said McKenna, who was in the lead. "Hey, you!"

William glanced languidly at an expensive wristwatch. He yawned with gentle emphasis behind a well-manicured hand. "Yes?," he said incuriously.

The hostile group closed round him. "What was the idea o' reporting that fella?," demanded McKenna.

"What fellow?," William asked mildly.

"Fella——," McKenna paused uncertainly.

"Watkins," said Stan helpfully. "W. G. Watkins. Elsie heard him too." "That's right," said Elsie with a glance of disdain at the imperturbable William.

"Come on," shouted McKenna. "Don't act dumb. The fella that got a job at Blackdepth's yesterday. That fella you just reported to the Manager as a Communist agitator."

"Ah yes. Chap called Watkins. The Manager informed me that he signed on on Friday to start Monday." The cool correctness of William's voice provoked the angry men to a low growl of infinite menace.

"Fat chance he's got o' starting on Monday now," said McKenna, "after what you done."

"I can assure you," said William, "that there is not the slightest chance of him starting on Monday. Or on any other day for that matter. His insurance cards, and a fortnight's pay in lieu of notice, are being made up now."

The cool effrontery of this took McKenna's breath away. Elsie, watching the men's darkening faces, moved backwards to the rear wall of the shop.

"You'll not be worrying, of course," McKenna's voice was a menacing hiss, "what that poor devil is going to do when the fortnight's pay is finished."

"On the contrary," said William. "The future of Mr. Watkins is a matter of very real concern to me."

McKenna stepped forward belligerently. "Are you trying to be funny——?"

"Just a moment." William's voice had a quality of quiet authority that would not be ignored. There was silence. William looked at them in faint disdain. "Follow me," he said, and walked across to the reception office with the group struggling curiously after him.

He said to the vision at the window, "Lucia, is my record card there?" "Yes," she said, and after a moment's fumbling drew it from a file.

He half turned and indicated his puzzled audience. "Would you very much mind reading out to these gentlemen the name on my card."

Lucia's lovely eyebrows ascended with practised ease to a pre-arranged spot on her flawless forehead. "But that's your name," she said with faint bewilderment. "That's right," said William patiently. "Please read it, in full."

Lucia slowly read out. "William George Watkins."

"Thank you so much," said William politely.

Mahomed Kham, the Pakistani mining student, saw it first. Saw in a single flash the whole perfect beauty of the plan. His brown, handsome face broke into a wide, happy grin. "Oh, Shabash Sahib! Shabash!" he cried. "Oh, wonderful, wonderful."

Afterwards he explained it to the others, except McKenna, who was indisposed. For McKenna had seen it too, and McKenna really was a Communist Agitator.

*   *   *   *   *   *   *   *

Part 3—There's aye a Road

"THERE ye are," lamented Sarah Brodie. "That's you left the scule for guid noo 'n ye havenae been recommended for a job in the office ava. Ah warnt ye what would happen. You an' your fitba' 'n runnin' awa' tae the juke-box in thon caffy."

Her fifteen-year-old son Colin shoved his shirt-tails into his trousers and sat down to pull on his thick-soled shoes. He quirked an eyebrow and surveyed his mother with affectionate condescension. He was short and thick-set, as became a lad off collier stock, with thick curly hair and big eyes that held a slightly disgusted expression.

His mother had long ago decided that her son would not go "doon the pit," but her desire to see him better than the neighbours' laddies did not blind her to the fact that he lacked application, and though possessed of a certain natural mental agility, was anything but an intellectual. The examinations, and the road that led to a colliery manager's certificate, were therefore closed to him as were all careers which depended on academic brilliance. This left the pit office, which recruited its future clerks from colliers' sons who had distinguished themselves at mathematics while at the local school, and this had been her hope for the lad who now stood before her.

"If Ah've telt ye once," she sighed, "Ah've telt ye a thoosan' times, there's nothin' got in this warl' withoot wark—ay an' sacrifice tae. But you couldnae see it."

He shook his head determinedly. "You're wrang, Maw," he told her. "It is possible tae get things withoot warkin' for 'em; look at the pools, 'n the quizzes on the telly. Folk walkin' awa' wi' fortunes 'n never done a stroke for it. Ah'm no fussy aboot the office job. Ma dad wis a collier 'n if he hadnae been kilt in Burma he'd be a collier the day, but if it'll mak' ye happy"—he smiled at her worried face; a sudden wide, bright smile—"and jus' tae prove that ye can get things if ye've a mind tae, though it seems a waste o' time tae me when we're a' goin' tae get blewn tae glory ony meenit."

"What are ye goin' tae do?" she asked him doubtfully.

"Ah'm goin' doon the pit," he told her in a matter-of-fact voice.

"No!" she cried. "Oh, no," and her face showed her horror at this destruction of all her hopes.

66

He said flatly, "Ah telt ye Ah'd get an office-job. Tak' it from me, the pit's only a temp'ry thing."

She looked at him, her face dubious. "Well," she said at last. "It seems a long-windit way o' warkin' . . . doon a pit a' day an' then goin' tae evenin' classes at nicht. If you'd jus' put your mind tae your lessons while you were at the schule—Ach," she shook her head violently. "Ah canna mak' nothin' o' you young folk these days."

He put a comforting arm around her shoulder. "Dinna worry, Maw," he told her gently. "We're jus' the same sorta folks as you an' Paw wis; but we're mebbe no jus' as stupid. Well, Ah'm awa tae the caff." He turned in the doorway and said with the faintly cynical grin that never failed to delight, while at the same time disturbing her, "See 'n mind, Maw. There's aye a road for a guid horse."

The homely old saying had a strange sound in the faintly American accent that her son laid at times over his native Doric, and she stared with troubled eyes at his back disappearing through the door.

He kept his word, however, and the very next morning applied to become a trainee miner and was duly accepted. Together with the rest of his class he spent the next three months at the local training centre, his pay making a welcome addition to the household budget.

He then departed for his twelve-week course at the mining college, and Sarah's sole contact with her son was through his infrequent but exuberant letters which were little more than lists of football, boxing and running events in which he had participated with honour.

When he returned to the village he had filled out and seemed even more confident of the inherent superiority of his method. His mother was so glad to have him at home again that she protested no more. And when she heard that his "supervisor" for his first spell at the "face" would be Nicky McFish, the most highly-skilled collier in the village, an old workmate of her husband, she became almost reconciled to her son's choice of career.

* * * * * * * *

"What's your name, laddie?" Nicky asked the boy while they waited in the pit-bottom for the bogies that would take them to the distant section.

67

"Colin Brodie."

"Eh?" The little collier focussed the beam of his lamp and looked more closely at his small companion. "You're no Angus Brodie's laddie, are ye?"

"Ay," was the non-committal reply.

"Weel, weel," Nicky lapsed unguardedly into nostalgia. "Your Paw'n me warked at the coal the gither lang syne. Ay did we. He was a braw collier your Paw. By jings, but he could strip coal."

"Aye," said the youngster drily. "An' muckle guid it did him."

Nicky, himself a master of the apt phrase, bestowed a long, long look upon the boy beside him. "Aye," he at last conceded suspiciously. "You can say that again." He looked once more at this precocious imp and muttered darkly. "Keep close ahint me, an' when we get tae the 'face' dae just as Ah say—'n you 'n me'll get on braw."

For the rest of the arduous journey they dispensed with conversation; Nicky, stealing an occasional sideways glance at the small bundle of humanity that traipsed, with a marked lack of enthusiasm, at his heels.

The bogies took them the three miles from the pit-bottom to the end of the Cross-Cut Main, and from here they travelled as best as the local conditions would permit; stumbling, moist but upright, through the rustling waters of the half-flooded Twenty-Foot Level; then they made the long tortuous climb of the "Heading"; from here, after a bite of bread and a mouthful of water, they proceeded to navigate the low dark tunnel of the "face."

The coal spat and crackled angrily at their faces; the "waste" fell in roaring clouds of dust and debris; the roof chittered at their shoulders and even when all else was quiet a prop would suddenly emit an anguished creak, as though despairing of being able longer to support such a crushing burden.

They had crawled perhaps eighty yards and were approaching their destination when the boy suddenly stopped dead and declared piteously:

"Ah'm feart."

Nicky span round on his knees, leathery palms and steel-shod toes raising concentric circles of dust. "You're what? Ach, you're

68

richt enough. It's quiet the day . . . you wanta see it when it taks a seat."

"Ah'm feart," was the quavery reply.

"Aye." Nicky had never had to deal with a problem like this before. "We're a' feart if the truth wis telt but we've jus' tae stravaigle on. You keep close ahint me, a' in jus' a wee whiley you'll be ower busy tae be feart."

The boy shook his head. "Ah'm no' bidin' in this place," he said. "Ah'm feart." He threw himself on his back, rolled over, and when he once more rose to his knees he was facing in the opposite direction.

With madly scraping toes he set off at a rapid rate. Nicky swallowed his disgusted surprise and sped after him. It says much for the suppleness of youth that the boy had reached the deputy's station at the foot of the thousand yard "Heading" before the little collier, who was himself nimble enough, caught up with him.

"This is some carry-on!" Nicky informed the Deputy, before that worthy had properly emerged from the manhole wherein he was wont to pass his time. "Cleart aff the 'face' an' run like a hare doon here. Ah've jus' catched him . . . says he's feart."

"Feart?" The Deputy's eyes assumed the shape—they were already the colour—of mushrooms. "But-but," he gasped. "Ye canna be feart. Can get hurt," he repeated the contingencies to himself as a means of reassurance in a world that was crumbling about him. "You can be no weel. No," he shook his head with complete finality, "ye canna be feart."

"Aye, can Ah," insisted the boy.

"Well." The Deputy carefully tore a page from his notebook, and producing a well-chewed stub of grimy pencil began to suck it. "Ah canna gie ye a line tae get up the pit for bein' feart, for naebody ever heard o' that complaint. Ah'll jus' say you're sick."

"Oh, no, you'll no. Ah'm fit enough. A' that's wrang wi' me is that Ah'm feart."

"There ye are," Nicky said disgustedly. "That's a braw yin, is it no?" And he directed a look of scornful reproach at his charge. The Deputy put his stub of pencil carefully away and scratched his chin. "Ah'm takin' nothin' tae do wi' it, anyway," he announced. "Tak' him back tae the bottom where ye got him. Ah'll ring up 'n

69

let 'em ken you're comin.' The Under-Manager can handle this yin. He's paid for dealin' wi' major problems."

Nicky spat. "Come on," he said, and followed by the Major Problem set off for the Bogie Station.

$$* \quad * \quad * \quad * \quad * \quad * \quad * \quad *$$

"He's what?" demanded the Under-Manager when Nicky, fed up with the whole affair, had finished his tale.

"He says he's feart," Nicky repeated, "'n he'll no' bide on the face ava. His een never stop rollin'. The meenit a prop creaks he's aff."

"Where is he?" asked the Under-Manager, seeking hopefully to postpone the admission that he was secretly baffled by this previously unheard of situation. Nicky led the way from the little office. "There," he said, and pointed across the pit-bottom to where, in front of the red-painted fire-fighting equipment, the youngster squatted like a small black Buddha.

"H'mm," said the Under-Manager, "Hhh'mmmH," and as an aid to cogitation swung his lamp by its cable. "Ah think Ah'll let the Manager deal wi' this personally. He'd due doon the pit ony meenit, 's bringin' a coupla the high heid yins o' the Coal Board doon . . . the Area General Manager 'n the Area Public Relations Officer. Hhh'mm." He teetered to and fro on his heels and stared with undisguised curiosity at the Major Problem. The latter, nothing loath, stared back with undisguised irreverence.

At that moment the bells at the shaft-bottom signalled that men were descending, and with a sigh of relief the Under-Manager prepared to welcome his superior. The Manager, accompanied by the two Coal Board officials and the Miners' Union Delegate, and anxious, no doubt, to impress, opened hostilities while still several yards away.

"Is that man hurt," he wanted to know. "Why isn't he up the pit?"

"No, sir," said the Under-Manager. "He says he's f . . ."

"Why is he sitting down if he isn't hurt?" inquired the Manager, "and you, Nicky . . . what're you doing off the 'face' in midshift?"

Nicky, tired of repeating his unlikely tale, said in a bored voice, "Ah had tae come oot wi' him. He run aff the 'face.' Said he wis feart."

"Nonsense," said the Manager testily. "Rubbish."

"Is it," Nicky snapped, bemusement giving way to impatience. "Well, jus' you try 'n get him back."

"Come here," said the Manager forcefully. "What's your name?"

"Brodie. Colin Brodie," the slight figure informed him.

"First time on the 'face'?"

"Ay."

"Bit nervous, eh. Poof. We a' felt like that on our first day. A coal face is an eerie place when you're no aquaint wi' it. Nothin' tae be ashamed of. Felt the same masel' when Ah wis a laddie. Dinna feel upset aboot it, no one will think any the less of you. Get awa' back now with Nicky here 'n we'll say no more aboot it. Richt," he nodded to a sceptical Nicky McFish, and turned with a knowing smile to his companions.

"Not on your Nellie," said a youthful voice from behind him and the Manager's mouth opened to its fullest extent. The Under-Manager flinched away from the blast to come but, recollecting his

71

company, the Manager shut his mouth again sharply and stared with awful fascination at the small black figure that confronted him.

"But you'll have to work, my boy." The Area General Manager took things into his own hands. "Are you aware how much money it has cost the country to train you for the pit?"

"Ah'm pairfec'ly willin' tae wark," said the beneficiary of his country's munificence. "But Ah'm no' goin' back tae thon 'face' place cos Ah'm feart. In fac' Ah'm feart a' the time Ah'm doon here."

"This is a pit." The Manager once more asserted himself. "You have been trained—at great public expense—for pit wark. If you're no' prepared to work in the pit—you'd better lift your books."

"It's hard lines gettin' sacked when Ah havenae done nothin' wrang." The boy's voice would have melted granite.

"You've re . . ." The Manager angrily erupted and subsided as suddenly, with a sound of whistling air, the A.P.R.O.'s elbow dug savagely into his ribs.

"No," hissed the A.P.R.O. with a warning glance at the closely watching Union Delegate. "You can't sack the boy for being afraid . . . think of the adverse publicity, and at a time when we are trying to recruit youngsters for the pits."

"Ah canna help that." The Manager, lungs refilled, had recovered his voice. "Ah'm no' payin' him wages tae sit 'n scratch hissel." He turned purple with horror at the thought. "They'd a' be oot here in a flash if he got awa' wi' it," and he nearly fainted at the picture the idea had conjured up in his mind.

"What a to-do about nothing at all," said the Area General Manager. "Give the boy a job at the pithead. Surely?" he asked them pityingly, "that is the obvious solution."

"Aye," said the Union Delegate. "But that means a reduction in wages. You're no' goin' tae penalise the laddie for tellin' the truth, for that's what it biles doon tae." "Of course not," said the A.P.R.O. soothingly. "Wouldn't dream of it." He looked appealingly at the Area General Manager. "Ah ken what Ah'd dae tae him," the Manager said softly, and the Under-Manager nodded devout agreement.

"That's soon settled." The Area General Manager was tiring of the affair. "Give him a job at the pithead an' pay him underground wages."

"A splendid idea," said the delegate with an admiring glance, and the Area General Manager smiled complacently.

The Manager turned white and reached for the support of a nearby girder. "Are ye aff your heids?" he croaked, and the Area General Manager's smile faded abruptly at his tone. "The rest o' the pitheid warkers'd be oot on strike the meenit they kent. An' the colliers'd a' be wantin' fresh air jobs in the pityaird at 'face' wages. Na, na, that'll no tak' a trick."

The Delegate's face fell and the Area General Manager said with a note of exasperation in his voice: "As you are so good at pouring cold water on all other suggestions, and as you are, after all, the Manager of the pit"—the voice was now dripping with sarcasm—"perhaps you will favour us with your solution. . . ."

The Manager frowned horribly and the Under-Manager, who was sensitive to sudden rises in temperature, took two paces to the rear. "Well," demanded the Area General Manager. "What's to be done with him. He's afraid to work down the pit; he can't be employed at the pithead. For policy reasons he can't be sacked and there's nowhere else you can put him. Perhaps you will favour us with some indication of your intentions?"

"Aye, there's one place yet." The Manager spoke slowly as the great idea blossomed fully in his mind. "And like it or no', that's where he's goin'—an' you needna try tae interfere," he told the Delegate, "for it's nothin' tae do with your union." He turned to the Under-Manager.

"Gie him a note to the Chief Clerk. He'll stairt in the office."

The Delegate said regretfully, "Ah'm sorry, son. But you see . . . wi' you bein' feart o' the pit. But see an' mind . . . if you're no' wantin' it. . . ." He looked round threateningly. "There's nae laddie goin' tae be shanghaied intae a job he doesna want while Ah'm Delegate o' this pit. Jus' say the word, son"—he glared at the Manager—"an' they pitheid wheels'll stop wi' a jerk. Ah'll no' let them tak' a len o' ye."

The boy hesitated. There was a long aching silence. He said at last:

"Ach, Ah'm no' wantin' tae cause nae bother. It'll just have tae do Ah s'pose." With an offhand nod he took the note from the Under-Manager's hand and sauntered away to the shaft.

* * * * * * * *

"Hello, Sairy," Nicky said when the widow Brodie confronted him in the pityard at the shift's end. "Nicky," she cried. "Where's Colin? What's wrang he's no' with you? Ah heard he'd been seen up the pit afore lousin' time an' Ah wis feart he'd been hurt."

"Hurt!" Nicky grimaced at her. "It's me that's been hurt the day wi' that laddie o' yours." He jerked a grimy thumb to where the pithead buildings nestled beneath the shadow of the endlessly spinning wheels. "He's been shoved in an office job," he grunted, "for being feart. A collier's son tae," he added in a voice of deep disgust.

"But, Nicky," she said quickly, "he wantit tae work in the office— at least," she blushed, "Ah wantit him to. But ye see he didna do awfy weel at the schule"—her face brightened and shone with pride. "He said he wouldna disappoint me," she murmured as Nicky's eyes grew wide. "And he hasna."

Nicky's jaws opened. At last he managed to speak. "Are you tellin' me," he croaked, "that he wantit a job in the office?"

"Of course," she said brightly. "That's why he went doon the pit in the first place." Nicky fumbled for the support of the yard wall.

"Ye ken, Nicky," Sarah assured her stunned companion, "he's nae fule, ma Colin."

"You can say that again." Nicky found his tongue once more. "He'll go far, thon laddie. Why," his face puckered with the growth of final enlightenment, "he's mastered the secret o' the age . . . how to make Nationalisation work . . . for him."

"Nor has the darkness changed; it is there still, ever ready to devour the slender beam of his lamp; so thick and palpable a thing as to seem almost solid. No drawing of the collier at work can suggest this ever-present darkness."

CHAPTER FIVE

NEVER A MINUTE

THEY had gone out at five, in the grey dark; as soon, in fact, as the dock gates were open. Now, it was after eight o'clock and they were headed once more for home before the gates again were closed.

Tommy Balgetty, short, slim and fiftiesh, stood spraddle-legged in the stern. He swayed easily to the rolling lift of the yawl; his left hand gripped the tiller, his right lay carelessly along the engine box, near the controls. His bright eyes in the sharp-featured face were half-closed against the hard sheen of the Autumn sunshine on the shining waters. In the forepart, Joey Balgetty coiled the last of the lines into the basket; flushed out the bait can over the side; sat down on a thwart and looked aft at his father.

"That's them all cleaned, Dad," he said in his clear schoolboy voice. "There's nineteen codling. Two of them are big and the rest fair. Seven fair-sized flounders and a plaice."

"What about the flatties?" asked Balgetty senior, as he savoured the sun-sprinkled air. He doted on his fourteen-year-old son; but when about the boats, or in the presence of other colliers, never deigned to notice him. The boy, a first-class scholar at the local High School, loved his 'canny' little sire, who, after forty years in the mining industry, had been flung aside like an old boot as the result of policy decisions made in a London office. Loved this wiry little man and admired his ability to survive in a world that offered few prospects for survival.

He could understand the contrary nature of his father's behaviour —this conscious ignoring. It was like a game which the two of them played together against the world; a secret game of hidden emotion in which the boy delighted as much as the man. He understood that this repudiation was a part of his father's pride in him; sensed, with the clear wisdom of a boy, that to have him ever at heel, as it were, silent and unquestionably obedient, was something of a salve to his father for the tricks that life had played on him, the blows it had dealt his pride and independence.

"Twenty-six," the boy answered the last question. "I flung back a dozen; they were too wee."

"We'll drop them aboard the 'Laurel' as we go up the fairway," said Tommy. "See and have them ready." He had not looked at his son, his eyes were on the piers, growing rapidly out of the sea as the yawl surged towards the land. Joey bent to the fish; astern he could hear his father softly humming a tune and the boy's face was suddenly all asmile with contentment and joy.

"I kent the codling were running," Tommy soliloquised to the breeze. "The others wait till October every year, and then greet because they've missed the best of them. To listen to them, you'd think fush kent the dates and worked by a calendar. Na, na. Whenever the watter gets cold enough—that's when they come—aye, s'posing it was June. We'll need to get out again this evening, and every other tide while the weather lasts and the cod are running. We're that AFFLUENT in Fife there's aye folk about the doors that'll give half-a-crown for a six-pound cod, and what's left, the old wife can salt down. . . ."

He turned his gaze from the channel ahead, his eyes ranging the hills beyond the shoreline, the shimmering sea and the lavender vault of heaven.

"I looked for rain the day," he muttered. "Must be moving more slowly than I thought. It'll be night afore we get it here. Better get they berries in the day, just in case." His eyes lighted on the grey-brown waste of beach, below the old pit bing, to the west of the harbour, and he demanded suddenly, "What like's the coal-cellar at home?"

Joey grinned to a wave-tip: his father always knew more about the state of the coal-cellar than he ever did; but he answered correctly.

"It's no bad, Father," he said, "but you could mebbe get a bag or two in."

They were through the piers now and Tommy eased the throttle and swung the yawl to starboard to close the line of moored lobster-boats. As they passed the 'Laurel,' Joey hailed, "Ahoy there, Mr

Gourlay!" and threw the bundle of fish. From the hold of the fishing boat a voice called, as though from the deep, "Is that you, Tom?" And Tommy, without turning his head, called, "Aye, Geordie."

With the yawl once again moored in its usual berth in the old dock, Joey got his bicycle from where it leaned against a rusting coaltip, hung the fish from the handlebars, and awaited orders.

Tommy, his pipe going now, sat on the engine box and looked with unsmiling eyes at his son. "Seeing as it'll be raining the morn," he said, "I'll have a bit hour at the seacoal. You get away home to your breakfast. Tell your Mother to make up a flask of tea and a couple of rolls and jam; get four sacks outa the cellar and bring them down to me on your way to school. Oh aye, and tell your Mother to hand those two big codling to ole Mame Macpherson—there's no muckle feeding in the Old Age Pension."

Joey suggested diffidently—they were alone or he would never have ventured to question—"What about the berries, Dad? Mum said. . . ."

"They'll keep till you and Chrissie get home from school: it's daylight till near seven yet. We'll no be long in filling a couple of pails at this place where I'm taking you." He glanced at the clock on the wall of the Harbourmaster's Office. "Away you go," he said sharply. "No be late for school."

When Joey returned, just before nine, he transferred his burden to the boat, and said, "I'm away, then, Dad."

Tommy, hunkered on the quay in the pale sunlight, and deep in talk with two of his cronies, only jerked his pipe-bowl in a gesture of dismissal.

At two that afternoon the little collier leant the bicycle, which he had built himself, against the back wall of his house. His hands were dark with grime and his eyes watered still from the keen bite of the wind along the beach.

"This is a fine time to come home," said his wife. "I was needing tatties, but when you never showed up I just lifted a row myself."

"I hope you've cleant that gripe."

"It's cleant," she told him, "and back in the shed, and that's the last of the tatties."

Working in a narrow seam in very unfriendly 'country.' Wooden props keep the roof up while the miner wins his coal from the reluctant 'face'

"Aye." His hands washed, he dropped into his chair and settled his lap for the waiting cat. "That's why I just put in a few mid-season ones this year. What's the use planting them when the house is full of tatties all winter. I've beet in; and kale, and sprouts; they're more use to us.

"When's the tattie-picking starting?" he asked; his fingers deep in the cat's fur, his eyes half-closed as he felt the pleasure of his warmed slippers.

"Next week," she told him. "Start Monday morning. Meg Dunsire was round no long since. I'm in her squad this year. I gave her some fish away with her for that sister of her's whose man's in hospital . . . We're to get twenty-six bob a day this year," she prattled on, "and Chrissie and Joey 'll be out with me at the week-ends, so that's over ten quid a week for two months. With your dole money we'll be doing no bad. . . ."

He yawned pleasurably. "Aye," he agreed. "It's a good lift each Autumn. But—ach . . ." he said slyly, provokingly. "You just spend the money you get. We're never no farther for'ard. . . ."

"Spent on the house," she reminded him sharply, "and on clothes for the bairns; what mair are you wanting? And I never saw us start a winter yet without half a ton of tatties in the shed. . . ."

"I ken," he said softly, placatingly, "fine I ken."

She bustled to and fro, a plump, nimble woman with shrewd eyes and an expression of perpetual benevolence which more than sufficed to take the bite from her sharpest words. She eyed him now, curiously, as he rose from the table and reached, not for his pipe, but for his boots.

"Where 're ye off to now?" she wanted to know. "You're aye running off some place. The mair you flee," she warned him, "the less you see."

"Away and boil your heid," he advised her affectionately. "I gathered four sacks of seacoal the day: I hope you think they'll walk up here from the harbour on their own. I'll need to get the car out and go down for them. I left 'em lying at the side of the sea wall. Charlie Mackenzie, the Dock Gateman, is keeping an eye on them for me."

"You're an awfy man, Tam," she admonished him admiringly, "you'll no bide still a minute."

When he came back the children were home from school and finishing their tea. The coal was dumped in the cellar and the four of them piled into the car and set for the spot on the uplands where Tommy had marked a rich cluster of elderberries. When they returned, the sunset was turning the house windows to gold and the growing dusk had a quiet, a melting loveliness. Old Jean Donaldson came to the door of the next house.

"I've a lobster and two partons for you," she said. "They're in the sink, in my scullery: the fella Gourlay handed 'em in. He said to thank you for the bait."

"Oh, that's good," said Tommy's wife. She held open the gate while her son and daughter carried through the full pails of berries. "You'll be right enough for your drop elderberry wine this New Year again, Jean. How did you like the bramble jelly I made ?"

"It was braw. . . ."

"Where's he away to now ?" cried Tommy's wife, as her son ran through the gate and jumped into the already moving car. "I never saw sic'. . . ."

Christina joined her mother. "They're away out in the yawl to set lines. Dad said he's no wanting to miss a tide while the codling are running. . . ."

"I hope he kens that Joey's to do his homework," snapped her mother, and Christina, taking the hint, retired red-faced to the house.

"No word of a job yet?" asked Jean in her cracked voice.

Mrs Balgetty laughed shrilly. "Job?" she cried. "Na, there's little hope of that now that the pit's been shut down. Na, he's fifty-four; that's ower old to start new trades; he'll be idle now till he dies. But that's what this Gov'ment wants. It tells you that on the Tee Vee. The Economy can only be stabilised if there's half-a-million unemployed, 'n anyway, they're no wanting folk to get jobs and bide in Scotland. That's why all the work's down south. After all, it's only natural; who's going to build factories in the Front Line. See and mind, there's nae Polaris Bases in England."

Old Jean nodded in sage and sad agreement.

"Na, na," Mrs Balgetty let her gate swing to with such an air of awful deliberation she might have been shutting the door on all human hope: "there'll never be nae work here again. And we're ower old to go traipsing off to England. I'm just waiting on the bairns

80

getting through their Highers and they'll be off, and you canna blame 'em.

"There's nothing here for 'em; but it's bliddy hard lines that our men had to get shoved on the dole and our fam'lies bruck up and our bairns go off to England jus' to give the Yanks time to smoke a last fag. Na," she sighed, "my man 'll never work again—less there's a war." She brightened at the idea.

"Ye ken," the words she had heard so often from T.V. speakers slipped all unconsciously from her lips, "just a bit of local unrest that could be settled with conventional weapons. Like K'rea," she said hopefully. "A lotta men woulda been flung outa work back in the Fifties if it hadna been for K'rea. But the big wars was the best," she spoke the words slowly from out of her thoughts; "that was the only time us working folk felt safe and secure . . . during the two big wars . . . there was plenty of work then."

There was a pause; the two women stood like dark images lost in thought in the soft twilight. "Ah, well," Mrs Balgetty sighed, "I'd better away in and get his supper ready for him coming back from the lines."

"I'll give you that lobster and the crabs over the fence," Jean told her friend.

"Never mind the partons: we've enough fish as it is, and I ken you like a bit crab. Just give's over the lobster and I'll do it for his supper: he likes a bit white meat now and again."

It was her first question when, at eight o'clock, her husband and son entered the house. "Will I sort that lobster for you now, or when you come in?"

"When I come home." He was already washing and spoke through the soapsuds. "I've no time now," he told her on his way upstairs to change, "I'm due at the garage in twenty minutes."

It was almost midnight when he returned and found his wife dozing in her chair by the fire.

"Where've you been till this time of night?" she asked sleepily. "That Garage job was supposed to be just a couple of hours from half-eight till half-ten, looking after the petrol pumps from when the mechanics go till when the pubs shut."

"That's all it's supposed to be." He drew off his boots and sighed with luxuriant relief. "But a fella came in with a flat tyre just as I was shutting up; so I stayed on and sorted it. He gave me a half-note for my trouble, too. . . ."

He was at the sink now washing his hands, and she stood at the stove preparing his supper. Their backs were to each other; but she could sense a note of quiet exultation in his voice, and she waited.

"Guess who he was—the fella with the puncture ?" And, before she could answer, "The new Manager of the big pub at Balawney. He's just got a seven-day licence, with this new law, and he's offered me a spart-time barman's job on Sunday nights; and driving home customers that've had a drop ower much—in the pub car. It just fits in braw."

He settled himself at the table and smiled contentedly at his wife over the lobster. "Sunday was aye the night when I never kent what to do with myself. . . ."

"See and no be all night over that fush," she admonished him. "Let's away to our bed: you've the Dole to go to the morn, ye ken."

"Aye," he moaned, "it's a cussed nuisance, that Dole, twice a week. You'd think they'd 've invented an easier way of working it by now. Fellas fleeing through Space," he grumbled as he ate, "yet I've to cycle six miles every week in the year to sign my name on a bit paper.

"I dinna have time for that caper," he told his wife. "What for can they no send the money, same as on the National Health?"

"*It has always been the tragedy of the miner that no one sees him at work. Even in this world of mass communication his life remains very much a closed book except to those who are near and know him well.*"

CHAPTER SIX

A NICHT WI' BURNS

IT had been a wild half-shift, the roof continually threatening to
close about us and huge masses of coal bursting off the 'face',
making us leap away in terror.

Now thankfully we were through the 'bad bit' and enjoying our
piece in the Heading, before returning to the face for what would be
the more or less straightforward job of cutting the rest of the coal.

"Ma knees is sair," said Heelplates McSobb, the leading propdrawer, "wi runnin'."

"It's ma ears that's tired," said Nicky McFish, the leading cutterman and my 'neighbour.' "They've been stannin' up like an Alsatian's a' nicht, listening' tae every wee crack."

"What eedjit invented coalpits onyway?" asked Beetle McSair,
who was Heelplates's neighbour. "They're nae use—'cept for growin'
muscles."

"Monks," I told him, "long ago."

"Well, Ah dinna wish 'em ony hairm," said Heelplates dolefully.
"But Ah hope they're a' fryin' at this meenit. Monks ... monkeys
Ah'd cry 'em."

"It's us that's the monkeys," growled Beetle. "Lettin' oorsel's get
chased aboot in a den like thon. Did ye year the Bomber when Ah
cried him a big ape ?"

"Don't worry," Nicky put in sourly. "We dinna hae enough brains
tae be monkeys, we talk ower muckle. The monks is ower fly tae
talk in case they get cried humans, an' sent doon a pit tae wark.
That's oor trouble, we talk ower muckle. An' onyway you wis
askin' for trouble when you cried the Bomber an ape. He had a
lotta trouble wi' yin once an' he's never forgot it."

"Tell us about it," I said.

"Well," said Nicky. "Akshully, it wisna ma monk at a'. It belongit tae the Bomber's brither, that wis in the Navy, an' the fella wis awfy fond o' this monk. He comes home on a fortnight's leave an stays wi' the Bomber. Well, it seemed that he couldnae tak' the monk back wi' him, 'cos he was goin' tae a diff'rent ship. So he asks the Bomber tae mind it for him. But the monk an' the Bomber didnae get on ava, the Bomber wis aye haein' a sly kick at the monk, an' the monk wis aye tryin' tae get its teeth intae the Bomber's hide. An' the Bomber flatly refuses tae hae onything tae dae wi'it. So the sailor fella comes marchin' in tae me. We wis next door, an' at the time the wife, ole Maggie, wis awa tae the guild meetin'.

" 'Ma ain brither,' " he says. " 'An' he refuses tae look after ma wee monkey while Ah'm awa in ma boat. If you will give it a hame,' " he says, " 'Ah will put you in ma will.'

"Well, Ah wis that fascinated starin' at the ferocious gorilla that he ca'd a wee monkey, that Ah wisnae payin' muckle attention, but when he says 'will' ma ears wis stannin' up on the tap o' ma heid like flagstaffs. But Ah kent whit old Maggie would say, an' Ah still wisn't too certain, then the monk decided the thing for me.

"Ma wife's toyteeshell cat wis lyin' asleep in front o' the fire. That wis the cat that nearly ate me an' the Bomber yince when it attacked us in the Laird's woods. Well, while Ah'm wunnerin' if a fortnicht o' the Bomber's wife's cookin' 'll prove fatal tae this fella, the monk grabs the cat by the tail an' awa up tae the mantelpiece.

"An' it sits there on the mantelpiece swingin' Fluff-Puff by his tail, an' tryin' tae drap him through the wee roon hole in the tap o' the stove.

"Why," Ah says. "Ah will be delighted tae have your monkey stay in ma hoose." An' aff he goes, as pleased as a pooch wi' a pullet. " 'He's a playfu' wee monkey,' " he shouts back. "Aye," Ah shouts. "Ah can see that. We're goin' tae get a lotta free entertainment aroon here wi' it.

"By jings, Ah never spuk truer words in a' ma life. Ah wis awa oot on the nichtshift when Maggie come hame so Ah dinna ken hoo she got on wi' her new guest, but Ah think they musta fell oot 'cos she wis waitin' at the pitheid for me the next mornin' an it wasn't no social call, 'cos she has an iron kale-pot in her haun. Ah had an awfy job gettin' her calmed doon, but when Ah telt her aboot the will she wis game tae gie it a try, 'cos she kent mair aboot the Bomber's wife's cookin' than Ah did.

"By jings, thon wis a queer creature thon monk. Ah dunno whit it liked. But we wisnae lang in gettin' tae ken whit it hated, an' fust on its hate list wis cats, wi' the Bomber a close second.

"After a week or twa, when it wis let oot in the mornin', it used tae mak' a beeline for the claes pole in the garden, an' a' you could see roon aboot wis the hintends o' a' the cats in the village disappearin' over wa's an' fences or fleein' tae their ain back doors howlin' tae be let in. An' his nibs up there on the claes pole surveyin' the scene like the Lord High Admiral, a' he needed wis a telescope unner his oxter. Ah could mebbe a' got money for thon beast frae the fillums," Nicky sighed reminiscently.

"Cos'," he went on, "Ah had a wee bit proposition lined up in connection wi' the monk. Whenever the wife wis oot, Ah was gettin' the lads in an' lettin' them see the stove trick wi' Fluff-Puff an' they wis a' layin' bets wi' me that the monk 'd never dae it. But Ah see that it got plenty o' practice. Ah wore oot a pair o' boots runnin' after thon toyteeshell tae fetch it back for the next attempt, an' the monk wis aye improvin'. Ah tell you, there wis a lotta money tied up on thon beast yin way an' anither.

"Ah think the Bomber musta still been giein' it the odd sly kick tae, 'cos it wis aye layin' for him. There wis one day Ah went oot in the garden an' whit dae Ah see but the monk sittin' up on the edge o' the Bomber's roof, wi' a big slab o' redd in it's arms like a tombstane. Well, Ah sees the Bomber is just comin' oot so Ah waits in case there's an accident."

"And was there?" it was Heelplates.

"No," said Nicky sadly. "It missed him, 'least it scraped a bit skin aff his nose, and bent the steel tae caps o' his boots doon over the edge of the doorstep."

"He wouldn't be very pleased at that," I said.

"Pleased," said Nicky. "He went an awfy length. Cairtainly, his taes wis inside the boots, an' they got bent a bit tae, but he didnae need tae greet like thon. Tae sorta pacify him, Ah telt him they wis makin' taes every day. Holy smoke!, it's a good job he wisnae able tae run, if he'da' catched me, Ah wis a deid duck, Ah'll tell you.

"Well, anyway, everything wis goin' alang fine an' the monk is aye in trainin' for the hole in the stove trick, the toyteeshell wis beginnin' tae get a far-away look in its een, but me an the monk wisnae worryin' aboot whit a cat thocht. When here, be jings!, does the monk no smash the wife's Tee-Vee. She's aye been in the habit o' leavin' it on when she went oot, so the cat wouldnae weary. Well, o' cos', Ah'm nichtshift an' Ah'm asleep in the room, an' the monk an' the cat's in the kitchen watchin' the Tee-Vee.

"The fust Ah kent aboot it wis an a'michty screitch o' rage. Ah comes fleein' oota the room in ma shirt just as the monk belts the Tee-Vee screen wi' the coal-hammer that had been lyin' in the fender. Ah tell you, thon beast wis aff its heid.

"It seems that there wis an animul programme on, an' a picture o' a big monk sittin' eatin' bynanys an' laffin' a'ower its pus. Well, o' cos', oor monk only got cat for its diet, an' it never had ower muckle tae laff aboot, whit wi' the wife screitchin' at it in oor hoose, an' the Bomber beltin' it wi' a garden spade when it went next door. He couldnae kick it 'cos his taes wis still sair. The pair beast must a got jealous when it sees thon Tee-Vee monk pushin' bynanys intae its pus an' laffin'.

"By jings, you should a heard ole Maggie when she come in, 'n sees a' the wheels an' springs stickin' oota her Tee-Vee. An' me dancin' aboot the flair tryin' tae haud baith feet at the same time. When the monk had feenished wi' the coal-hammer he flung it doon, an' ma bare feet wis where it landed.

" 'Ah'm leavin' the morn,' " she says. " 'Ah'll not bide in the same hoose wi' thon beast anither day.' Well, that wis yin bright spot onyway, so Ah puts ma feet back on the flair an' hurries tae gie her a haun tae pack afore she changes her mind. She could be rotten enough—after gettin' me a' built up—Ah kent that.

" 'Your not leavin' thon gorilla in this hoose wi' me the nicht either. Me an' Fluff-Puff 'll hae peace on oor last nicht onyway.' "

"Ah canna stay aff ma wark," Ah tells her.

" 'Then you can just tak' thon savage cat-eater wi' ye,' " she says. " ''Cos it's no stayin' here wi' me.' "

"Well, you canna argue wi' old Maggie. Ah fund that oot lang ago, so that wis that, an' Ah wisnae goin' tae lose a shift over no monk.

"By jings, that wis some nicht Ah'll betcha. The monk wis richt enough till Ah got it intae the cage. An' then it musta tumbled tae where it wis goin' an' it bites Big McFatt stannin' next tae me. Well, you ken yersel's, Big McFat's no whit you'd ca' a friendly sorta fella, an' he clonks the monk over the lughole wi' yin o' they big hams o' his.

"Well, that calmed the monk doon, cairtainly. But when its heid stopped spinnin' aboot half an hoor later the only one aroon wis me, so it took aboot half a pund o' steak aff the tap o' ma breestbane. By jinks, if Ah coulda just got aholt o' a pickshaft, Ah'da gie'n it what for, Ah'll betcha. It wisnae playin' when it bit you, thon monk wis a serious animul, Ah'll tell you. An' Ah'm no fat tae stairt wi'. Ah canna stan' lossin' half punds at a go.

"Well, o' cos', a coalpit's no a place for fun an' games at ony time an' the monk wis quiet enough for Ah had it tied tae a girder in the Headin'. Holy smoke, the Bomber's wife musta been feedin' him up for somethin', 'cos he's got a bynany in his piecebox. Here, does the eedjit no haud it oot for us tae see afore he eats it. Ooooh! Whit a carry on. Ah tell you this, by the time we gets the monk awa, half the Bomber's arm wis doon its neck, never mind the bynany.

"He got a fricht, Ah can tell you. He went straight tae the telephone an' reported me. Claimed the monk had bit him. That wis reedeecilous; hoo wis the monk tae ken where the bynany stopped an' the Bomber stairted.

"By jings, thon monk took an awfy notion tae the Bomber after thon. It musta thocht he wis a bynany tree, it followed him roon like a dug.

"Well, when we gets up the pit who's waitin' but the Manager an' the polis. Whenever Ah sees the reception committee, Ah lets the monk go an' walks past as if Ah kent nothin' aboot it, an' o' cos' the monk jumps up, flings its arms roon the Bomber's neck, an' tries tae kiss him in front o' them a'. An' the last thing we hears as we goes over the gangway is the Bomber screamin' tae the polis tae get him oota 'this gorilla's mooth.' Ah thocht the Bomber woulda got the sack for sure, but na, nothin' happened, 'cept tae me. It wis me that got a' the sufferin'.

"What happened ?" asked Heelplates sympathetically.

"Well," said Nicky, "in the fust place, the monk deed. O' cos' Ah expected that, wi' it biting the Bomber. Ah shoulda sued him for pisenin' a valyuble animul, but ole Maggie come back wi' thon Fluff-Puff, an' ma spirit wis bruck. Then the next thing is, Ah get took tae court for subjectin' a dumb animal tae unnecessary sufferin' by takin' it doon a coal pit . . . Ah got awa wi' it though an' just got admonished."

"Oh, but Nicky," I put in. "In that case there should be a Society for the Prevention of Cruelty to British Miners."

"Aye," said Nicky. "That's whit Ah telt the Beak, an' it just bears oot whit Ah wis sayin' aboot monkeys bein' ower fly tae talk. He says he'd changed his mind an' the offence was mair serious than he had at fust thocht, an' he fines me a fiver, an' follers that up by givin' me fourteen days for contempt o' court.

" 'You're no goin' tae stan' there gie'in me a lotta lip,' " he says.

89

"In a world of people anxious, nay, determined to force their opinions on us, the collier remains silent; not because he is inarticulate, but because he is humble. Daily, he comes face to face with the imponderables of death and the tomb, and the result is a quiet unassuming man."

CHAPTER SEVEN

THE END OF THE STINT

Methil, October 1967

So the last shift has been worked at the Wellesley, the last coal has come up the shaft!

The closure is to be complete for, when emptied of all that can be salvaged, the waters are to be allowed to rise. A couple of pumping stations only will be kept going underground to control the level and supply water for the huge washer at the pithead which still handles most of the coal produced in the East of Fife.

For the rest, a dark tide will swirl through the places we knew so well and the far-ranging subterranean galleries will be given over to final oblivion. I find this hard to comprehend for underground the Wellesley was like a great city; a city which, with its outlying suburbs, covered an area of more than twenty-five square miles.

From the brightly-lit pit-bottom, where many lines of tracks converged upon the shaft, long straight roads ran out to the distant sections; and beneath these roads were older roads and their adjacent worked-out coal measures; and above, yet other roads, long since abandoned unless retained as travelling roads or aircourses. And, as in a city above ground, there were known landmarks such as the Big Light and Carbide Alley; and familiar buildings, pumping stations and loco sheds and new-built transformer houses and old stables.

And the sections, like the suburbs of a city, lay miles apart, each with its own distinctive atmosphere. The Dip Mine, where the stour lay thick as satin on the throat, and whence men carried always the half-moon of black beneath the lower eyelid to tell where they had 'wrocht'; the Dip Mine, where a whiff of gas could set serious men cavorting like drunken fools, and where there was always a fire burning somewhere. The Dysart East, where I have lain on my back and stared at the widespread, clawlike wings of a pre-historic bird-lizard clearly etched on the roof two feet above me; the Crosscut and its maze of workings far 'oot unner the sea,' and deep below it, the Basin.

Here the steep 'dook' of smooth stone, hidden by ankle-deep torrents of water, was 'sair tae walk' and the officials wisely turned a blind eye when we—in flagrant breach of mining regulations—rode the Mother belt for more than a thousand yards; half-naked bodies pressed close against the hot rubber as we rushed upwards through the silent darkness with, at each barrel end, the relished thrill of terror as we soared through eyeless space before landing with a reassuring 'plump' on the next belt to resume our upward flight. And the Basin Dook was but one of the great dooks spidering down into the farthest recesses of the Pit.

And everywhere we went about the workings there would be traces of other men on other shifts, or of other times: men we knew and had laughed with; others long dead and 'done wi' pitwark.' A rusted pickhead dug out of a reopened old working; a man's head beautifully carved—the work of months—on the stone pillar fronting a deep-set pumphouse. An old section where, long ago, there had been a bad 'fall' and where I found rails, haulage motor, and seven full tubs of coal which would never be brought out. Still faintly decipherable on the first tub was the message: "What time is it, Will?"; and I wondered who Will had been, and whether time still mattered to the writer of those words.

And there were glimpses of men—these stalwart men, the salt of the earth, which I shall always treasure. I remember one morning as I was coming off-shift, I arrived at the shaft as a cage descended with a load of dayshift men. Staring-eyed, fumbling with lamps, they stumbled noisily past me. Last to come were two young strip-pers. Their helmets were pushed carelessly to the backs of their heads and at each slim waist hung the heavy lamp battery, but the lamps were draped over their shoulders and lay across their chests, each lamp, suspended from its cable, throwing a pool of light about their feet.

Moleskins, buckled in at the knee-pads, flared again above the heavy boots, giving the two youngsters a strangely taut and graceful appearance. Each carried in one hand his steel box of gelignite; the other arm of each was flung about the shoulder of his neighbour. I pressed back to the side of the road and watched them stroll past, each smiling face turned to something he saw in the eyes of his friend. They did not see me but I have long remembered them and the glimpse of mutual trust and true companionship which they afforded me.

Another revelation of human nobility happened after a bad roof fall. Several men had been extricated but two were still trapped and one had asked for the consolations of his faith. When the priest arrived at the Main Level I was among a party taking in supports, who accompanied him to the scene of the fall. It was a bad journey, and if I ever saw terror in a man's face it was in the face of the priest.

But his concern for another was greater than his fear of the strange, dark, frightening world wherein he found himself, and he uttered no word. I last saw him crawling into a narrow hole below a tottering mass of rock, and it was not such a place as I should have cared to enter. I never heard the name of that young priest; but I have never forgotten his courage.

There is another scene that will always remain with me. This was when I went into the great winding engine house on the 'bank,' or pithead, in midshift and saw the winding engineman enthroned like a god at his controls.

At that moment I became suddenly aware of the power and the isolation and the awful responsibility that was his, whose hands drew up and lowered the flying cages with their freights of men and materials and coal. The shaft was fifteen hundred feet in depth, yet eight tubs of coal were whisked from bottom to bank in fifty-four seconds, and this speed of operation was maintained for sixteen hours out of the twenty-four that make a pit working day.

Underground, the Wellesley maintained a vast network of roads: when I first went to work there, as a rope-splicer, there was more than thirty miles of flexible steel wire haulage rope to be looked after (there had been more) and these haulage ways were little more than a third of the total travelling roads. Walking such roads brought experiences that ranged from the uncanny to the plainly farcical.

After 'lying on' (the miners' term for overtime), the long tramp out to the pitbottom could be an eerie business. Occasionally, at some isolated crossing, we would be hailed by a solitary laddie, anxiously awaiting 'tim yins' as the empty tubs are called. Later, walking in single file through the dripping reaches of the Sea Mine we would first hear the tubs—they were as yet unseen in the darkness —then would follow the strange sensation as thirty or forty of them, unattended, but firmly clipped to the haulage rope, splashed noisily past, brushing our bodies; on the first tub there would be scrawled in chalk some cryptic message such as:

'What's wrang in there, Donal', the phone's no' ringing?'

'Watch it, the Manager's doon the Pit.'

'Flask of watter in second tub, Eck; tak' your piece after this race.'

At 'lowsin' time,' miners generally are seized by a craving to escape, a sort of frenzy of impatience, the result of perhaps an unconscious, but cumulative claustrophobia. It is an impulse that sometimes results in tragedy; but I would rather mention an incident in lighter vein which well illustrates this anxiety to 'get up the pit,' and which at times is so strong as completely to change a man's nature.

It was a Saturday, and three of us had been cutting a coalface in a distant part of the North Mine. It was in the more recent period and 60 h.p. diesel pugs had supplanted the rope haulage. The deputy, arriving to tell us that there was little time left, delayed departure till we had finished; then the four of us crawled-ran-slithered and stumbled down to the loading point in the Main Level just in time to see the rear light of the pug disappearing round a far-off bend— no doubt the pug driver also 'wanted up the pit.'

Cursing, for we were now faced with a long tramp and were already exhausted, we set off at our best speed. I, the third man in the cutting team, happened to be in the lead, followed by Old Bob, the leading man, a highly-skilled, staunchly independent Scots collier: there was a slight gap, then came the second man of the cutting team, an Englishman. He was a meek, rabbity little man, lacking any sort of individual spirit and too ready to accord respect to deputies to suit us; for to colliers the deputies, since they accepted responsibilities for wages as well as safety, are anathema.

The Englishman was particularly subservient to the deputy who now brought up the rear; a brash, newly-promoted young fellow who thought it smart to bedevil old colliers with his authority and who, oh, anathema upon anathema, wore a wristwatch at the face.

We limped on in weary haste. A shining smear of water loomed in the lamp beam directed from my bowed head: I had already splashed or waded through a thousand, but . . . there was something about this one.

I shouted a warning and swiftly turned aside. Bob, his senses ever alert, followed me round. Then, suddenly from behind, came a loud splash followed by a scream of terror which turned into a prolonged howl of bitter anguish.

We spun round and watched in amazement as the Englishman's head appeared above the surface of that filthy pool, the deputy focussing his lamp to give him light as he clambered out.

He was choking with rage and frustration; glaring about him like a wild beast. Discovering that the deputy was the only person near, he subjected that worthy to a stream of such blistering invective it should have reduced him to ashes where he stood. Then, clutching his dripping rags about him, he hurriedly set off once more . . . and plunged straight back into the same hole . . .!

Even as the life of the Wellesley bridged the changes that took place in forms of transport, from ponies to diesel pugs, so also did it span new developments in lighting and the use of explosives. The miner's lamp is the only illumination at the coalface. In the early days of the pit the colliers used the 'tally' lamp.

This was a coffee-pot-shaped container made of thin metal and fixed to the cap. The miner brought tallow and wick and made up the lamp as required. I don't know what light it gave but I have heard the older men speak of the volumes of smoke it produced, which fouled the already none-too-clean air, and nearly asphyxiated the wearer.

In the twenties the 'tally' gave way to the brass carbide lamp with which I was, myself, familiar. Depending on its age and condition, it required replenishment with carbide and water about three times in a shift of eight hours. It gave a good light but over a restricted area, blew out when shots were fired, and was a prey to dust obstructing the jet. In bad conditions a carbide lamp could become as temperamental as a prima donna and I can remember many a time when a collier, after losing patience, clashed his lamp to the pavement, jumped on it with his heavy boots, and sulked in the dark for the rest of the shift.

In the fifties, however, the introduction of the electric cap lamp brought an era of better illumination.

When explosives first came into general use underground they were called powder, and were in cake form with a centre hole, and were ignited by a fuse knows as a 'strum.' Each man took several yards of strum with him each time he went below and cut off a length as required—in judging this experience was the only guide—attached it to the powder, lit the frayed end, and retired smartly to a place of refuge.

A bad moment resulted (as frequently happened) if the strum went out after burning for a while: the hushed wait, the half-fearful return to the shothole, and the awful problem of whether to relight the now shortened strum and 'chance it.' No easy choice for a man with a wife and bairns and a wage of from five to eight shillings a shift; for, then as now, the collier was paid only on results.

Today the modern electric exploders can fire whole rounds of shots, with delayed action effects if such are required in difficult or inaccessible situations. When first introduced, however, the electric exploders were treated with some suspicion. I remember one particularly hair-raising experience. This occurred when an older collier was sent to blast down and remove a 'nose' of coal weighing several tons which was obstructing the 'face.'

He stemmed the shot with wet clay as was usual, connected up, and from a place of safety, twirled the key of the exploder. Instead of the roar of the explosion there was complete and utter silence. Later, the deputy arrived on the scene to be told by the complaining collier: "These new ways dinna work, ava;" and the man pointed to the thin wires trailing away into the darkness.

"You should have checked the wires to the shothole, and tried it again," said the deputy.

"I did," replied the collier, "three times I've tried the cussed thing."

"Four times," said the trainee.

"Three times," snapped the collier, brushing him aside. "D'ye think I canna coont!"

"Four times," the trainee insisted. "I gave it a try while you were checking the wires at the shothole!"

But, joking apart, few people realise that on a hand-stripped face—most faces were hand-stripped until recently, and in Scotland many still are—the average collier will carry underground and use daily the contents of a four-pound box of gelignite. At the magazine on the pithead, men drawing their quota of 'stuff' would gaze thoughtfully at the caged canaries kept there in case of emergency: they are carefully, lovingly, tended; for the life of one of these little yellow songsters can save the lives of many men should gas roll through the darkness.

I walked round the Wellesley pithead the other day and found it greatly changed: it was almost deserted and given over to silence and the dust of memories. The production board at the side of the old check office in the pityard gave the figure of 300 tons for the last day. I have known the time when the figure was nearer three thousand tons; then, in every twenty-four hours, two thousand five hundred men went underground and returned again, at shift's end, to the surface.

Looking back now, it all seems like a dream; a dream of many inter-related fragments. Queueing resentfully at the lamp cabin in the dawn light and drowsily awaiting the cage; then, at 'lowsin' time,' the blessing of the baths and hot soapy water, followed by a race across the road to 'The Goth' for a pint; or a noggin of Stewarty's famous jungle juice: to lean gratefully on the bar, drink in hand, with the sunlight streaming through the coloured glass of the windows, listening to Stewarty, ex-stoker in a crack destroyer flotilla, telling tales of Papeete and Hiva Oa, while, from the corner by the door, would come the gruff rumble of dear old Angus Cameron as he collected 'horsey lines' and paid out the winners.

Then, and only then, could one relax and let aching limbs find an easement and parched throats a liquid compensation.

Going down on the backshift, perhaps, on a golden afternoon with the heartbreaking sight of a bright sun shining in a clear blue sky; and in the pitbottom the half-guilty hope that a dispute would start . . . and there'd be a strike . . . and we'd get back up the pit and get a bit of that sun. . . . But there was no strike, and one went grudgingly to work; to discover at shift's end that it was almost as good coming up in the cool velvet of the early Summer dusk to hear a blackbird singing his heart out.

Or the leisurely pause for pithead gossip before the nightshift in still, frosty weather, and the last look up at the stars so seeming-close above the cage wheels, so that, mingled with a dread of what lay deep down was a glowing sense of wonder that the world could be so beautiful: and the moment would be harshly broken by the sudden clang of steel bars about us and, to the stroke of a clear, sweet bell, we would have our last frantic glimpse of the banksman's face-belt-boots as we dropped into the shaft.

But it must not be thought that it was all misery underground; there was a joker in every group, and I have also been delighted by flashes of repartee from quarters where it was least expected. As I heard in the cage one morning. We were packed in even more tightly than usual and, as we hurtled downwards, a sarcastic voice instructed from the whirling darkness, "Even numbers breathe in!"

Another occasion was at the face. My neighbour was rubbing his head and complaining bitterly to the shotfirer about the injustice of fate.

"That bit stane's been hangin' there for fifty million years," he growled, "but it has tae drop just when I appear!"

"It musta been waiting for you," snapped the unsympathetic official.

This lugubrious note persists at all times underground, but on the surface the miner is more carefree, and it was in the baths that one heard the best examples of Wellesley humour.

I remember an oversman walking through the baths passage on his way to the canteen. He walked slowly, consulting his notebook, oblivious to his surroundings. A naked, blue-scarred collier stopped soaping his neighbour's back to mutter suspiciously—"What's that basket doin'?"

"He's mebbe writin' a buik," suggested his neighbour after due consideration.

"It'll be a horror comic, then," said the first, "if he's come in here for his material."

My favourite memories of the baths, however, are of Sunday mornings when, empty of miners, the buildings were unofficially given over to the children from the nearby 'garden city' of Denbeath, where the houses are without baths.

For these little ones, to bathe was not enough; the hot water seemed to infect them with a sort of delirium of joy so that they romped and scampered madly in and out of the showers, small feet pattering noisily on the wet tiles and the slapping on damp bodies and shrieking all the while with such hilarious, such echo-rousing delight, that the baths attendant could no longer pretend not to be aware of their presence and had, perforce, to go into the pityard and smoke a pipe that the proprieties might be observed.

In other years it would have been accepted that these children should follow their fathers down the Wellesley. That is no longer possible and, in the case of most pits, the immediate—and natural—mining response would be, "An' a guid thing, too!"

In the present instance I am not so sure of that reaction, and this doubt is, in its way, the best tribute of all to that special relationship of place and the men who serve it, which was called The Wellesley.

However, in these days of frequent pit closures, it is impossible not to experience a feeling of sadness each time we hear of a once-busy mining village left derelict and dispeopled.

It may relieve our disquiet a little if we reflect that such closures have always been part of the natural order and are no new thing. Given that a seam of coal be worked long enough, it must at last become exhausted ... the people move away, the buildings fall or are demolished, and the land goes back to grass or the plough.

It is an old story—the oldest in the world. Man takes a profit where he can and then moves on. I have gathered the material for this article in much the same fashion, gleaning a little here and there as I went upon my journeyings in Fife. It has proved a scanty harvest, for in olden times few records were kept, and, unlike the baronial castle and village church, the ruin of an ancient pit is not often suffered to remain. A pity, this, in my opinion, for it was frequently the pit that made possible both keep and kirk.

In many instances the place name, with its telltale prefix—Coaltown, or Colton—is not only the sole indication of what once was, but also all that remains. Sometimes there is physical witness of mining activities, such as the turf-clad declivities and humps that tell their own story; or there may still be left a fragment of a long-disused pit building—the Klondike at Methil is such a case. Often there is no more to go on than the talk of an old collier retelling the tales he heard from the greybeards of his youth. But books are the best of all.

How often have I not, when leafing through some old volume, found a reference to mining in an area where, by reason of its sylvan beauty, I had never otherwise suspected such a possibility. The note of the value of the ancient Balcarres Coals, which I will mention later, is an instance of such good fortune.

However, the faintest, most evanescent of the leads which enabled me to pinpoint an area of old workings was vapour—no more, in fact, than a thin wisp of smoke seen one evening from the Standing Stane Road about three miles from Cameron Bridge. At this spot there is a lonely stretch of moor and thicket, newly set with plantations. Fearing that boys had kindled a fire near the young trees I left the car and set off on foot to investigate.

After half a mile of rough going I rounded a grove of saplings to find pasture and a flock of blackfaces. With the sheep was a tall, well-dressed man with keen grey eyes and a dark-skinned face.

"Ye'd see the smoke," said the elderly stranger, and nodded understandingly before I could reply. "Aye, every time the old waste sparks up I get folks coming across from the main road to put the fire oot. Even had the polis once. There's little hope of putting this fire oot," he confided with a smile. "See——" And, walking a few paces, he squatted near a liplike hole where two great slabs of rock, canted almost to the vertical, closely overlay each other.

"Thon's an old pit waste," he told me. "Whiles it's quiet and ye'd never ken it was here; then all of a sudden it'll start to smoke again. But it never does nae harm, and there's never nae flame—nothing here that would burn, anyway—just smoke and heat.

"Feel that rock," he said, and, when I hesitated, "Go on—it'll no burn ye. It's just warm. I'd show ye, but I'm a' cleaned. Me and the wife go to the bingo in Kirkcaldy on a Saturday," he explained, "and I like to come up here for a last look at the ewes while she's getting ready."

Encouraged, I let my hand rest gingerly on the smooth rock. As he had said, it was warm to the touch.

Little more than a mile away was the site of Wellsgreen Pit. I asked him if there was a connection.

"Och, no." He seemed shocked by the suggestion. "Wellsgreen was a modern pit. I doubt if Wellsgreen was mair than a hundred years old. It was the Coal Board closed it down. Na, na, these are old workings frae lang syne." He paused and took thought. "Mebbe the monks," he volunteered at last.

Recollecting the curses levelled at the heads of the poor monks by generations of Fife colliers for discovering coal, I forbore to comment. We talked a little longer and then parted, the patriarchal old shepherd to go to the bingo, I to go home and make yet another note.

The mention of monks brings me to the Balcarres reference of which I spoke earlier, for it is dated soon after the charter to mine coal given in 1219 by Seyer de Quincy to the monks of Newbattle Abbey. The Balcarres note is from an old record dated 1293 which lists the lands and appurtenances of the estates of Balnacrois in the Schyra de Ryras, held of the King of Scotland by Duncan, son of Colburn, late Earl of Fife, and which were at the time held by the King of England on behalf of Duncan, son of Duncan, then a minor. The estate was managed by Walter de Cambo, and the coal pits were valued at 4s 5½d per annum—a considerable sum in 1293.

The discovery of this note was a matter of great elation, but, oh, to know just where those old pits actually were! Landale, in his essay on the East Fife coalfield, says that the trap of Calcarres Crag must be partly overlying, as coal has been wrought from beneath it. No one today, looking at the wild loveliness of that sequestered spot, would believe such a thing.

Yet there is good reason for belief. This was once all coal country that is now a bosky pastureland, tree-capped, and slashed and cut by slithering drops and brambly-dark defiles. They were small pits, no doubt, worked perhaps by a score of men and women, some manned by no more than two or three families. And they are hidden now, these tiny borings made by man into the crust of Earth, hidden, lost, and all forgotten; but we who have hewn coal in these comparatively easy modern times know full well what mighty efforts must have gone into such seemingly puny delvings.

Some had a short life, others lasted a century or so; but there were many that refused to die and blazed the path to modern times.

101

One such example of longevity was the Pirnie at Methilhill, not closed until the 20's of this century. It was first worked by the great David, second Earl of Wemyss, in 1677, when he records that to open up his "New Mhynd at Methilhille cost 10,000 lib." Yet it is a scant couple of years since the reeking bing was finally levelled and houses built upon its site.

Another ancient sinking that survives is the Wellesley Colliery itself. It stands near the site of an 'ingoing eye' which Earl David first drove in Denbeath in 1671, and which he called the Happy Mine. It ran through the metals for six hundred fathoms to the Kirkland of Methil, where he had at that time seven pits in full production. From my window I can still see the tottering ruin of the Manor House he built upon the braeside above the river, that he might the more conveniently oversee the workings.

The coal from these pits was carried to the surface by women bearers, but the water which gathered continually underground was removed by pumps driven by the River Leven. When, as in times of drought, the level fell and production was threatened, the Earl would arm his collier serfs, and, fighting their way to Loch Leven, they would break down the banks to release a better flow.

Another interesting facet on the lawless habits of the times, and on the scant respect such men accorded to the property of their fellow peers, is a letter from a later Earl to the factor of the coleheughs at Methil. He writes, "And if you see it for my benefitt, and that there is work and room for more people below ground, why don't you get some of Balbirnie's colliers who are now in different parts of the country and nobody's property?"

But Earl David was a great innovator. Traces of his advanced experiments in mining methods came to light when the dock was built at West Wemyss; but now they, and the dock also, are buried. At Methil, the harbour of which he was so proud lies beneath railway sidings, and the 'grete dubble house' he built upon the harbour head—that, too, has gone, and there are only old books to tell of it, and the memory of the passing stranger.

Such a one was the indefatigable Daniel Defoe, who said of the colliers of nearby Leven: "Partly from their poverty and the black hue which they get from the coal, they make a frightful appearance." Later, in 1760, another traveller, Richard Pococke, Lord Bishop of

Golfers playing over lovely Lundin Links on the Fife east coast little realise that below the fairways lie the old workings of Durie Pit. Records claim that 'Lundie Coals' were being worked in 1770

Meath, said of Leven, now a popular holiday resort: "Great coal pitts and many waggon roads from them to the sea; there is plenty of coal in these parts."

But the coal referred to by my Lord Bishop has been worked out. In Leven now only the name Wagon Road remains to tell of what the Irish cleric saw, and there were older workings forgotten long before his time. How many of those who play golf along the shore towards the pretty village of Lundin Links know that the roughness of the course, the many hummocks and hollows and bunkers, are the turf-clad debris of old mines. Cunningham quotes Dr. Landale as saying that he met in 1836 two men who sixty years previously had worked the 'Lundie Coals.'

A little farther along this lovely coast is St. Monance, the village where everyone smiles. It is a bright place, and given over to fishing and boatbuilding. Yet here—and I can think of no place where such an industry seems less likely—a writer lists six coals that once were worked, and names the seams as follows:—

The Fore coal, the Back coal, the Parrot coal, the Brassie coal, the Foul-nose coal, and My Lord's coal; the same writer asserts, moreover, that the pier of the harbour is built upon an outcrop of the same mineral and that the harbour is part of a coal basin worked out long since. A more easily verifiable fact is that the farm to the east of the village is called Coal Farm, and beyond that again the ruins of Pittenweem Priory remind us of yet other monks who held a charter to mine coal. Westward, as far as Elie the sedate, were mined the famous Strathairly coals—basis of many a local fortune.

Even beautiful Largo, sweetly nestling in its wide bay, was once the site of important coal workings. Largo, which I always see as green and gold, once supplied the heating for the King's bedchamber in Falkland Palace and His Majesty would have no other coals.

On another occasion, when kings were out of fashion and lords protector were the thing, Cromwell's garrison at the palace, in 1654, made repeated demands on the overseer of the coleheughs at Largo. Lamont tells us, "Fifty loade of coalls were but a fortnight's provision of fyre for the garrison." One can detect a note of outrage in this comment by the trugal-minded old Scots diarist.

So it goes on. Everywhere in this south-east corner of Fife the local history is based on coal, and, though one may leave the coast

103

and turn inland, the story of the past has the same sable emphasis. I have written already of the Balcarres coals; beyond, at Largoward, a village set squarely in an agricultural area, coal was still being worked in 1907. The bing of one pit remains in a field behind the little church. Nearby is a red-roofed row of miners' cottages, and, incongrously enough, among the pastures of Cassingray protrudes the tall, dark 'lum' of another old pit. An old friend who died recently at a great age started work as a boy, driving the pony that turned the gin at Largoward Pit to wind up the coal.

North-east, at Lathones, black-streaked hummocks and quarry-like depressions below the thin turf of the wide, lonely fields are the only physical evidence, but history tells us that when Hackston, of Rathillet, met his fellow-conspirators at Magnus Moor for the second time, on April 11, 1679, it was at Lathones "in the house of a collier."

To the west, high on a furzy heath above Ceres and at the end of a rutted lane that bears traces of having been a road built of pit-rubble, there is no more than a couple of cottages to mark the grandiloquently-named Coaltown of Callange—a cottage, and wavering lines of nettles, to show where stood the rows of collier homes.

In my wanderings about the 'Kingdom' I seldom cross the Eden—in the present case there is little need, for coal is never found to the north of that river, and so I turn south again to New Gilston, the highest village in Fife and built to house colliers, but where today one would have difficulty in mustering one such person. On now by the bare, ribbon-like road to Woodside and Teasses, where there are trees and grass and prospects fair—a solitary land of tree-whorled knolls, thorn-thick ravines, and sheep with wind-combed fleeces. Yet, when, in 1840, the Parliamentary Commission on Child and Female Labour took evidence here, there were as many as sixty-five people employed at the coalpit.

The Lessee stated, in answer to a question, that boys drew the coal in carts from the working faces to the pit bottom. In his evidence, a boy of sixteen said that there were no rails and that "the pulling wis sair." Such human misery, where now there is only bird-song and the bleating of blackface lambs.

And with such thoughts in my head I came to Montrave, the verdantly beautiful. It is a name that makes me think instinctively of farming and fox-hunting and of all rural pursuits. Were it not for old Jacob Gordon's map of 1645, I should not have known that this was once the Coletoun of Monthryve.

It was in much the same fashion that I discovered that nearby Kilmux was also once the scene of mining activities. I came upon this clue while browsing through *The Favourite Village*, an old book which had been lauded by a friend but which I thought of small merit. There was, however, something to be gleaned.

Writing of a severe winter in the early years of the last century the author tells us that the road to Kilmux colliery had been blocked by a snowstorm. James Fernie, laird of Kilmux, and owner of the coalfield, sent word to Kennoway to raise a body of men to cut a road through the drifts: a drummer announced the message, and, to cheer the workers, two gallons of whisky were sent. There is scant trace today of that coalfield unless three twisted thorns above a mound of shaggy hummocks tell of its location.

In the same book, the writer describes a much-relished pleasure of his boyhood; this was to visit the pit at Smiddyhill, near Windygates. Here, within the shaft—a great open mouth in the earth—rude wooden buckets swung wildly on chains.

From the rim of the shaft the pit bottom was plainly visible and, standing there, the boys were able to watch the colliers at work and see the pit ponies drawing forward the tubs of coal to fill the buckets. I frequently pass Smiddyhill. The smiddy still stands, though much dilapidated, but the great shaft has disappeared nor could any of my old mining friends decide on just where it must have been.

Some of the workings I have mentioned were no more than mines, but many were true pits, with ladders for the coalbearers or with some system of haulage. And so I have come home, full circle, having missed more than I have found, no doubt, for such is ever the way; and I am once again where Earl David drove his 'Happy Mine' three hundred years ago. Sometimes, looking back on the days when I worked underground here at Denbeath, I think that I, too, was happy, though I grumbled just as bitterly as did my neighbours.

One of these I remember well; a thin man with a thin face and sad eyes; he was tall for a collier and possessed a remarkably soft and engaging voice. I recall him particularly because he exemplified for me an uncanny instinct, inherent in the man who is collier-born and without which no pit could be 'wrocht.' The instinct to which I refer is the ability to divine the whereabouts of mineral-rich strata.

He confided to me on one occasion, that, during the 'great strike,' he had risked prosecution by illegally mining coal on a stretch of beach near Lundin Links. Using driftwood to secure the roof, he 'howked' the coal by night, and sold it by day.

"How did you know where to dig?" I asked him.

"Ach." He shrugged. "I kent where there wis coal."

"But how?" I persisted.

"Och, Chairlie!" He frowned, impatient at my lack of understanding. "I dinna ken hoo. There's things ye just ken——"

When a pit is shut down a whole community is forced to change its way of life and abandon the habits and customs of centuries. The Scots collier has always been more conservative than his English counterpart. Because of the early days of slavery and the segregation that went with it, the Scots mining village is an integral and self-contained community.

Considering the revolutionary changes demanded of the men thrown out of work, one would expect regret, but the feelings engendered were well expressed in the words of Sandy, an old collier:

"It's not afore time, Chairlie," he said, "but it'll come too late to save us. Aye," he reflected, "we wis born too soon: that's our tragedy, Chairlie—we wis born too soon."

One does hear an occasional word of regret born out of a backward-looking longing for things past; this is only natural. All expression must contain something of nostalgia: of what else can we speak but what we know; of what else tell but what we have ourselves experienced; each man is the unconscious mirror of his life and of the world he has known.

For the miner that world has changed more violently in the last few years than in the previous five hundred, for mining is not only a job but also a way of life. When the collier is taken from the pit and his familiar world he is, in very truth, like a fish out of water. His first reactions to the change are physical.

His supple muscularity, bred through the centuries and, like his keen, native caution, developed since boyhood, is of less use, and as the relaxation becomes permanent his sinews slacken and warp till he becomes subject to aches and pains—and sometimes actual physical disablement. This troubles and upsets him, for his body was always his pride.

He misses the daily dehydration, when the last drop of fluid, or so it seemed, was leached from his straining over-heated flesh. At the factory bench, his body slackens; he develops a paunch and is discontented. He grumbles at the loss of his strength and the agility on which his safety once depended.

He smokes at work now, for now he can; and feels it in his stone-roughened lungs, and in his pocket. His eyes, accustomed to darkness, are at first ill-at-ease in the glass-walled palace of light which is a modern factory.

He, who knew only the silence of the underworld, whose ears were trained—where eyes were useless—to heed the warning of a creaking prop, is bewildered and deeply distrustful of the clangour of the conveyor belt and the frenzy of *Music While You Work* from a dozen loudspeakers.

When the tea-trolley comes round, twice—or thrice—in every day, the novelty leads him to eat more than his tough frame requires: more than is good for him who, for most of his working life, was content for his twenty-minutes break to perch on a glacier-chilled stone with a flask of tepid water and a 'piece.'

Even if he stays, his old haunts, his surroundings change; the scenes he has known since childhood. No longer in the forenoon are the pavements silver-streaked where the keen dawn air has caught at ravaged lungs. No longer can he find the groups of his familiars—the nightshift and the backshift—gossiping on their hunkers at the corners. The huge bing, there before he was born, growing bigger as he grew, seeming as immovable as a mountain, is now carted away for making bricks and roads. As it disappears, shabby houses are revealed which have never caught the sunlight on a window.

A pub closes and the Bowling Club winds up; and the Miners' Institute is offered 'For Sale or Let.' The dog track deteriorates into rusting iron sheets and flapping boards which the first winter gale will utterly demolish.

The 'Band,' that central, joyous exultation of colliery life, begins to lose musicians and finds it hard to recruit youngsters. Now that

107

the 'weekly penny' from countless pay-packets is no more, there is little for uniforms or new instruments. It was the miners' weekly penny—or threepence—which built the band and lovingly maintained it, and a vicarious pride was found in its achievements. The 'Band," always a great worker for the Kirk and for charity, is no longer seen and heard at 'Summer Occasions,' and good causes suffer.

Not seldom now, one sees the saddest of all sights, an empty church, now disused or abandoned to secular activities. In the limited surroundings of my own small burgh, ten pits and five churches have closed in the last forty years. Small consolation to reflect that the members are worshipping in the other lands to which they have taken their faith together with their skills.

As men and their families leave for Canada or Australia or England, whole streets fall vacant. The bulldozers move in among the close-ranked, narrow streets of back-to-backs. In a little while only rubble and the melancholy of emptiness remain.

To me, the most distressing part of this wholesale destruction of dwellings, poor though they are by modern standards, is that all knowledge is thus destroyed—all memory of the generations who lived upon this spot and went from here each day to hew coal; who endured back-breaking toil, heart-breaking conditions and derisory wages, yet were withal content: happy with simple things; 'hame' with its great collier fire roaring up the lum, the family; humility and courage and comradeship and the staunch faith of their fathers.

All this is lost except where it lingers in the memory of some pensioner, soon himself to depart, or where some fragment can be deciphered on a mossy stone in the bleak, stane-dykit little kirkyard.

For those who emigrate, certainly life will be easier; it could not be harder than what they have known. I like to hope that life will be more rewarding; this they deserve, for they have been betrayed too often. I remember how the best of them laboured and struggled, the efforts they made, when, believing empty promises, they 'wrocht haird and sair,' that the pit might be kept open.

I recall a scene underground some years ago. An old collier argued fiercely with a group of younger, more cynical men, when we were first told (incorrectly as it turned out) that it was up to us whether or not the pit was to shut.

At Woodside, near Largo, Fife. It is difficult to believe that these idyllic acres were once festooned with pit buildings

Opening up a new 'face' in a desperate attempt to 'get' coal we had run into trouble: heavy water, roof falls and severe geological faults.

The methods being introduced to cope with the problems involved no little risk, and the men hung back. "This pit has tae be wrocht," declared old Sandy, waving his short, light, miner's pick, and preparing to take the lead. "If we canna work it the one way, then we maun try anither; but this pit's our breid and butter. It has tae be wrocht."

He is dead now, old Sandy; his blue-scarred body and oft-broken bones sleeping peacefully in the shadow of the kirkyard dyke.

I would give much to know what he is thinking, now that the pit to which he gave his life has closed.

THE COALFACE

Here the unquiet voices
Of the deep and lustful earth.
Pulsate upon the thick, the stifling air.
The soul is muffled, lost.
In the dust of shattered time
And fettered with the fretted strands of care.

Within the unhappy dark
Of a thousand sabled nights
The virgins of the rocks are whispering drear
And dreadful symphonies.
While all about sings putridly
The stark, unlovely stench
That wraps the pallid pulse of private fear.

CHAPTER EIGHT

NICKY FIGURES IT OUT

NICKY McFISH, coming up the pit off the backshift, threw his check into the bowl as though severing his connection with mining for ever, and marched across the pityard.

He paused to sniff appreciatively at the mild air of the spring evening and it was then that he saw the two blue-uniformed figures in the shadow of the yard wall. Jerking his head angrily, he hurried into the baths and demanded of Magnus McAra on the seat opposite:

"You're no goin' doon the pit on the nightshift are ye?" And his voice was equally compounded of scorn and horror.

"Aye." Magnus emitted an indifferent grunt and inserted his right leg into the left leg of his moleskins. Trying to retrieve the error while his left foot was still off the floor, he collapsed in a heap in Nicky's arms.

"What're ye bletherin' aboot, man," he snapped bad-temperedly. "Ah michta bruk ma neck then, listenin' tae you." He hobbled back to his seat and once more concentrated his attention on his toilet.

Nicky, till that moment speechless with contempt, now found his voice. "You should think shame!" he exploded. "Ah never thocht ah'd live tae see the day. Polis in the pityard an' colliers linin' up for the cage—you should think black burnin' shame o' yoursel's," he informed them. "By the hokey, but things is come tae a bonny p——"

Magnus, hunting for a lost knee-pad, lifted from under the seat a face that was already black, and said wearily, "Oh, Nicky, haud your wheesht, will ya, 'n gie's peace. What've the polis tae do wi' us goin' tae oor work?"

111

"They're no nuthin' tae do wi' us," Wull McAan said from farther along the cubicle. "They're after three young fellas that robbed a bank some place. They're supposed tae have headed this way."

"Ohh," said Nicky, not attempting to hide his disappointment. "Ah see the polis, 'n thocht the pit wis on strike—'n pickets—'n polis—'n a' that——" His voice tailed sadly away and then rose again excitedly, as he asked, "Hoo much did they get?"

"Fifteen thoosan' accordin' tae the evening papers," said Magnus, who, having found his knee-pad and strapped it on, had now discovered that he had forgotten something to suck in place of the forbidden tobacco.

"See a pan drop," he begged.

"Guid luck tae them," Nicky said enviously, handing out a poke of sweeties. "Canny noo," he urged. "Ah'm no paid tae keep the nichtshift in pan drops."

"Aye, lucky devils." Wull McAan sighed heartfelt agreement with Nicky's remark. "They'll be whoopin' it up richt noo."

"They're safe enough here in a colliery village, did they but ken it." Nicky, naked now, looked something like the last of the Ten Little Nigger Boys.

"Ach." Magnus rose to his feet with a marked look of enthusiasm. "They'll be miles awa by noo. Thae boys dinna hang aboot."

"The polis'll get nae help from us, anyway." Nicky cast his towel about him like a toga, and, clutching a bar of soap, prepared to depart.

"They ken that weel enough," Magnus grunted from the end of the passage. "That's why the place is pollutit with 'em. They ken that if they wanta catch crooks they'll need tae do it theirsel's—aboot these parts, anyway."

"Fifteen thoosan' quid in a oner." Nicky sighed ecstatically, and made a sudden grab at his slipping sarong. "There's hope for us yet. Ah'll need tae tak' a walk doon the Brae the morn an' have a keek at oor wee bank. Why—ah'm mebbe knockin' ma sowlcase oot down a hole in the grund when ah'm no needin' tae." And, so struck was he by the horror implicit in this dreadful thought, that his towel fell, unheeded, to his ankles, and he was only brought back to awareness of his position when an unsympathetic bath attendant's broom slapped heavily on his bare flesh.

"Watch what ye're daein' with that broom," he warned, and gathered his garment about him, but his thoughts were far, far away.

"Where the devil hae ye been?" his wife demanded, as he entered the door some time later. "Last nicht ye wis in here at twenty tae ten because there wis boxing on the TV; the night it's twenty tae eleven when ye come waltzin' in." She bustled into the scullery. "Hoo am ah s'posed tae gie ye a hot supper when ah dinna ken——"

"Awa an' bile your heid," Nicky advised her affectionately, and maliciously dropped his empty piece-box on the sleeping cat.

"Let that beast alane," she shrilled. "What's goin' on? The place is alive with polis. You monkeys are no on strike again, are ye? Ah thocht you said there wis kindlin' ready chappit in the cellar?"

"Aye, there's kindlin'." Nicky answered the last question first. "Na," he then added regretfully, in answer to the first question. "Lookin' for young fellas that bust intae a bank——"

"As you're so sure there's kindlin' ye'd better go doon n' bring it up," she said. "Ah hunted, but ah couldnae find it, an' ah'll be needin' it the morn. Ah've turnt the gas up under your supper, so ye've just got time. What are ye needin' the axe for?" she demanded. "You said it was all ready chappit——" But he was gone, and, with a conspiratorial nod to the offended cat, she put her husband's baffies to warm for his return.

At the foot of the dark steps Nicky heard the soft rustle of sound as his hand reached for the coal cellar door. He stiffened, his wiry body dropping into a half-crouch and the axe-shaft sliding more comfortably into his hand. He flexed his shoulder and arm muscles, pulled the cellar door open and spoke into the silence.

"Come oota that," he said in a cold, quiet voice, "an dinna have me comin' in after ye." Nicky McFish was not very big, but, as a working collier, he was as strong and agile as a fox, and moreover was utterly fearless.

"Come on," he said again. "Ah'm no giein' a monkey's jump who ye are or what ye are, but ah've an axe in ma hand, 'n if ah've tae come in there after ye ah'll tak' your heid aff at the angles——".

"No," a trembling voice said from the depths of the cellar. "Wait Dinna——" Nicky stared at the hulking youth, who, with his hands raised as though at gunpoint, emerged and stood hesitantly before him.

"What're ye doin' in ma coalhoose?" Nicky wanted to know.

"Ah was hidin'—no doin' no harm—the p'lice——"

Nicky gasped. "Wait," he said with desperate urgency. "Are ye the fellas the polis is after?"

The figure said with pathetic simplicity, "Aye, my pals an' the money got caught, but I got away. They're after me."

"Up thae stairs," Nicky commanded. "Up thae stairs, 'n quick," and he almost lifted the stranger on to the first step so anxious was he, and so excited, with this, his first personal contact with a real criminal.

"Wha's he?" said Rina, narrowing her eyes and pursing her lips and staring at her husband's companion.

"Sssh!" Nicky shoved his captive into the kitchen. "This is him that the polis is after."

She stared at him aghast. In his home the collier is master, a compensation, no doubt, for the harsh disciplines imposed by the

114

pit, but this was too much. "What're ye bringin' him in here for then?" she asked in a voice of apprehension.

This flummoxed Nicky, who had been so obsessed by far from clear quixotic notions that he had hardly given serious thought to what he was doing.

He coughed importantly and noticed the steam rising from his own supper which had that minute been placed on the table. "Haud your wheesht, wumman," he asserted his authority, and gave the back of the bank robber a friendly shove.

"Sit doon," he said, "an' wrap your lugs roon that plate o' grub while ah think."

He saw Hectorina's mouth open and said hastily, waving the axe like a banner. "We'll hae to gie the laddie a bite o' meat, Rina." And this statement not only silenced his wife, but consoled his own uncertainty.

Hectorina, though no more lacking in generous motives than her husband, saw only a long-haired youth with a flabby face and shifty eyes wolfing her man's supper.

"Wha are you wummanin'?" she snapped. "Ah've a hann'le tae ma name. An', another thing—what's tae be done wi' him when he's fed. He's no bidin' here," she glared at the two men, arms akimbo. "Ah'd never close ma een if ah kent he wis in ma hoose. Wha's that?"

"Through there," Nicky barked, and dropping the axe, which was still, inexplicably, in his hand, he sat down in the vacated seat, as the 'room' door closed stealthily behind their visitor.

"Oh, Rina, have ye a shillin' for the gas?" They both heaved great signs of relief at the familiar ring of the voice of their neighbour Sophia McAdam.

"Ah dinna ken, Suff." Hectorina hunted through her purse to produce a ten shilling note and—a shilling. "Aye, you're lucky." She gave Sophia the shilling and put the two sixpences and the note back in her purse.

"Ta," Sophia said. "My, what a polis a while back there. Ah wis feart, wi' ma man awa oot on the nightshift——"

"Ye're no needin' tae be lonely." Nicky made to rise to his feet.

"You sit doon, you," Hectorina ordered her husband. She said to Sophia, "Nicky says fellas robbed a bank. If ye're lonely come up an' sit wi us."

"Och, no," Sophia's black eyes flashed. "Ah wouldnae see polis in ma road. They're awa noo onywey. Well, Ah'll need to flee afore the bairn gets hame frae the dancin'."

"Wha's awa, Suff?" It was Nicky who put the question.

"The polis. They catched twa an' got the money back, an' they're a' aff tae Balawney in their Hurry-up waggons after the third yin. He's s'posed tae have been seen there——" The door shut behind her and Nicky, sharp ears alert, heard her out to the street before calling his guest back to the table.

"Did ye hear that?" he asked the youth. "They've got your pals an' the dough. What're ye going tae do now?"

"Are ye goin' tae gie me up?" The bank robber looked quickly from the little collier to his wife.

"No me," Nicky said with engaging simplicity. "Ah'm no paid tae do the polis's wark for them. Na, na, there's naebuddy in this place'll split on ye. But you're better makin' tracks afore daylicht. Balawney's no that far awa, 'n they micht come back. Feenish that grub an' then Ah'll see the coast's clear for ye tae get awa."

He watched with fascinated eyes the eating habits of the guest. Then, with a preliminary, depracatory cough, he asked—"Where did ye learn the bank bustin' wark. Ah mean——"

"Fellas Ah met in the Approved School learned me," the youth said from a full mouth.

"What like places are they?" Nicky, devoured by an awful curiosity, did not intend to miss a moment of this golden opportunity.

"Places where they keep us," was the answer; "the Gove'ment runs em."

"Oh, aye," Nicky said affably, and nodded at Rina. Then he had a sudden thought and his brows contracted ferociously. "The Gov'ment?" he enunciated slowly, as if he were chewing the words before speaking them, "but—that's taxes—that's us—the warkers, an' taxes an'—by the hokey," he breathed and his fingers reached longingly for the axe, still beside his chair. His guest saw the move and prepared for flight.

116

"The poseeshun is, then," Nicky said unbelievingly, "that ye have tae rob banks tae live because ye'll no wark. But Ah've tae wark every day in a coal pit tae pay taxes to keep you in an approved schule where ye can be taught how tae rob banks——" The whole monstrous irony of the thing burst upon him for the first time and he leaned back in the chair, his eyes asparkle.

"Here, son," Rina pressed the ten shilling note into the young man's hand and shoved him relentlessly towards the door. "It's a' Ah have, but it'll keep ye goin' a wee whiley. Go on," she pushed him out into the darkness. "If ye're still here when ma man's feenished figurin' oot what Ah think he's figurin', ye're a deid duck."

She watched him slither furtively down the steps and then bolted the door behind him. It took a long time, for collier's doors are never locked, and the bolt had rusted into its socket.

Nicky said defensibly, half-angrily. "Ah s'pose ye think Ah'm daft—bringin' the likes o' him in?"

"Na." She smiled a bright smile. "You wis nae waur than me. Ah gied him ma last ten bob. Oh!" she put her hand to her mouth. "What'll ah do for your dinner the morn? An' ye've had nae supper the nicht."

He shook his grey head moodily. "Ah'm no hungry, Reeny," he told her.

She poked the fire, but without interest, and sat down, the poker still in her hand, and stared thoughtfully at the leaping flames.

"Ah couldnae but feel sorry——" she began.

"Dinna turn on the watter warks," he told her gruffly. "Ah'll gie ye your ten bob back. After a' it wis me that brocht him in. It'll be worth it at that," he murmured to himself. And in his mind he saw himself in the pub on Saturday, the centre of a cleared space, the focus of every eye; leaning nonchalantly on the bar and retelling casually, for the fiftieth time, how he, Nicky McFish, had helped a hunted criminal to evade the polis.

He got to his feet, his eyes glistening with joyous anticipation. "Aye," he said perkily. "In fact, ah'll just gie ye that ten bob richt now."

"On a Wednesday?" she shrilled. "Where'd you get ten bob on a Wednesday?"

117

He opened the 'room' door and grinned back at her over his shoulder. "Ma Wembley money," he told her proudly. "Ah've nearly fourteen pun' plankt in a vase on the mantel-piece," and with a smile, he left her.

He was back in a flash. "The polis!" he roared. "Ohh! Quick, the polis—ah've been robbed!" and he collapsed, howling with rage and frustration, in the armchair on top of the cat.

"*Many misconceptions prevail about the toilers in the darkness. Perhaps that which is most commonly held is that colliers are, as a class, irreligious. Nothing could be further from the truth. Not only is the miner aware of God in the way of all who pit their strength against nature and attempt to control elemental forces; men such as seamen, hill shepherds and mountaineers; but he has a more vivid comprehension of 'a power strong to save.'*"

CHAPTER NINE

COGS IN THE WHEEL OF TIME

MY name is Jan Ladislav and I am a Pole, but I have applied for British naturalisation and I had planned, when my papers came through, to call myself John Leslie. Now—I do not know——?

During the war, the Polish unit to which I was attached was based at Invermuck. And after the war and demob, I came back to the little Scottish mining village. I found lodgings among the collier people and work at the big Motley Pit, on the beach nearby.

I have always wished to be a writer and last year, in furtherance of this desire and also to improve my English, I set out to write a history of this place. The local Librarian, with whom I shared a warm love of books, helped me to get access to old documents and records. Poring over these I found it would be impossible to write a history of Glenmuck without also writing a history of the Vogel family who were so much a part of the district. This strange family haunted me and at last, after many false starts and fruitless plans, I put my notes away and turned to other things. I could not write a history of the Vogels and the ghostly Vogels would not let me write a history of Glenmuck. I returned the documents, through the Librarian, to the Laird's factor and tried to forget the matter. I have no contact with the Laird, who is a Marquis and a Director of the newly-formed National Coal Board.

A fortnight ago, however, something happened which caused me to take out the bundle of notes and read them again—and again——.

*   *   *   *   *   *   *   *

The earlier part of the history of the Vogels is only to be found in the old documents in the records chest of the Laird's Castle, and from the dusty registers of the Parish Kirk. In the later stages, information

120

can be gleamed from the newspapers of the time and court records.

In 1580, during the reign of Philip the Second, a Flemish ship was wrecked in the Bay of Invermuck. There was but one survivor, a huge young man with a white scar on the ball of his left eye. After a time he obtained wood and built himself a boat and a hut on the foreshore. Here he set up as a fisherman and a year later took as wife, a bond-serving wench from the Castle. His name was Adam Vogel.

In 1602 the old Laird died and his son, anxious to develop the coal seams that lay beneath his lands, took all his people into bondage, naming them vagabonds for the purpose. Vogel resisted and with his wife and two eldest sons was killed. His third and youngest son was taken by the Laird's men. A metal collar inscribed with his name was fixed about his neck and he was put to work in the mine that the Laird was driving up towards Muckburn, the village that lay a mile inland on the other side of the low hills that fringed the coast. Adam Vogel was fifteen when he was taken into slavery. There is a copy of an overseer's report, dated 1605, which records that the "collier Vogel, him of the white-scarred eye, continues obstinate and must be whipped almost daily."

The mine, however, seemed to be successful. For in 1610 the Laird writes in his accounts, "that the Motley Mine was being wrought by both day and night."

In 1623, the Laird received from the King—of his great love—permission to build a harbour at Invermuck. In 1627 the Laird records in his diary that on the twelfth of June "I sent from my new harbour at Invermuck a brig lading of coles to Leith, where they were much loved, being fine coles and which were sold there for five pounds scots. To the brigmaster I paid seventeen shillings scots for the carrying of them, and to one Adam Vogel collier, twopence scots for the winning of the coles."

Later this year, the Laird wrote from Edinburgh to his overseer that "as Adam Vogel is of such strength and size and his son also, by the woman he hath with him, it would be well that he be bred to as many of the collier women as ye think may be to my advantage."

This attempt at selective breeding proved a failure. Vogel failed to fertilise any of the women he was put to, and by his own woman had but the one son.

In 1640, the Motley Mine, now nearly a mile long, drew too near the river at Muckburn. Water broke into the workings and both Vogels were drowned. Adam junior left a daughter aged ten and already working as a collier girl. There was no male offspring.

Now, for the first time, appeared the phenomena which was to be repeated at roughly hundred-year intervals—the persistence of the Vogel strain and characteristics; huge frame, white skin and blue eyes, with one eye always marked by a white scar.

In 1670, a gentleman of the district returned from the West Indies to retirement in his native place, bringing with him a negro slave. After a year's sojourn, the slave approached the local minister and asked to be baptised, claiming that in this country he was no longer a slave but a free man and wished to become a Christian.

The minister supported the negro, but his master refused to accept the slave's claim and sought his return. The negro found refuge in the 'sink,' an area close to the harbour wall where, amid the reeking salt pans, clustered the filthy hovels of the collier people. One aspect of the affair which was remarked upon at the time was the fact that money was subscribed for the negro's defence by the half-starved colliers who were themselves slaves and with no hope of freedom to lighten their horrible lives. While waiting for the case to come before the Court of Session, the slave's master died and the matter was forgotten.

The negro lived in the hut of a collier woman named Vogel, and as he had no name of his own the minister gave him that name and baptised him Adam. Having taken a bond collier woman to wife, the negro had lost his own freedom yet again and became a collier and the property of the Laird.

Among the collier folk, "the small, dark people" of the cole heughs, the negro soon ceased to attract attention. But when a child was born to him and the woman Vogel, all were amazed. There was a slight broadening of the nostrils, perhaps, but no darkening of the skin and no thickening of the lips. The child was unmistakeably a Vogel. As the minister records, no one would have credited him with having a black father.

The records continue—"In 1701, the Laird sold to the Provost and Magistrates of a neighbouring town—for working at the cole—one Adam Vogel, his woman and his child Adam. Before payment was

Women bearing the coal, bag by bag, up the pit shaft. These toiling creatures cried like children under their loads

made the sale was hurriedly cancelled and the Vogels were returned to their original owner, as being savage and unruly folk who, tho working well at the cole, do but stir up unrest and discontent among our own collier people."

In 1728, the Laird wrote from Edinburgh to his overseer at the Muckburn Cole Heughs—"and see that the collier Vogel and his woman, who ran away the day after my leaving, be recovered and brought back, for if they once they get into England there will be no getting them back. And see to it that they be soundly whipped."

In 1743, a neighbouring Laird offers to buy some colliers of the Laird. But stipulates in his letter—"that he will not receive one Adam Vogel, of the scarred eyeball, nor his ilk, for much is known to me concerning his wickedness and troublemaking———"

About this time there were five pits at Muckburn and another two on the crest of the hill at Muckridge. The Muckridge pits used horses and gins to wind the drainage water to the surface. Muckburn, however, was near the river and here water power turned the pump wheels to drain the pits. The coal, of course, was dragged underground and carried to the surface by half-naked collier women and children.

Hugh Miller, writing of the collier women of these times, states— "it was calculated that a day's labour of one of these poor, overtoiled creatures was the equivalent of carrying a hundredweight from sea level to the top of Ben Lomond. No wonder that they cried like children under their loads. They were marked by a peculiar type of mouth . . . wide, open, thicklipped, projecting equally above and below . . . like savages."

The collier people became, in the words of another writer, "Savage and brutal of manner, destitute of all principles of religion and morality, unknowing of and perfectly indifferent to the opinion of the world."

Over the years Invermuck had grown in importance and was now a busy, though still small harbour. Houses were being built along the Eastern side for the merchants and coalshippers. But west of the harbour still festered the 'sink' of slave hovels, a place where no-one not of the collier people might set foot. A steady flow of ships sailed in for the Laird's coal. Some of them brought flax from Russia for the sailcloth mill that the Laird had built at Muckburn.

In 1760, three interconnected pits at Muckburn were flooded when the pump engine broke down. And one hundred and sixty-two of the colliers and their families were trapped and drowned. There were, in fact, but three survivors, an old woman employed in the shaft, a collier boy who was "nailed to a stoop" in the pit bottom (the punishment for running away), and a seven-year-old collier girl named Vogel, who freed the boy and escaped herself. She was the only survivor of her family, her parents and brothers being drowned.

She was severely injured but must have recovered, for it is recorded that the brig *Duchess*, a ship of Invermuck returning from Russia with flax, was wrecked within half a mile of her home port. This happened during a great storm on the night of the twenty-eighth of January 1775. Of the ship's company, but two were saved, the Mate, one Alex. Durie of Leith, and a young man with oriental features who, said the Mate, was found hidden in the ship when she cleared her port of loading. They were shorthanded and the young Russian was taken into the crew.

Ashore now in Scotland and friendless he, being a castaway and a vagabond, was taken into bondage by the Laird for service at the Muckburn Cole Heughs. The overseer put him to live with the young woman Vogel, who was without issue and having no man of her own. This woman was of a family of great repute among the people of the Cole Heughs and was thought by some to be a witch. For one of her eyes from birth bore a white scar. She would not tolerate the advances of the colliers—"and none of them durst approach her for fear of her savage temper."

She must have shown less aversion to the young sailor from the Black Sea, for not much more than a year later the Minister writes: "Was visited today by a collier woman and a foreigner, almost Chinese in appearance. They brought a new-born child, male, which I baptised Adam Vogel after the woman's own father, for the man had no means of telling me the way of his own, outlandish name and could not write it down. Both woman and child are unlike the most of the collier people, being fair and with blue eyes. And both are scarred with a white crescent on the ball of one eye, but the eyes of the child are shaped like almonds after the style of his father."

This Adam Vogel was born technically free. For the so-called emancipation of the Scottish colliers had taken place in 1775. No doubt it was lack of alternative employment that forced him back to the hated trade of his mother's people. For we read that in 1800, at one of the two remaining pits at Muckburn, colliers broke through into the workings of an old mine driven by the fourth Laird in 1603. All but seven of the men escaped and among the list of survivors we read the name of Adam Vogel, mine driver or brusher, aged 25 years.

In spite of repeated attempts, the obsolete pumping machinery could not cope with the ever-increasing flow of water. Two years later, in 1803, the last pit, Muckburn No. 5, was abandoned.

Adam Vogel is one of the names on the list of 'Good Workmen' who were offered employment at the one pit still open at Muckridge. The ancient wagon road, which wound from Muckburn up over the brae and down to the harbour, became a neglected weed-grown track, its heavy wagons derelict, its teams of snorting horses employed elsewhere. The Laird refused to invest more capital and in the great gale of 1812 the East harbour wall collapsed. The Laird could see no profit in its repair, and Invermuck was doomed.

In 1830, it was reported to the Laird that Adam Vogel, a brusher, while driving a stone mine through a fault at Muckridge had come upon a rich and exceedingly thick seam of coal. It was not reported to the Laird that Vogel had been ordered to stop the mine a month before, as the wall of stone seemed endless, and had persisted at his own risk and without wages because, as he said, "he kent the coal was there waiting." It proved, in fact, to be the old "Motley" seam worked and then forgotten, centuries before. It lay less than five hundred yards from the pitbottom and might be easily worked. Invermuck was saved. The wagon way was cleared and rails laid down to ease the labour of the horses. A branch road was cut and extended to Muckridge. The Laird obtained a government grant for the repair of the harbour.

These were wild days, however, the early days of the long-drawn-out and bitter fight by the miners for better wages and conditions. From now on most references to the Vogels are to be found in court records.

In December 1842, a striking miner, one Adam Vogel, was sentenced to transportation for life for killing a blackleg during a riot. In 1850, a woman Vogel, wife of a striking miner, and her

125

daughter Euphemia, aged twelve, were sentenced to be whipped and imprisoned for six months for stealing potatoes from a field. For the defence, it was stated that the Laird had evicted the strikers from their hovels. They were camping in gangs by the roadside and their children were starving in bitter winter weather.

To break the strikes the coalmasters imported squads of starving Highland and Irish labour. Then, when the men had been forced back to work, the anti-papal drum was beaten to such good effect that the colliers were confused. And, losing sight of the real enemy, blamed for their troubles King William of Orange or The Pope of Rome.

In 1859, a number of collier women were sentenced to various terms of imprisonment for attacking and severely wounding another woman named Euphemia Vogel. She had taken in as a lodger an Irishman and Papist, a man named O'Hara, who had been a blackleg.

Within a month O'Hara was killed in a pit explosion. And when later a bastard child was born, it was called Vogel after its mother and she called it Adam, after her own father. It closely resembled its mother, even to a white scar on the ball of one eye.

In 1880, the Yeomanry were ordered to fire upon rioting strikers. Among those wounded and taken by the troops was "One, Adam Vogel, a notorious agitator."

As a result of favourable survey reports in 1904, the Laird decided to sink a new pit on the shoreline in order to tap the rich seams lying under the sea. The shaft was planned for the centre of a group of miners' hovels, and for refusing to obey an eviction order and for assaulting a Sheriff's Officer by striking him with his fist, Adam Vogel, mine driver or brusher, aged twenty-four years, was sentenced to six months' hard labour.

In 1916, Sergeant Adam Vogel, D.C.M., Royal Artillery, was reported "Killed in Action." In her distress his wife informed the authorities that her son, Private Adam Vogel, M.M., Black Watch, had enlisted at fifteen and was still but sixteen and a half. His immense size had helped to deceive the recruiting officer. He was sent home to his mother and the Motley Pit.

In 1923 were married in the Parish Kirk of Invermuck "Adam Vogel, Miner (brusher or mine driver), and Katherine Muir, pithead worker. Both of this Parish."

126

NOTICE.

NO FEMALES

Permitted, on any account, to work under ground at this Colliery; and all such is STRICTLY PROHIBITED, by Orders from His Grace the Duke of Hamilton.

JOHN JOHNSTON, Overseer.

REDDING COLLIERY, 4th March, 1845.　　　　　J. Duncan, Printer, Falkirk.

The practice of employing women and children as a form of underground transport in the pits only ended with an Act of Parliament in 1842. No longer could a pit accident claim the entire family.

During the six months' strike of 1926 Adam Vogel was sentenced to six months' hard labour for stealing coal, the property of the Laird of Invermuck. It was stated in Court "That the accused, a striking miner, in company with others and working only by night, had driven a mine up from the foreshore under the golf links, securing the roof with drift wood from the beach." Asked by the Sheriff how in the first place he knew the exact spot where coal could be found, accused replied his instinct "telt him where it was," and appeared surprised at the question.

The *Edinburgh Evening Echo* of June 5th, 1936, reports: "In an accident this morning at the Motley Colliery, Invermuck, two miners were killed by a fall of roof. The first fall took place shortly after three a.m. burying Alex. McAttie. The leading man of the team, Adam Vogel, was attempting to extricate McAttie whose feet could be seen, when a further fall took place and both men were entombed.

"McAttie was without family but Vogel leaves a wife and two children, a daughter aged eleven and a son aged sixteen who is employed in another part of the same colliery."

In 1942, a case was heard in the Sheriff's Court in which Sergeant Adam Vogel, V.C., Royal Marine Commandoes, was charged with assault upon the Marquis of Glenmuck, Laird of Invermuck.

The previous autumn, while walking in the woods that formed part of his estate, the Laird was accosted by a trespasser and ordered him off the estate.

Vogel was stated to have replied, "Yure land! Who the bliddy hell said it wis yure land. Ah expec' yure blasted ancestors stole it in the fust place."

The Laird replied that his ancestors had had to fight for it.

"Richt," said Vogel, removing his battledress. "If yu want tae keep it ye can muckin' well ficht fer it again." He then made an unprovoked attack upon the Marquis.

The Sheriff's Clerk reported that Vogel had been on leave and had returned to his unit. The case was therefore adjourned for further enquiries to be made.

Two weeks ago, my neighbour, as we miners say, was killed while attempting to enter a gas area after an explosion. He had done this in the belief that I was there. I felt the tragedy more keenly than

127

others, for not only did we work together but I lodged with the man, Adam Vogel, and his unmarried sister Euphemia.

Unlike the swarthy-skinned, dark-haired women of most mining villages, she is a tall, stalwart girl of an almost exotic beauty, the faintly Mongolian cast of her features contrasting strangely with her broad, clear forehead and laughing, grey-blue, Irish eyes, on one of which is a small, crescent-shaped scar.

Frequently, since her brother's funeral, I have noticed her studying me with an air of grave pre-occupation. And yet—she can know nothing of her family history—surely.

"In 1841, a girl aged 15, giving evidence before a Royal Commission, told them that she had wrought underground for three years and worked from 6 a.m. till 6 p.m. 'It is guie sair, sweating work.' She had to make 14 races (a number of coal hutches coupled together made a train or race) before porridge time—the distance being 600 yards from incline to pit bottom; 14 to 15 races between porridge time and piece time, and another 15 races afterwards. 'We get 1s 3d a day, but the men drive us, and many girls have left and gone to the fields.' "

CHAPTER TEN

THE BOMBER'S ROMANCE

THE caustic voice of Mistress McFish was well known in the mining village and I was not surprised, one day in early Spring, to hear her serenading her husband.

His sweating back was bowed over a spade as I passed his garden fence and, as he dug wearily, a flow of acid comments came through the scullery window. But that night down the pit he was his usual irrepressible self and at piecetime he was anxiously awaiting the advent of the Bomber, our section deputy—a mournful man who had suffered much at the hands of his small tormentor.

One of the ties that secured the power cable of the coalcutter to the girders overhead had been broken, and a big loop of cable hung down across the road at the height of a tall man's chin. Nicky was waiting to see the Bomber catch it, and with Nicky McFish's assistance he did.

He came lumbering down the Heading from the coalface, his sad face drooping. "See an' watch your feet there," said Nicky, sharply, officiously. In spite of himself Bomber Brown's eyes fell to the rough, rock-strewn pavement, and a second later he was swinging gracefully through the air by his chin lodged over the cable loop, only to fall a second later at our feet.

"By the hokey," said Nicky, assiduously massaging the Bomber's throat and nearly choking him in the process. "Ah've aye kent you wis born tae be hung, but Ah never kent you'd do the job yoursel'."

"Shut your pus," croaked the Bomber, staggering down the Heading, and brushing Nicky off as though he were a fly.

"I don't know what fun you get out of tormenting him," I said. "There's no challenge or battle of wits about it. He just doesn't have a chance against you."

"Don't you believe it," snapped Nicky. "He's a fly boy the Bomber. Don't you worry, he can tak' care o' hissel. He got the better o' me yince onyway. An' Ah've never been allowed tae forget it."

"When was that?" I asked, settling my back against a girder.

"Och, it's a good while back, certainly," Nicky explained. "But still, if he could dae it yince he could dae it again. Ah woundnae trust him. We wis young fellas at the time, an' at that age a' you think about is runnin' after the lassies. Well here, aboot that time the Polisman in the village retired an' anither yin comes wi' his dochter. He wis a widower. He'd a braw job tae, 'cos there's nae crime in a mining village. Yeur ower tired after a shift doon here tae want tae go aboot burglarin' or murderin' folks—'cept mebbe a gaffer here an' there. Some o' them could dae wi' murderin'. There wis a bit poachin', o' cos, but only the Laird bothered aboot that, an' Lairds is fair game for colliers.

"Man, she wis a braw bit stuff, the Polis's dochter. Ooooh! she wis a smasher wi' lang black hair doon to her knees, an' twa big black een. Her een wis like two chunks o' the Dunfermline Splint, pitch black an' a' shinin' an' glitterin' like diamonds. Well, o' cos, me an' the Bomber mak's a beeline for this. An' afore lang it gets aboot that we're courtin' her.

"But she couldnae mak' up her mind atween us. Ah think she likit me, but Ah'm just a wee fella, an' she'd aye been used tae big Polismen like her Paw, an' the Bomber wis big enough for twa Polis. He wis mebbe at the back o' the door when they wis dishin' oot the brains, but they gie'd him a big enough carcase tae mak' up for it. Well, does this lassie, Margaret her name was, no hae a big cat that she thocht the warld o'? Toyteeshell she cried it, an' it had a pedigree as lang as McFett's Dook.

"Well, this cat goes a missin' at aboot the time I'm talkin' o' an' we baith kens that whoever finds it an' gies it her back would be Margaret's hero.

"Well onyway, we're goin' tae oor wark this day on the backshift. We had tae go through the Laird's woods tae get tae the pit, that wis afore they made the road. Well, nat'rully the place was mobbit wi' rabbits an' some o' the wickeder o' the colliers used tae go after 'em. Well, we stops in the middle o' the woods tae attend tae a wee bit business we had on there, me an' the Bomber. An' a' of a sudden there's an awfy kefuffle in the bushes nearby an' the Bomber dives in tae see if it wis mebbe a rabbit or somethin' that had got hurt an' wis needin' assistance.

" 'It's Meg's cat,' he shouts a meenit later, 'wi' its foot catched in a snare. Ah'll hae it oot in a coupla shakes.' A coupla shakes? It wis mair near a coupla hoors, but o' cos he wisnae well aquaint wi' the cat at that stage. By jings, that wis some carryon. A short-haired toyteeshell she ca'd it. Its teeth werenae toyteeshell onyway. Ah've kent blunter razor blades, an' its claws wis langer 'n its pedigree, Ah'll betcha. Thon cat cussed near eat me an' the Bomber afore we got it in a sack.

"If he'da let me alane Ah woundnae a' been lang in quietenin' it, 'cos quite by chance me an' the Bomber both has a half-dozen rabbit snares in oor pooches, an' if Ah could justa got yin o' they over thon beast's heid . . . But na, he's determined that thon cat's no tae be hurt—apart o' cos from giein' it a bit clump aside the lughole noo an' again by way o' restrictin' its minoovers. An' by jings, it had some minoovers, Ah'll tell you.

"Ah never kent a cat that had a nature as cruel as thon beast; it wis wicked the way it carried on. Me an' the Bomber wis swimmin' in bluid—his. In the end Ah took aff yin o' me pit boots. 'Let me at it,' Ah says. 'An' Ah'll gie it a wee shot o' morphia.'

" 'Puss, Puss,' says the Bomber. 'No, no, naughty pussy.' An' tae me, 'Put that boot doon, you brute. D'ye ken wha's cat this is?' Well, o' cos, that wis richt enough, but Ah keeps the boot in ma haun just in case the cat wins an' starts on me. Pussy . . .? by jings, that's the fust time Ah've neard a man-eatin' tiger ca'd a pussy.

"After a wee whily the Bomber says, 'Ah've got it, Nicky,' an' he comes crashing oota the bushes haudin' this creature. Well, he mebbe thocht he wis winnin', but by jings if there'd a'been onyone aroon tae tak' a bet ma money woulda gone on thon toyteeshell. Ooooh! Whit a carryon. 'Ah've got ye, Puss,' shouts the Bomber. Well, mebbe he had, but the cat had mair o' him, Ah'll betcha. There wis nothin' but lumps o' steak danglin' frae its claws . . . Bomber-steak.

" 'Here,' he says, 'haud it a meenit while Ah examine ma wounds.' 'Oooh,' Ah says, 'Ah'm sorry, but Ah'm just puttin' ma boot on.'

132

You shoulda heard what he cried ma boot, an' he shoves thon savage beast into ma arms. Well, Ah s'pose it musta been tired wi' a' the strugglin' an' wrastlin' 'cos Ah just happened tae tap its heid against a tree trunk an' it went tae sleep richt awa.

"Well, there wis nae mair nonsense after that. We shoves it in a sack an' hides it in the ole bothy at the pitheid where we kept oor gear. An' we decides that at lousin' time we'll tak it hame tae Margaret the gither, an' let the best man win.

"Later on, when we wis workin' awa doon the pit, we has a prop tae set an' it wis too short, so we has tae slice up a bit wood tae jam atween it an' the roof. The Bomber hauds the wood an' Ah tak's a grip o' ma pick.

"'See an' watch what you're doin' wi' that pick,' he says. Well, o' cos, Ah'd been wrackin' ma brains a' shift hoo Ah could get up the pit aheid o' him, so Ah dunno if it was that or if it wis him speakin' just when Ah wis takin' aim, but here dae Ah no miss the wood an' get the Bomber's leg. Oooh! the howls o' him. Ah thocht he wis deid for sure, the roars he lets oot. Holy smoke, Ah says tae masel; Ah've kilt him. Aye, but he gets up on his knees an' Ah wis that glad tae see him livin' Ah drappit the pick.

"Folk says," Nicky chewed reminiscently on a small piece of coal, "that you canna run on your knees. It's s'posed tae be a physical impossibility. Don't you believe it. Ah went doon thon run like a Pooderhall sprinter thon day on the backshift, an' nothin' but the Bomber's hot breath on the back o' me neck tae keep me movin'. It wis enough though, Ah'll tell you. It wis ma ain fault onyway, Ah should never a' let go o' the pick."

"Did he catch you?," I asked with interest.

"Dinna be daft," Nicky snapped impatiently. "D'ye think Ah'd be sittin' here talkin' tae you the noo if the Bomber 'd catched me thon day on the backshift. Aye, that'll be richt. Ah tell you this, if he'd a' gotta grip o' me Ah'd a'been killed aff in the fust bloom o' ma youth. Na, na, there wis twa steel props set close the gither at the bottom roadheid an' Ah nips atween 'em, an' o' cos when the Bomber follows he gets stuck. By jings, he musta fetched up wi' an' awfy jerk.

"His false teeth went fleein' past me like bullets an' disappeared doon the dip-side. He wis foamin' at the mooth. It wis a peety he lost his teeth, he coulda nashed 'em.

"Well, the dep'ty an' the three brushers wis in the Level. It wis a good job tae, 'cos Ah could never a' stood listenin' tae language like thon on me lonesome, it wis awfy. Well, he wis jammed solid atween the twa props, an' the only way we could get him oot wis by easin' the props oot. So we sets a security prop an' then Ah tak's grip o' the mash tae tap oot the props that wis haudin' the Bomber. But whenever he sees me swingin' the mash an inch from his lug he throws anither fit, so tae quiet him, Ah gies the mash tae the youngest o' the brushers. Ah kent the laddie didnae hae muckle experience, but he'd shoulders on him like a coal wagon. Anyone woulda thocht he wisnae a good shot wi' a mash, the way the Bomber carried on.

"Well, the young fella ignores the screitchin' o' the Bomber an' gies the fust steel an a'michty swipe wi' the mash. Nat'rully the prop flees oot, nothin' coulda stood a blow like thon. Ah wis gettin' ready for the off once the Bomber wis free. But Ah couldnae bear tae leave thon place. Ah tell you, it wis fascinatin' watchin' thon brusher laddie swingin' that heavy mash roon the Bomber's ugly pus. Ah just couldnae tear masel awa. Well, the prop—an' them steel props are no very licht—drops on the Bomber's fingers on the

134

pavement. Holy smoke! Whit a day. An' a' the time he's suckin' the fingers o' his left haun his een is rollin' roon lookin' for me. So Ah decides it's time Ah'm awa. If he'd a' been a reasonable sorta fella that you could explain things tae . . . but, na, na.

"Ah wis slidin' awa doon the Headin' when the brusher laddie wallops oot the ither prop. Ooooh, whit a calamity! Does it no drop on the fingers o' the Bomber's richt haun that he wis usin' tae steady hissel. By jings, Ah'll tell you, Ah never kent afore that there wis words like thon, an' o' cos he's on his knees, so when he yanks up the second haun tae suck his fingers, he fa's flat on his pus in the dirt!

" 'Ah've had enough,' he shrieks. 'Ah've been eaten alive wi' savage beasts, an' stabbed wi' a pick, an' ma knuckles bruck wi' steel trees.' Ooooh! He wis a fly cuss the Bomber, Ah'll betcha. 'Get the stretcher,' he roars. 'Ah'm hurt.'

"Ah seen whit he wis up tae, o' cos, an' by jings if Ah coulda got a grip o' thon mash he'da been hurt a'richt, Ah'll tell you. An' me stannin' there like an eedjit watchin' him tryin' tae suck twa sets o' fingers wi' yin mooth. Ah tell you, Ah needed ma heid looked! He wis a fly customer the Bomber, Ah'll betcha.

"Well, o' cos, the dep'ty wis a' puffed up wi' importance at haein' an injury case on his hauns an' he starts orderin' us aboot, me an' the three brushers. By jings, it wis somethin', Ah'll tell you. But we gets thon fly cuss loaded ontae a stretchy an' he wis that pleased Ah thocht he wis goin' tae bust oot an' smile, then he'da' really hurt hissel.

"Here, did he no hear me tryin' tae persuade the dep'ty tae dope him up wi' morphia for his sufferin'. Whit a length he went. 'Ah've tae go oota here wi' a' ma faculties unimpaired,' he roars. 'Ah wouldna trust thon McFish no tae drap his corner o' the stretchy an' droon me in the gorton.' Ye ken, he'd an awfy evil mind, the Bomber. Ah'd nae intention o' droonin' him. Ah wis goin' tae slip him under a passin' race o' tubs!

"Well, we lugs him doon the Headin', an' then we stairts up McFett's Brae, seven hundred yards, wi' a gradient o' one in fower. Mountaineerin'? Ah tell you, thon Everest carryon wis naethin' tae this, ma tongue wis hangin' doon tae ma boots. Then the Bomber stairts greetin' that ma corner o' the stretcher is saggin'. Nae

135

wunner, he weighs mair stanes than Ah weigh punds. There wis mair than the stretchy saggin', Ah'll tell you. Ah could see ma ain een stickin' oot six inches in front o' ma pus. When we gets ower the napp o' the Brae we puts the stretchy doon for a bit blaw, an' we cussed near fell doon flat on tap o' it.

"The Bomber gets up an' throws aff the blanket. 'Ah'm feelin' better noo,' he says tae the deputy. 'Ah'll manage masel. These lads can get awa back tae their wark. See an' mind an' tak thon stretchy back,' he shouts tae us.

"It's a cussed good job Ah didnae hae nae breath or Ah'da sizzled his lugs."

"So he beat you after all," I said, with a smile.

"Aye," Nicky grunted. "He's a fly customer the Bomber. When Ah gets over tae Margaret's hoose at ten o'clock thon nicht him an' her are sittin' a' lovey-dovey on the settee. An' she looks at me as if Ah wis somethin' thon cat had brocht in. Ah kent Ah wisnae very welcome, so Ah sits doon in the chair for spite an' stares at the Bomber. His battle scars is a' lipstick, an he has a glaikit sorta look on his pus.

" 'Darlin' William,' she says, 'has been tellin' me hoo you were there when he rescued ma precious Fluff-Puff from that wicked rabbit snare, Mister McFish.'

" 'Aye', Ah says. 'Is it no dreadful. Men settin' such horrible traps for pair dumb animals.'

" 'Did you see ma teeth aboot the run?' asks the Bomber.

" 'Aye', Ah says. 'Ah've brocht up everything you lost,' an' Ah drops the teeth an' half a dozen rabbit snares in his open haun.

"Holy smoke!, thon lassie lets oot yin screitch an' the next meenit she's sittin' on ma lap howlin' for her Paw. Well, o' cos, he couldnae pinch the Bomber for sittin' in the room wi' snares. There wis nae proof he'd ever used 'em. But he orders him oota the hoose, an' by jings wherever the Bomber went after that, thon copper wis trippin' over his heels."

"What happened to the romance?" I asked.

"Och," said Nicky. "Ah had a clear field after thon."

"But, Nicky," I put in, "you said the Bomber had been too clever for you that time."

"An' wis he no?" Nicky demanded glumly. "Aye, he wis too clever by half. An' Ah've been reminded o' the fact every day for the last twenty years. You heard her yoursel' the day," he added sadly.

"According to agreements made among the colliers a boy under 13 ranked as a 'quarter-man,' at 13 he became a 'half-man,' at 16 a 'three-quarters man,' and at 17 took his place as a 'full man.'"

CHAPTER ELEVEN

LIKE THE OLD WHORE SAID

IT was five to nine when he finished making up his snack. He packed the two slices of bread and cheese in the rat-proof metal box and added a threepenny packet of sweets. He put on his shabby overcoat and his old bonnet with the broken peak. Taking the box, he put out the scullery light and walked slowly into the living room to stand waiting on the carpet in front of the fire.

Big Ben chimed nine o'clock and the announcer began the news. He bent down then and checked the fireguard in front of the fire. Satisfied, he switched off the radio and the light and stepped into the passage. At the foot of the stairs he paused and called.

"Ah'm awa then, Sairy."

"Aye, Tom, Aye." His wife's reply came thinly down from the bedroom.

Walking down the road in the brisk chill of a February evening he thought he could detect a faint promise of Spring in the air and his nostrils dilated like those of an old war-horse. Below him, at the foot of the brae, lay the shoreline and black-limmed in the orange glow of the dock lights was the wheel-crested pithead gear of the "Motley." Behind it all was the backcloth of star-spangled, wind-rustling waters.

In the "clean end" of the baths he took his towel and soap from the locker and laid them on the bench. He stripped and locked up his clothes. Walking down to the "dirty end" carrying the snack box, soap and towel, he became one of a stream of naked men, all on the same errand.

His back was covered with black hair and heavily muscled, his shoulders ribbed with ancient gashes and blue scars. In bare feet, the limp of his crushed and broken leg was more pronounced and he stumbled a little as he walked. He took his pit clothes, dust-thick and

139

stiff with dried sweat, from the locker and replaced them with his soap and towel. He had the weak, unused legs of the collier, a man always on his knees. He was sixty-five and he grumbled a little in his chest as he bent to pull the thick moleskin trousers over his feet.

He was buckling up the straps of his kneepads when his neighbour appeared at the end of the passage. He carefully finished what he was doing, adjusting the top strap to allow for the cramped position he would soon be assuming. Only when he was satisfied did he look up and nod.

His neighbour gave him his usual greeting. "What a muckin' existence," he said with a lugubrious grin. "Still, like the old whore said, 'It's sair, but we need the money!' "

His neighbour, Benny, had been transferred to the Fife coalfield many years before from the dying pits of the West. He was a small, wizened, wiry man of forty-five, with puckish face, quick wits, and a ready tongue. Benny had neighboured Old Tom for two years and in spite of the older man's quiet almost morose nature they worked well together. Tom was one of the older, more conservative school of colliers and had little understanding of his "communist" neighbour's frequent battles with officials. Though there was no doubt where his sympathies lay, for like all colliers he had been too often betrayed by coalowners to have any faith in lavish promises.

The two men filled their water bottles and drew their lamps. Then, after submitting to a search, they waited with a crowd of others for the "cage."

Before their eyes the vibrating steel cable rushed heavenwards and the cage, with its slatted iron gates, emerged from the depths. The safety lock shot home, a bell rang, the gate clanged. And a mass of black, sweat-soaked flesh pushed and shoved its collective way through the waiting nightshift.

Words were flung and hurried questions caught.

"Has it been rainin'——?"

"What won the three o'clock——?" and from a young but cynical voice, "Oooh, yu lucky people!"

A bell rang vibrantly, the banksman waved, and they surged forward into the steel box dangling on the end of its slender thread. Behind them, others continued to push and soon they were packed like sardines. They heard the "snack" of the safety lock being with-

140

drawn. Again a bell rang and the cage dropped swiftly into the damp, dripping darkness.

Somewhere in the crush a humorist said, "Even numbers breath in, odd numbers breath out."

The whirl of flying metal against the guides became a tormented, howling shriek which died slowly to a rattling dirge and stopped. The cage hung motionless, then it suddenly dropped and stomachs reached crazily to throats. "What does that bastard think this is," demanded a plaintive voice, "a muckin' yo yo?" Then somehow it was all over and they were walking up the firm, concrete pavement of the brightly-lit pit bottom.

At the outer end of the Sea Level the two propdrawers switched on their lamps and, accompanied by the two cuttermen, settled down to the long, stumbling, slipping, clutching, twisting, splashing, crouching journey. Five thousand weary yards later they reached their own Section, where the deputy awaited them.

"Yure coalcutter's picked an' ready tae go," he said, and waved the two cuttermen up the heading. Then he turned to the prop-drawers. "Ah'm told it's pretty bad up at the top end o' the run, Tom," he said to the old man. "So watch what yure doin'. But fer Christ's sake get me oot. Ah'm told that this new Manager's a bastard, so try no tae lose any props or there'll be hell tae pay."

"There'll be none lost if we can help it," Tom said steadily.

"An' neither o' us'll be lost either," snarled Benny with fire in his eyes. "We're no chuckin' oor lives awa fer the sake o' a ten bob prop. Ah'll gie yu that, richt now. Yu mebbe aint discovered it, but them muckin' days is over."

The deputy said bad-temperedly, "That's yure job unt it? That's the job yure paid fer, yure the steeldrawer o' this section."

Benny opened his mouth for a devastating reply but Tom silenced him with a look. He turned to the fat deputy with a glance of arid disdain in his eyes. "We ken what oor job is," he said in his dour, hard voice, "an' it's a job you'll never be able tae do as long as yu've a hole in your ass."

The deputy looked confused as Tom turned away and, followed by Benny, scrambled slowly up the narrow heading.

The deputy said sourly, "That's a miserable ole bastard, that. 'Ve yu ever heard him laugh?" Then he sat down and opened his snackbox. "He'd hurt hissel' if he laughed," he said, before anyone could reply.

The shotfirer said suggestively, "His only son got killed wi' the Argyles in Korea."

"That's muck all tae do wi' it," the deputy snarled. "Korea wis only a few years back. That old bastard's been like that as long as Ah've kent him, an' that's twenty years if it's a day."

It was three in the morning and near the end of the shift when Tom and Benny reached the "bad bit." Slowly they had worked their weary way up along the hundred yard face, drawing props from the waste and throwing them over to the face to be used again the next day. As the last prop came out of each "drift" the roof collapsed in a crashing roar of rock and rubble, making them leap frenziedly for the comparative safety of the face. In the centre track, the long snake-like, steel conveyors wound away between lines of standing props.

The next day the face would advance and the conveyors would be shifted into what was now the face track. Where they now crouched watchfully on the conveyors would have become the waste. And the props that sheltered them now would to-morrow night also have to be drawn. An endless cycle, ever to be repeated, until the seam was worked out or reached the "boundary" or struck a "fault."

Down the face they could hear the rumbling clatter as the low, steel-clad monster crawled deliberately along the face in the care of the two cuttermen, its whirling picks tearing into the hard, glistening, diamond-bright glitter of the wall of coal. Snarling, growling, spitting and cracking as though in an insane rage. ·

They crouched together in the darkness and soberly surveyed the "bad bit." Several of the props had been forced more than a foot down into the pavement under the relentless pressure, and in the bulging roof were ominous, dripping cracks.

Benny popped a sweet into his mouth. "This is where the muckin' fun begins," he grunted. He dragged off his black singlet and wrung it out in wiry hands, the sweat forming a pool on the pavement. He slipped the cold wet garment on again and it began to steam the moment it came in contact with his heaving body.

Tom rubbed a corrugated palm over the sweat-matted hair on his old naked chest. There was a sound nearby and the second cutterman

142

stopped beside them. He turned on his knees and began to haul the heavy power cable, coiling it between his own body and the coalface.

Tom and Benny started gingerly, cautiously to the withdrawing of the props. Frequently they paused to listen and stare around them. Twice Tom tapped the roof with the shaft of his pick and listened attentively to the resulting, all-revealing sound. Finally there was but one set left. Two steel props supporting a huge wooden bar, nine feet long, a foot wide and six inches thick.

Willie, the cutterman, threw down the last coil of cable with a sigh of relief, wiped the dribbling sweat from his eyes and looked about him. "Christ," he began, "this is a braw bit, Ah don't thi——"

Tom's suddenly-lifted hand silenced him. The wooden bar cracked as though it were matchwood. Then there was a tomb-like silence. Benny took the end of the short chain, crawled carefully into the menacing waste and fixed it gently around a prop. Once it was secure he hurriedly rejoined Tom and, getting as far away as the length of the chain permitted, they prepared to haul.

The cutterman, suddenly realising their intentions, got hurriedly to his knees. "Just a meenit," he cried, "yure no goin' tae draw that set, are yu?"

"Aye," Tom told him doggedly, "aye, it has tae come oot."

Willie crawled rapidly down the face.

"Let me oota here," he shouted, "yu bastards can bury yusel's if yu like, but yure no goin' tae happ me up. Ah've a wife an' weans at hame." They heard him shouting to his neighbour to stop the machine, that the steeldrawers were going to "shut the bloody, muckin' place."

Tom and Benny strained to their work. The prop moved slightly. As it shifted, so the bar and the roof it supported sagged even lower. In his black face Tom's white, protruding eyeballs stared unwinkingly at the prop, with the bar and the threatening roof looming above it all.

Benny sucked frenziedly at a sweet. "Christ," he said. "Ah could do wi' a smoke." Then, miraculously, the prop was clear, the roof sagged down and the bar cracked again, protestingly, but somehow it held.

Benny sighed with relief. "Ah do believe we're goin' tae get awa wi' it after a'," he said softly.

They waited apprehensively for several minutes, ears and eyes straining, then Tom inched forward over the conveyors and reached for the prop, which in falling had jammed on the waste side. As he strained at the stubborn steel Benny, with one eye on his neighbour's safety, began to pull in the slack chain.

A thin trickle of flour-like whiteness drifted down from the roof· Benny roared a warning and flung himself away. Tom hurled his heavy body backwards as there was a thunderous, crashing rumble above them and an avalanche of rock smashed down on the steel conveyors, buckling and twisting them.

The remaining prop lurched crazily. The bar, under its shattering load of stone, drove into Tom's back, pinning him like a fly to the pavement. There were a few lesser rumbles and then a deep, deep silence.

Benny flung himself on the mound of rock, tearing wildly with his bare hands and screaming madly to where the two cuttermen were waiting below him in the darkness.

It took half an hour to dig Tom out and not only was he alive but he claimed to be unhurt. "Ah'm richt enough," he said brusquely, struggling to his knees.

"Are yu sure?" Benny was not convinced.

"Ah'm right enough Ah tell yu, just that ma back's a wee bit sair."

They helped him from the cramped space out to the comparative roominess of the "top road" and as they emerged from the face the deputy appeared on the scene.

"What's up?" he demanded.

"Yu an' yure muckin' props," snarled Benny, "an' yure muckin' bad bits, pity it wisnae that muckin' Manager that got this. But nah——," Benny was almost in tears. "The bastard'll be lyin' snorin' on his wife's shirt tail the noo."

The professional instincts of the deputy were aroused. "Let's have a look at yer back, Tom," he said.

"Ah'm richt enough," Tom told him, but in spite of his protests the deputy lifted the newly donned shirt. "Christ, man," he said aghast. "D'yu ken what sort o' a bliddy mess yure back's in? Benny——," he turned to the small man, "awa oot tae the telephone at the end o' the road an' tell em tae get a stretcher up here."

144

Hydraulic roof supports have replaced the old wooden props in the massive mechanisation programme which has made pits safer and more productive

"Yu'll get nae stretcher fer me," Tom said loudly. "D'ye hear." His eye fell on an old pickshaft lying at the side of the road. "Gie me that fer a stick," he said, "an' Ah'll get a hand off Benny if Ah need it."

They stared numbly at the lines of determination round the strong old mouth. Benny gave him the shaft and one of the cuttermen took their two water bottles and snack boxes.

"Ah'm telling yu——," the deputy began again irresolutely.

"Yure tellin' me nothin'," Tom said. "Come on," he growled to Benny. And the deputy, nonplussed, watched the little procession stumble slowly down the heading. He followed them at a distance and when they were clear of the section he phoned the nightshift oversman in the distant pit bottom.

"Ah've an injured man comin' oot," he said. "Old Tom McCoffin. No, he's walking, wouldnae tak' a stretcher. Aye, it's serious, warn the first aid room, an' hae an ambulance waitin' at the pit head. Aye, it's serious. Ah'm tellin' yu, his back's like a lump o' muckin' steak, but the ole bastard'll no gie in tae it."

The rest of the nightshift were long away when Tom and Benny came over the gangway from the pithead. A white-coated man stepped out of the first aid room and with him was another man in a blue uniform with silver buttons. Through the pit gate they glimpsed the not unfamiliar sight of the ambulance.

"You, McCoffin?" began the first aid man.

Tom brushed him wearily aside. "Ah'll come in when Ah'm washed," he said gently. "Ah'll mebbe get ye tae put a bit dressin' on it fer me."

"They'll wash you at the hospital," the man said.

Tom staggered and breathed thickly, leant against the wall. Through the twisted face of pain, his eyes shone with what looked like fear.

"They'll wash me where?" he demanded.

"The hospital."

Tom McCoffin seldom swore but now he said, "Ah'm muckin' sure an' they'll no. Hospital, na, na, there's nothin' wrang wi' me that a few hours in ma bed'll no fix." Then he said suddenly, "Wait, is that ambulance fer me?" and his voice was ripe with apprehension.

"Of course."

"Then tak' the muckin' thing awa again. Ah'll no be needin' it," his voice rose hysterically. "D'yu hear me. TAK' THE MUCKIN' THING BACK WHERE IT COME FROM."

The ambulance driver said gently, "You nee'nt go to hospital unless you want to, but if you like I'll wait and run you home."

"An' scare the bliddy life oota ma wife when she sees an ambulance coming up the street," roared Tom. "Tak' the muckin' thing back where ye got it." He stumped away heavily to the baths. Benny looked quizzically at the other two men. "What a muckin' carryon," he muttered and hurried after his neighbour.

"That's a hardy old cuss," the ambulance driver said.

With infinite gentleness Benny helped Tom to strip and bath. At first the hot water was torture on his bare flesh, and the old man writhed in silent agony. Afterwards, however, he felt fresher and submitted quietly while his back was dressed in the ambulance room.

"It will be a wee while before you are back again," the attendant murmured conversationally as he worked.

"Ah'll be at ma wark the nicht," Tom said stubbornly.

The young man smiled sympathetically. "Bet you twenty fags you won't," he said. "Remember, you have been on the move all the time since this happened. When you get home and go to bed your back will stiffen. You won't be able to move when you wake up."

"Ah'll be at ma wark the nicht," Tom insisted. "Ah canna afford tae lie aboot idle."

The dresser looked closely at the deeply-lined, hard-eyed face before him. The strong mouth and grizzled, rock-like chin.

"Well," he said, "I'll tell you one thing. If you are here to-night look in and I'll dress it for you before you go underground. But quite frankly, I don't expect to be seeing you."

"You will," Tom said from the door, "——an' thank you."

It was not until he saw the bottles of milk on the doorstep that he realised how late he was. He was usually home before the milkman arrived.

"You're late, Tom," his wife called from the bedroom.

"Aye," he called back. "We had a wee bit bother an' the job took longer."

He went into the scullery and put the ready-filled kettle on the gas. While the water was boiling he cleaned out the fireplace and

146

emptied the ashes. He was chopping sticks when the whistle of the kettle warned him. The teapot and two clean cups were ready. He made the tea and took a cup up to his wife. When he had kindled the fire he drank his own cup of tea and laid the table for breakfast. It was daylight by then and he switched off the light and drew the living-room curtains. He took his wife up a second cup of tea and when he came down he heard the noisy laughter of school children in the street. He switched on the wireless and when the sound came through he tuned it to the Light Programme and stood waiting with the alarm clock in his hands.

He was frightened to sit down in case he was unable to rise. When the nine o'clock Greenwich Time Signal came through he checked, set, and wound the alarm. He watched it for a minute and then put it back on the mantelpiece. He adjusted the radio for Housewives' Choice and went slowly upstairs. He pulled the covers gently back from the small, warped body of his wife and, leaning over the bed, tried to slip his hands under her body.

She drew back with an expression of annoyance on her white, wizened face. "What's this?" she asked shortly.

"Och," he said casually, "Ah just thought Ah'd carry yu doon in ma arms the day——fer a change."

"No," she sulked back on the pillows, "I want it like always."

He hesitated a moment then turned and sat down on the edge of the bed. She twisted her body round behind him. When he felt her thin arms about his neck he put his hands behind him and slipped his big, rough, coal-pocked palms beneath her small buttocks. His grip secure, he straightened up with a stifled groan and limped slowly to the stairs.

"Hurry," she said petulantly, "I'll miss Housewives' Choice."

He put her down in the big chair near the fire and went to the scullery for bowl, soap and towel. He brought her clothes and put them over the fireguard to warm while he washed her pallid face and hands. When she was ready, he took off her nightgown and began to dress her.

"Where's my blue dress?," she cried, pushing his hands away. "You know this is Doctor's day."

"Ah forgot, Sairy," he said, "I'll get it."

147

While they were at breakfast he heard a van outside. He went out and bought fish for dinner. He came back to find a cup lying broken on the carpet and a large stain of spilt tea.

"Yu shouldna try tae feed yursel', Sairy," he reproved her gently. But she had already forgotten the cup and stared vacantly about the room, ignoring him.

When the doctor left Tom walked to the door with him. "Well, Doctor," he said, "this year again?"

"I'm afraid so."

"How long for?"

"At least three months, you see she would derive no lasting benefit from a shorter stay. Will you be able to afford it again, Mr. McCoffin?"

"Och aye," Tom said. "We'll manage it all right."

The Doctor nodded thoughtfully. "Good," he said, and got into his car.

Tom went back into the scullery. He stood perfectly still in front of the sink and let the pain of his injured back rage savagely through him. After a little while he peeled potatoes and cut them up for chips. He took the fish from its wrapping paper and laid it between two plates. It had been dressed by the vanman and was ready for cooking.

His wife asked for a glass of milk and when she had drunk it he made her comfortable and began to tidy the house. Within an hour he was brought hurrying from bedmaking by his wife's shriek. Mrs Dale's Diary was on and she complained that she could hardly hear it. He turned up the volume and went back to his work.

Mrs McGabbie arrived after dinner while he was washing the dishes. Mrs McGabbie sat with his wife for four hours every day for an agreed sum. He got to bed soon after one but it was some time before the raw pain in his back would let him sleep.

The alarm clock woke him at a quarter-to-five. At five o'clock, still struggling to dress, he heard the front door slam behind an impatient Mrs McGabbie. Somehow he managed to stumble downstairs and give his wife her tea.

After the six o'clock news he took a shovelful of live coals upstairs and kindled the fire in the bedroom. He was tidying the bed when his wife called him to take her to the lavatory. Even this short journey left him trembling with pain and weakness and he dreaded

148

the effort that would be needed to carry her upstairs. His wife once more installed in the big chair in the living-room, he went upstairs again to look at the bedroom fire. He leant over the bed for some time resting his body on his hands and staring at a portrait on the wall. It was a large photo of a well-built young man in kilt and battle dress with a sergeant's stripes.

The short rest eased his back a little and after supper he got his wife up to bed without too much difficulty. He undressed her in the warmed room and put on her a clean nightgown. He combed and brushed her hair and folded her clothes on a chair. Before he left he put the fireguard in front of the fire and looped the string from the light switch over the bedpost where she could reach it.

He was buckling the straps on his kneepads when his neighbour appeared at the end of the passage. He carefully adjusted the top straps to allow for the crouched position he would so soon be assuming. His neighbour gave him his usual greeting.

"What a muckin' existence," Benny said with a lugubrious grin. Tom slowly straightened his back and nodded.

Benny said, "Ah didna expect tae see yu the night." Tom stood up and grasped his water bottle. "Come on," he said in his deep voice.

"Aye," Benny turned with him. "We'll hae tae go an' face it. Like the old whore said, 'It's sair, but we need the money.' "

THE CAGE

We stand, close packed and waiting
Where the sun-bespeckled dust
Makes mad and merry moments, thro' the bars,
That lap our voiceless thrust
To freedom, light, the witching distant sky,
The anxious, waiting moon, the sun-locked stars.

But we are trapped and fall
Through golden air, that henceforth we must
Memorise
Past dazzled beach,
Where blue and laughing water sighs.
But this we do not hear
If we are wise.

CHAPTER TWELVE

THE BANANY CAIRT

DURING the nightshift a part of the "face" had "closed." We cleaned up the fall and secured the broken, crumbling roof. But by then it was too late for us to complete our "task" or contract and cut the full hundred yards of coal.

"Will you lay on and cut it out?" begged the nightshift deputy. The Bomber we called him for he always brought bad news.

"Ye ken, Ah'm no keen on overtime wi' a' this redundancy," said Nicky McFish, the leading cutterman for the Seven West section. "Neither's ma neighbour here," and he nods to where I crouched against the coalcutter. "Anyway, we'd never manage it oorse'ls noo, it's too late."

The Bomber looked at his watch. "It's half-past four," he said. "The dayshift get doon the pit at six. It'll be seven onyway afore they're in here so that gies you twa an' a half hoors. An' the steel-drawers are finished. They've promised tae stay an' gie you a hand if you'll bide."

"That's different," Nicky said. "Four o' us ull mebbe manage it." He looked at me. "Aye," I said, "I'll stay."

"Here's the prop drawers noo," said the Bomber, with undis-guised relief. Old Paddy McClory and his neighbour, a young Glasgow lad, hunched down beside us. Paddy, I noticed, was, as usual at the end of a shift, black and sweat-streaked, but his neighbour seemed almost unmarked. I had heard Nicky say that the youngster would never make a collier. From the appearance of the two men it was obvious who was doing the work in that team.

He took off his helmet and carefully smoothed back his hair. "Ma Tony Curtis is gettin' ruined doon here," he said. "After me going through tae Glesga last week-end, special tae get it done."

"What do you call it?" the Bomber demanded.

"A Tony Curtis."

"Hellfire and pestilence," said the Bomber, his eyes goggling. "That's the fust time Ah kent a haircut had a name."

"It's the style, ye see," said the young Glaswegian. "Costs eight and six tae."

The Bomber's face turned purple. He reached his arms above his head and knocked his knuckles on the black shining roof. "The heavens have mercy on us," he said in a strangled voice. He lowered his hands and shook the roof water from his wrists. "Haud ma hands, Lord," he beseeched the surrounding darkness, "afore ah dae thon thing an injury."

He watched the Teddy Boy as he crawled sideways to avoid a sudden stream of water. "Are you telling me that you paid a fifteen bob fare to Glasgow an' then eight an' six for a barber?"

"Glesga's the only place you can get your hair done prop'ly."

"Awa," snarled the Bomber disgustedly.

"Ah'm tellin' you the truth," said the Teddy Boy gently. "It takes an oor fer ma hair."

"By the Holy," said the flabbergasted Bomber. "You believe in haein' yer eight an' a tanner's worth."

"It's no the money," the Teddy Boy explained graciously. "Ah canna let him hurry in case he makes a poor job of it." He seemed quite oblivious of the fact that he was putting the Deputy into a state bordering on apoplexy.

The Bomber stared at him as though he were some incredible monster. "Ah'm cussed if Ah can see what he's done tae ye that's worth eight an' a tanner," he said slowly and thoughtfully. "Your a scruffy little wart at ony time an' as fer your heid—it's like naethin' sae much as a duck's behind!"

"Shampoo," said the Teddy Boy. "Sings, friction. . . ."

"What the bliddy hell is a friction?" roared the Bomber. The Teddy Boy looked at him pitingly and we nearly choked with stifled laughter.

"It's a machine," explained the youth, "that they put over your scalp, an' it makes yure hair curly. That's the wust of it," he went on sadly. "You come doon here and yure hair gets a' knocked aboot again with sweat and this safety helmet." He took off the helmet and looked at it disparagingly.

152

"What are you doin' in a pit onyway?" asked the Bomber in wonderment.

"Ma National Service," said the youngster, quite unaware of the effect he was having on the nearly hysterical official. "You see, in the Army yure no allowed tae get yure hair cut hoo you like. So Ah came to mining instead. Anyway the pay's no good in the Army an' they get you up at all the hoors of the morning."

The Bomber hardly heard this last remark for he was talking to himself. "Friction," he mumbled softly. "By all that's holy," he breathed. Then his headlamp focussed on the Teddy Boy again and he seemed to come to himself.

"De'ye ken whit Ah'm goin' tae tell you," he growled. "If you dinna put some friction ahint that shovel AH'LL mak' yure bliddy hair curl, an' Ah'll no need a machine tae do it wi'. Yure nothin' but a lazy little cuss." He took a deep breath. "An' that's a' ye are," he finished.

"No," said the Teddy Boy. "Ah've changed ma mind. Ah'm going hame, this place is too wet. Come on," he told the open-mouthed deputy. "Ah'll lead the way." And he crawled away down the face.

"He's going to lead the way . . ." The Bomber was almost dribbling at the mouth. "That eedjit couldnae lead the three blund mice tae a moontain o' cheese. Ah'll awae after him," he said, "afore he kills hissel. You fellas'll manage, eh?"

Paddy rubbed a filthy hand over his leathery old chest. "If we could manage before," he said with a grim smile, "we'll manage noo; that thing leaving'll no make any difference."

"Richt," the Bomber sighed with relief, and hurriedly crawled after the disappearing light of the Teddy Boy.

"Ah thocht the top o' the Bomber's heid wis goin' tae blow off there," Nicky laughed, as he turned to the controls of the coalcutter. "He wis steamin' like a chip cairt."

It was seven o'clock when, with the coal cut and the cables disconnected, we crawled wearily over the bench of the roadhead and stretched our aching muscles. At the side of the heading several strippers were already sitting on lumps of coal or rejected props and mouthing over bread and jam or swilling from water bottles. Far down the heading we could see the lights of the remainder strung

153

out in ones and twos, straggling up the steep incline like a taggled flock of wayward stars.

I sat down with Nicky and leant my back gratefully against a girder. Paddy carefully unhooked an ancient, ragged jacket and drew it reverently over his shoulders.

"That jacket's hanging in shreds, Paddy," I told him.

"Aye," Nicky's pawky voice supported me. "He's had it since it wis a waistcoat."

"I brung that jacket from Ireland forty years ago," Paddy informed us. "Twas the only luggage I had. That jacket an' twa pairs of long-sleeved drawers with stainless tails." He sat down beside us, his eyes sparkling humourously. "They was hard days, them days," he said. "You was lucky if you got one week's work in four in the pits then. 'Tis no joke," he went on, "with bairns to rear and a wife to make a week's wages last a month."

"A month," Nicky exclaimed. "Mine canna mak' it last ten meenits!" And to the listening strippers, "Are none o' you miserable devils goin' tae gie us a piece?"

A burly young stripper handed over a sandwich from his box. "There's supposed tae be an egg in that," he said with glinting eyes. "But Ah dinna think the hen wracked her back layin' it."

Nicky opened the bread suspiciously. "Ah dinna see nae egg," he commented after a prolonged survey.

"She's mebbe just used the foty of an egg," said the young stripper.

"Aye," Nicky agreed, "an' it wis the negative." But he ate the "piece" with obvious relish. One by one the remainder of the men clumped up the steep heading to collapse with heaving chests and sweating flanks at the side of the road. Nicky, his wicked little eyes ripe with pawky humour, had a greeting for them all.

"Watch yer feet, Eck," he warned one man. "There's a big hole sticking up there." And to another, "Jings, Geordie, yure a' humpty backit. Ah doot yure wife hasnae been richt woken. She's buttoned yer troosers tae yer waistcoat."

"Man, Tam," he commiserated with another, who lay spreadeagled against a girder. "You look awfy tired."

"Aye," Tam agreed, "It's the lack o' beer."

154

"Yure needin' awae tae yer bed, Tam," Nicky told him, and added meaningly, "Alone! Look at him," Nicky appealed to us all. "He's bitin' his ain lip tae keep awake."

"Shut yure pus, Nicky," Tam growled. "'S a'richt fer you. Yure finished. We're no stairted yet."

"Dinna loss the heid, Pal," Nicky told him.

"Ah'm no lossin' the heid," Tam retorted. "But the only time Ah ever felt like laffin' at this time o' day was the mornin' that big McSwindle gie the canteen cat the mustard. . . . Ah whisht Ah could pick a winner on the Pools," he sighed feelingly.

"You couldnae pick yure nose," Nicky told him.

"What like is it up there?," Tam nodded towards the "face." His hands were occupied with a recalcitrant carbide lamp, a tin of carbide and a flask of water.

"Well, you'd better get that lamp sorted," Nicky told him cheerfully. "It's blacker 'n the Earl o' Hell's waistcoat."

The stripper called Eck rolled over disgustedly. "We've tae suffer that lamp a' shift," he mourned. "It's bruk mair hairts than Marilyn Munroe. An' he's his water bottle tae his mooth a' day yet he canna play a note."

"Awae an' bang yure heid on a girder," Tam advised him coldly. "It'll mebbe tak' the glaze aff yure een."

"Ah ken whas heid Ah'll be bangin' on a girder."

"Awae, twa o' you wouldnae mak a good plate o' soup."

"Haud yure tongue, man," Eck said, "an' no one 'll ken there's anythin' wrang wi' you."

"O-o-o-oh," Old Paddy sighed with relief as he eased off the second boot and emptied out a shower of small coal. He stared sadly at the holes in his socks. "Ah'll need tae buy anither pair of socks," he informed us sorrowfully.

"Och, Ah widnae dae that," Nicky said with hastily assumed concern. "Gie yure feet a good wash, you'll mebbe find an old pair."

"Yure boond tae hae plenty o' money onyway," Eck said. "Lyin' on after time doon a coalpit."

"Aye," Old Paddy told him with a chuckle, "and I also take in stairs to wash. I'm steaming with money."

"Yure steamin' a' richt," Nicky grunted, "but it's no wi' money. Fer Pete's sake put yer boots on."

155

"YOU'LL need tae mak' a will, Nicky," Eck said sarcastically. "It'll no do tae hae 'em fichtin' over what you leave."

"Don't you worry, Eck," Nicky laughed. "A' Ah'll leave is empty tumblers." At that point a breathless man stumbled the last few feet and flung himself down beside Nicky who said with a distinct lack of sympathy, "Jings, Pat, yure like a coo wi' a sair tae."

"Ah've near run a' the way frae the pit bottom," gasped Pat, who was Old Paddy's son. "The mair you flee the less you see," Nicky said sourly.

Old Paddy turned to his son. "Yure late, what wis wrang?"

"He wouldnae be able tae move," Eck suggested. "His wife'd be lyin' on his shirt tail."

"Missed the bus," gasped young Pat, "by a couple o' seconds. Too much traffic, Ah couldnae get across the road."

"Is that you growing a moustache, Pat?" asked Nicky, suddenly changing the subject. "Aye," young Pat said eagerly. "D'ye think Ah suit it?"

"Ah thocht you had a rat in yure mooth when you come for'ard there," Nicky told him unsympathetically. Tam, yawning hugely, reached for his pick and shovel. "Jings," he said, "Ah'm tired."

"So's the Agha Khan," Nicky put in quickly. "It wis in the papers. He's awae tae the Sooth o' France tae recup'rate."

"Must be wi' coontin' his money," Tam said. "It's no wi' wark."

One by one the strippers crawled up to the face, fumbling for picks and shovels and boxes of gelignite and cursing their lot and their lamps. An old man started the conveyors and we got to our feet and made for home. The shotfirer examined his box of detonators. "Ah'd better scramble awae up there," he muttered, "an' mak' sure they're no a' dead."

"You wouldnae be lang in hearin' 'em if they were," Nicky told him as we passed.

We tramped down the thousand yards of the heading and then up the seven hundred yards of McFett's Brae. In the Main Level we heard the unearthly screech of a deisel pug starting up. We quickened our footsteps, but as we pushed through the last soggy airscreen the pug was already well on its way and all that came back

156

to us out of the darkness was the faint rattle of the long train of coal tubs that the pug was towing.

"We'll just hae tae wait," Nicky said, and we plumped down on a pile of wooden props beside the main loading point and listened to the conversation of the two laddies that were in charge of it.

"Ah couldnae get tae sleep noway last nicht," said one. "Ye ken, ma mind's tae be a blank afore Ah can sleep."

"By jings," the other commented, "Ah can get tae sleep at ony time." "Aye," Nicky said deliberately, "Ah believe that." We became the target for two hostile pairs of eyes and the conversation died abruptly.

"Well," Old Paddy said, "we got it cut anyway." "Aye," Nicky agreed. "Yure neighbour goin' hame didnae mak' muckle difference. It's time you wis gettin' rid o' him, Paddy. Yure ower old noo tae be carryin' young fellas on yure back. You need a neighbour that's able fer his ain share o' the wark. A pit's nae place fer folk that'll no wark. See an' mind," he went on, with a look at the two laddies. "Dinna think Ah'm agin him just a' cos' he's a Teddy Boy. You canna condemn them oota hand as a class any mair than any ither. You get good an' bad in every group o' human beings. There's good warkers amang the Teddy Boys. Ah had one wi me yince in this very pit. Och, it'd be aboot five or six year ago, an' he wis sent wi' me as a trainee.

"He wis a richt Teddy Boy, Ah'll tell you, wi' a Tony Curtis hair-cut an' a'. He wis saft o' cos, but a' they non-mining folk are that. It's just wi' them no bein' aquaint wi' hard wark. Jings!, he wis thin. Ah've seen wider shoulders on a milk bottle, but he wis a willin' enough wee laddie wi' an awfy cheery face on him an' muckle, big een. His hair used tae hang doon his back like sweaty socks an' he wis nae higher 'n a pit boot.

"Well, he wasnae very strang but he wis willin' an' that wis enough. We wis on the strippin' at the time, doon the old Twenty Foot. Whatever Ah telt him tae dae he did it tae the best o' his ability, an' you canna ask mair than that aff naebody. Him an' me used tae get on fine.

"Ah, but there wis a gaffer in that section, name o' McPinch. We used tae call him 'Promises,' so you'll ken whit he wis like. When it come tae gettin' wark oota yer he'd promise yer the Kingdom o'

157

Heaven. But when it come tae payin' oot. . . . Plausible—Ah tell you, he'd a brocht tears tae a glass ee. Ticht . . .? He wis as ticht as a duck's ass an' that's watertight. OoooH!, he wis a sleekit wee devil.

"He only told the truth if a lie didnae fit. An' by jings, did he torment thon laddie. He just wouldnae leave him alone. An' it wis in a dirty sleekit sort o' way tae. No like the Bomber this mornin'. Bomber Broon losses the heid certainly, but he's genuine. He'll a' forgotten a' aboot it when he comes oot the nicht.

"But this McPinch wis different the way he used tae carry on at that laddie, Ah tell you, it wasnae here nor there. The kid couldnae dae nothin' richt fer him. Man, it wouldae made you weep. There wis one day Ah telt the laddie in front o' him tae draw his hand across 'Promise's' mooth. But the laddie wouldnae do it. He wis an awfy quiet wee soul. Ah tell you this, if McPinch had said a tenth tae me o' what he said tae thon laddie, Ah' da' knocked him as cold as a kipper.

"Well anyway, he's aye needlin' intae the laddie an' huntin' him aboot, it wouldae made yer sick tae watch it. One day the laddie's warkin' awae wi' me when up comes bigheid an' starts as usual. He tak's ma pick an' crawls up tae the top end o' ma place an' calls the laddie up aside him. He tak's the pick an' just tae show hoo good he is, by his way o' it, he hauls over a darn great nose o' coal that wis hangin'.

"Ah tell you it wis a nose that woundae fell doon if you looked at it twice. Ah kent that an' Ah wis keepin' the laddie awa till Ah wis ready tae deal wi' it. Well when 'Promises' hauls it over it busts, nat'rully, an' a big lump smacks the laddie in the pus. Fer a meenit o' cos the laddie didnae ken whaur he wis. Then he puts his hand up tae his face an' o' cos it's a' bloodin. Well the laddie wasnae a collier an' when he sees the bluid he gets in a panic.

"Ah'm a' bloodin," he greets . . . Ah'm a' bloodin."

"Well, wipe it aff," says 'Promises.'

"What wi?," the laddie asks him desperately.

"Wi' a hanfu' o' small coal o' cos," says 'Promises,' as if he wis talkin' tae an experienced collier. "Same as anyone else; you've surely got special bluid you."

158

"Well, by noo Ah'm up alongside 'em, an' Ah just lifts the pick an' wags it under McPinch's chin. 'Get oota here,' Ah says, 'or Ah'll nail you tae a prop this very meenit,' Well o' cos that wis that, an' aff goes McPinch wi' his tail atween his legs. The deputy come up the face an' we gets the laddie bandaged up. Then the deputy tells me tae tak' the laddie up the pit 'cos he thocht his een wis damaged.

"Well, they wis, so that wis the last we seen o' the laddie fer a while. He lived in Edinburry someway-doon at Leith. An' when he gets oota Hospital he goes hame an' stays there on compensation, waitin' fer his case tae come up at the High Court. It was a liability case o' cos. The laddie wis a trainee, an' 'Promises' shouldnae been messin' aboot in ma' place anyway.

"Well, the laddie wis nae fool. He kent he wis ontae a good thing an' he sticks tae it that he could hardly see at a'. So o' cos his lawyers wis claimin' a big sum aff the Coal Board. The laddie's een wis damaged o' cos. Naebody kent that better than me, but not as bad as he wis makin' oot——however, the laddie wis determined that the Coal Board wis goin' tae pay fer whit their official had done tae him.

"Holy smoke! You'd never believe the rotten luck. On the fore-noon o' the day the case wis tae come up the laddie wis haein' a quiet game o' darts in a pub in Leith when who comes snoopin' in but the bold McPinch. Well, o' cos, that wis the ba' bust.

"You canna plonk darts in the double one if yure blund. Man, it wouldae made you weep. Ah wis in Edinburry masel' o' cos. Ah wis a witness, like McPinch. But Ah wisnae snoopin' roon' Leith tae see if Ah could catch the laddie oot.

"Afore we goes intae court McPinch tells me what he'd seen, an' man, he wis fair gloatin'. He even described the look on the laddie's face when he saw 'Promises' watchin' him in the pub. Well, o' cos, it stuck oot a mile that if 'Promises' gets up in court an' tells that he'd seen the laddie playin' darts the day afore the morn there wasnae goin' tae be muckle damages going.

"Ah, but that laddie wis nae fool, Ah'll tell you. Ye ken, o' cos, that the tramcars in Edinburry is yella. Well, when we gets intae court the laddie's missin'. They waits fer a while, o' cos, an' then they decides tae adjourn the case. But at that meenit, wha's fetched in by twa big polis, but the laddie."

160

"What had he done, Nicky?," I asked.

"Jumped on a loaded banany cairt comin' oot a' Leith docks," Nicky said grinning. "An' insisted on gie'in' the driver tuppence fer his fare. Holy smoke! Whit a carryon! The driver o' the cairt thocht he had a lunatic on his hands, so he drives tae the nearest Polis Station an' roars fer help.

"Well, o' cos, after that there wisnae muckle McPinch could dae. S'posin' he'd seen the laddie threadin' needles nae one woulda believed him after the twa polis had feenished explainin' tae the Judge what had happened on the banany cairt." A deep orange glow appeared in the distance and we heard the pulsing of the powerful pug.

"What happened to McPinch?," I asked Nicky. "Is he still in the pit?"

"Nah," Nicky said. "He left last year; took that wee paper shop at the Crossroads. He's no in the shop much though. Let his wife run it. He spends maist o' his time sittin' on the seat in the park, tellin' stories aboot a' the wonderfu' things he did when he wis a pit gaffer."

The pug was drawing closer and, mingled with the throaty roar of its engine, we could hear the multitudinous rattles of a race of empty tubs.

"But, Nicky," I said, "I've been in that wee shop for fags. The man in there is almost blind."

"Aye," said Nicky. "That's 'Promises McPinch.' His eyes started tae go bad on him last year. Collier's nystagmus, the doctor said it wis." He spat luridly into the darkness. "That wis nae nystagmus," he stated firmly.

"What was it then?," I demanded, as we got to our feet.

"That wis a judgement," Nicky said darkly, climbing into the first empty tub. "That's whit that wis. A Judgement."

"*Certainly the miner is a brave man, for he daily faces that which he fears most. But he is also a humble man, aware as are few others of his own puny strength and of his utter dependence on God and his neighbour.*"

CHAPTER THIRTEEN

WEE FAT BASTARD

"WHY is it," I asked Nicky once, "that only the member of a sect such as, say, The Plymouth Brethren, is called a 'Christian' by the Scots miner?"

We had retreated to the shelter of the Heading while shots were fired in a projecting "Nose" that was obstructing the coalcutter. "After all," I went on, "there are fervent Catholics and Presbyterians in pits too, but they aren't regarded as being different or peculiar in any way because they love God. And no one ever thinks of referring to them as 'Christians.' In fact, that word 'Christian,' when applied by a collier to a collier, is almost an insult.

"It signifies, at the least, contempt, and at the most, dislike. It seems to denote a person not so much . . ." I hesitated for the right word—"below notice as beyond notice by the ordinary man." Again I was stuck for words.

"Oh!" I cried impatiently, "I don't know. . . . But it's as though in mining terms a 'Christian'—or at least the word Christian—means, when applied to another man, someone outwith the human family altogether, beyond this world and the comprehension of the men of this world."

"You've got the right word," Nicky said, "but the wrong meaning. When we refer tae a chap as a 'Christian' we mean that either he's afraid or he's no human, but only in the sense that the code o' life he follows, or claims tae follow, is so strict that it's past the hopes o' ordinary folk, more especially men who wark in the conditions we do. An' we ken that they are ordinary men, so we canna believe that they're honest in what they claim tae be, because we ken fine that we couldna manage it. We don't understand 'em, an' what man doesna comprehend, he automatically distrusts. It's only nat'rul——"

"Whited sepulchres," I suggested, but doubtfully.

"Eh?," Nicky said, wrinkling his black forehead.

"Everything nice outside but nothing but dry dust and bones within."

Nicky's eyes brightened. "Aye," he said. "That's mebbe the poseetion, though it's hard tae say what's inside a man till yu try him. But maist o' us think it's a' on the surface. It's like they T.V. adverts; they tell yu sae muckle aboot a thing being wunnerfu' that yu canna help thinking that it's really just a lotta muck, or it wouldn't need a' the bull. What wis that yu said?," he asked curiously.

"Whited sepulchres."

"Aye," he said slowly. "That's a braw description, that. Where'd yu pick that up?"

"Out of a book," I told him.

He grinned. "Ah kent yu never figured it oot yersel," he said impishly. "Wis it a blue book?"

"It was. Some say the bluest of them all."

"Oh," he grunted, "the Bible. Ah've aye been meaning tae read thon. They tell me there's some rare hot bits in it."

"Obviously," I said, "It's the story of human beings."

"Aah," Nicky nodded his head wisely. "Yu've got something there. But as Ah wis sayin', the folk we call 'Christians' are the ones who dinna do everything."

"Don't do anything," I corrected him.

"Ah mean everything," Nicky repeated stubbornly. "Take that wee, fat bastard, Davy Swordfish. He's ane o' they sect fellas. They dinna smoke, dinna drink, dinna swear, dinna argue wi' the gaffers, dinna go tae the flicks, dinna go tae the dancin'. They'll no hae a radio or a T.V. or let their wives cut their hair. If there's a war on, they'll no fight tae defend their muckin' sel's.

"They'll no join the Union or go on strike, but by the Hokey, they're no slow grabbin' ony extra wages we win wi' a strike. He's doon here on a Sunday forenoon 'cos he gets double pay fer it. An' Sabbath nicht he's up at the Crossroads singing hymns and cryin' doon hellfire an' damnation on the Teddy Boys an' their wee bits o' lassies. Ah yince heard somewhere that Christianity's a way o' life. That bastard doesnae live. Christ, his religion's nothin' but don'ts."

"Oh," I agreed. "You're right enough there, Nicky. Religion should be a positive force, not a series of negatives based on outward show."

Nicky said with a surprising show of tolerance, "'Cos not doin' a' they things is boond tae mak' it easier tae be really good. Ye ken what Ah mean, good inside."

"But where is the challenge then?" I demanded. "Surely Christianity should present a challenge."

"Mebbe it's easier tae be good inside," Nicky suggested with a mystifying want of clarity, "if yu dinna go boozin' an' chasing women around outside. Efter a', ye canna blame 'em fer pickin' the easy road oot."

"No, no, Nicky," I said, "that'll not take a trick. A man cannot claim to have conquered the temptations of the flesh and the devil, if at the very start he cuts himself off from the temptations of the flesh and the devil. That's what the old monks did long ago."

"Aye," Nicky snarled viciously, "an' it left 'em wi' plenty o' time fer pokin' their long noses intae what didnae concern 'em. Ah hope they're a' fryin' this meenit. They're the blokes that discovered coalpits. Hell roast 'em!"

A heavy explosion shuddered through the underworld galleries and, roaring with laughter, I got to my feet and followed Nicky back to the "face."

We shovelled the burst coal into conveyors and started once more to cut. We travelled another slow, grinding twenty yards when we were held up by Davy Swordfish, huddling incongruously against the "face."

"Are yu a'richt?" Nicky, all concern, switched off the coalcutter and grabbed the loose rolls of flesh on Davy's fat, naked chest. Davy Swordfish turned to face us, his white-rimmed, toad-like eyes glimmering obscenely in the darkness.

"Yes," he said thickly. "But I had to come away. The roof's all going near my pack. I came down here a bit until it quietened. I think it's going to close."

"What's wrang yu never stayed an' secured it?," snapped Nicky caustically. "That's what yure peyd fer, no fer runnin' awa'. Ah tell yu, this clown's goin' tae hae us a' bags o' nerves afore he's finished. Ah'll awa up an' hae a look at it," he went on. "Yu stay here wi' fatguts, one's enough tae risk."

He turned to the 'Christian.' "An' if yu've got the wind up at a wee bit scitter o' stane dust an' are haudin' us up fer nothin' Ah'll . . . Ah'll toss yu in the waste there an' cover yu up fer good." And he shook a small but solid fist under the wabbling double chin.

"Do not fear," he said with an assumed touch of jauntiness. "Do not fear, Nick is here." He crawled away from us, his lamp beam arching out before him in a swinging scythe of brightness that slashed a million diamonds from the lowering wall of coal.

In the sudden silence I fell to considering the uncouth lump of flesh that crouched beside me. Apparently he was aware of no sense of shame that another man should go and inspect his "working place." The mere suggestion of such a thing would have put any other collier into a state of almost insane rage. I couldn't help wondering if the derision he inspired in the other men was not caused as much by his appearance as by his religious beliefs and practices.

He was incredibly fat and ungainly in contrast to the tight-fleshed, smoothly-moving collier; a man whose whole life is spent in confined spaces, places that are sometimes so small that one wonders how the human frame can possibly be cramped into them. His flabby paunch was a thing unknown among the slim-bodied, hard-muscled miners.

His lower eyelids hung down, exposing the whites and giving his eyes the effect of being surrounded by thick, leprously-glowing rims. His face was blotched and unhealthy looking with thick, loose lips and broken, yellow teeth. Although all his life in the pit, he was regarded as an unreliable workman; one too nervous to be sent to any job of importance.

"It's no one of his muckin' false alarms this time," Nicky reported on his return. "They's twa bits that's pretty shaky. One of 'ems just below this bastard's pack an' the other's just aben it."

"Where's the rest o' the lads?," I asked.

"They're a'richt," Nicky said. "They're a' workin' higher up. I shouted to 'em an' warned 'em no tae come doon the way. No——" he said thoughtfully, "the bad bits are nearest tae this bloke's pack so they're his responsibility, an' yu ken what that means. We canna

166

cut past till the pack's in, an' fatty here'll sit a' nicht shiverin' wi' fricht lookin' at it. If ole Geordie, the regular packer, hadnae got hissel' hurt last nicht this eedjit woulda' been sittin' dreamin' at a conveyor button an' we wouldnae a' needed tae worry.

"However, Ah think the best thing we can do is tae gie him a hand. The three o' us'll no be lang gettin' the pack in an' then we can get cuttin' again, an' the quicker we're through that bad bit wi' yon coalcutter the better Ah'll be pleased. Them things cost a couple o' thoosan' quid o' the taxpayers' money an' Ah'm no wantin' tae loss it."

Turning to the 'Christian' he spat derisively. "This'll be richt up yure bliddy street, eh, yu fly bastard. Gettin' yure wark done fer yu. If Ah wisnae sure it wis that shot that shook the place up ah'd a thocht yu'd planned a' this oot an' mebbe drewn a few props tae start the place goin'."

"You have no right to say such a thing," Davy told him in a shocked voice, and then doubtfully, "Is it safe yet——?"

Nicky sunk his fingers in the thick belly while Swordfish squirmed away and tried ineffectually to free himself. "If *yure* workin' place is safe enough for me an' ma neighbour tae go into," Nicky snarled, "then Ah'm muckin' sure it's safe enough fer yu. Come on, get goin'," he growled menacingly. "Yu wee, fat bastard!"

As we passed the coalcutter we collected our picks and shovels and crawled up the face behind the reluctant 'Christian.' The roof grumbled and shook; flour-like streams of fine, uncannily-white dust filtered down through ominous black cracks; every now and again a steel prop would sigh and crunch down another inch into the soft, grey pavement, or a wooden prop would snap with a bitter crack.

"It's a hairy bit this," Nicky whispered, as, filled with the urgency of the moment, we tore into the job of building the pack. "Christ, this is no canny ava'." And as we worked like frenzied demons I watched Nicky's head continually turning as his sharp ears probed each revealing sound.

"Ye ken," he said, in what was for him an unnaturally serious voice, "Ah dinna like this. Fer twa pins Ah'd get tae hell oota it. This bliddy place is all on the move, Ah can tell yu."

167

Davy Swordfish blinked uneasily and said, "I think we'd better——"

"Yu shut yure muckin' pus," snarled Nicky badtemperedly. "Fine we ken what yu'd rather do. Well that roof's a' goin' an' it's tae be secured. If we muck aff an' leave it some ither pair bastard on the next shift'll get sent tae it, an' it'll be a muckin' sight wuss then. That's what yu'd like, yu fly bastard, fine we ken. Well it's no' goin' tae get left. Yure goin' tae stay here wi' us this time an' face it. Supposin' Ah've tae nail yu tae a prop wi' ma pick."

"Is it really bad, Nicky?" I asked him.

"Aye," he grunted, and his keen eyes ranged over the adjacent roof with the bitterly-won, professional wisdom of the experienced collier. "Aye," he murmured again, almost to himself. "If we dinna manage tae get a grip o' this bit quick it's gonna shut tight, Ah can tell yu that."

His last words might have been a signal. There was a sudden, thunderous roar of heavy guns punctuated by a series of whip-like cracks as props snapped with a sound like rifle shots.

"Doon the way," Nicky roared. "Go doon the way!," and we fled in terror at his bidding. Then again—in front of us now—the roof thudded down in masses of rock; the pavement heaved up as though in an earthquake—and the walls of our tomb thrust in amid a bedlamic din that announced the end of a crazed world, while the shrill shrieks of tortured, flying steel drove through our bursting eardrums like red-hot, naked knives.

I cannot describe it; to do so is impossible. All I can say is that for a hellish while there was a heart-shattering cacaphony of noise and whirling death and choking dust in an endless burning darkness.

Then—again as suddenly—it was very, very still, and lying across Nicky's legs in this deep other world of seeming stillness I listened to my neighbour's breathing. And it sounded to my straining ears like the anguished, noisy snoring of an empty dry-sucking pump.

"Holy smoke," I groaned when the three of us had gathered together our bruised bones and scattered wits. "What now——?" Then, as our position appeared more real and positive to my dazed and enfeebled brain, "Nicky," I asked, and I know there was a tremble in my voice. "Nicky, what chance have we got?" And the thick, clotting dust clagged my lips and tongue.

168

"Ah dinna ken," he said softly, slowly. "It a' depends on hoo much has fell . . . Ah, shut yure pus, yu mealy-mouthed bastard," he flung at Davy Swordfish, who lay prone in the dirt, gobbling sobs out of a grotesquely-twisted mouth. "We've enough tae worry aboot withoot yu lyin' there greetin' like an' ole whure that's dropped her bottle a' gin.

"Yu've a chance o' gettin' tae this heaven yure aye slaverin' aboot quicker than yu planned. Put yure light oot, yu useless bastard, an' shut up." He turned to me, "Put yure's oot tae," he said. "We'll just keep mine on tae start wi', there's nae point in using up the three batt'ries at once."

The simple words showed me more than anything else just how desperate our situation was and I began to tremble helplessly. Nicky's huge, all-embracing, miner's heart must have sensed my terror, for he said gaily, "Dinna loss the heid, Pal. We never deed in winter yet. Roll over an' put that fatty's licht oot tae. He's awa' in a trance, Ah think. We're goin' tae need the hurry-up wagon fer him in a wee while if he doesnae get a grip o' hissel'."

I reached over and switched off Davy's lamp. He lay groaning softly to himself, his thick body shuddering. The small action helped me to control myself and the trembling stopped and I could once more govern my limbs and my mind.

"That's better," Nicky said with a gallant attempt at a laugh. "Do not fear, Nick is here!"

As I grew easier I asked him again what our chances were. I was proud of my voice too. It seemed unnecessarily loud, but quiet, steady, and firm.

"Christ," Nicky said, "where'd yu get that squeaky voice? Yu soon' like a rat wi' a rock on its back."

I was crestfallen at his careless comment and once more my spirits dived into wild despair.

"It depends what's doon," he said again. "This bit's stannin', thank Christ; though it wouldnae a' been if we hadnae got that pack in. That's a' that's holdin' it. It's fell above an' below where we are." He paused a moment to consider.

"We're aboot the middle o' the face," he said thoughtfully. "An' it's aboot a hundred yards lang."   Slowly he swung his lamp round our refuge.

It was a rectangular box, ten yards long and six feet wide and perhaps three feet high. In front of us was the "face" scintillating in the light; behind us, the half-squeezed pack. Above us, a menacingly low, stone roof and beneath our feet the muddy grey slime of some prehistoric jungle. To the right and to the left was a wall of fallen rock and rubble.

"Well," said Nicky cheerfully, the survey completed. "If they dinna get us oot, it's a braw roomy tomb. That's a collier's life," he said, as though the word had reminded him. "Naethin' but worry, frae the womb tae the tomb."

Once more he squinted round our dusty, black box. "Aboot ten yards lang," he muttered thoughtfully. Then, with a swift spinning on doubled legs, he turned and faced me.

"It's this way," he told me gently. "There's aboot forty-five yards o' the 'run' above us, an' another forty-five yards below. Oor only hope is that they can tunnel a hole through tae us, securin' it as they travel. The big trouble is that they dinna ken exactly where we are, nor hoo we're fixed. If the hale length o' the 'run' is shut, then we've had oor chips. It'd take 'em weeks tae drive even a wee hole forty-five yards. But there's mebbe only twenty yards shut on each side o' us, or . . ." his voice rose hopefully, ". . . just ten. In that case we've a chance."

"Weeks to tunnel a wee hole forty-five yards——?," I said in surprise. "Why, three men drive a twelve foot by nine foot road at the rate of a yard and a half a shift. And there's three shifts in a day."

Nicky said patiently, "It's a wee bit different in this case, Pal. Fer one thing, they canna use the conveyors; we could be lyin' jammed in 'em. They don't know, so they daren't use 'em. Which means that a' the muck they excavate'll hae tae be shovelled back frae man tae man. An' every yard they gain is a yard farther fer the muck tae travel back tae somewheres where they can get rid o' it. Then again, they canna use explosives fer fear o' blowin' us into Hallelloojah Land.

"It'll hae tae be pick an' shovel wark, an' even wi' picks they'll hae tae be carefu' in case they stab one o' us lyin' buried in the muck. Ah tell yu, they'll muckin' near need tae wark wi' bare hands."

"We'll need to just hope for the best then," I said. And wishing

170

No longer is the coal gathered at the point of a pick. Today machines do the work

to—at least appear—cheerful, I went on, "Still there will be plenty of men at the job."

"Aye," Nicky agreed. "But there's nae time tae drive a big tunnel an' a wee one means that, mebbe, just one man can get warkin' at a time, supposin' there's a thoosan' willin' hands behind him. And there will be," he emphasised, "an' a' the equipment that's needed. Ah'll tell yu this, the rescue service has been expanded and equipped until it's prob'ly the finest in the warld . . . until they get us or oor corpses oota here this section'll be mobbed wi' skilled colliers that's ready tae wark till their soulcases drop oot till they get us. An' noo, fer the fust time in the history o' British Coal Minin' they've got every muckin' thing they need tae do it wi'."

"And for us," I said, "it's just a matter of hanging on." Then another thought struck me. "Nicky," I said, "what about air?"

"Ah 'spect enough'll seep through tae keep us goin'," Nicky said cautiously. "If not, we'll never ken. It's a braw death thon. Yu get droosy an' that, an' yu lie doon fer a wee sleep an' that, an'——well, yu just dinna wake up."

"No-o-oh," sobbed Davy in a long drawn-out howl of anguish. "To die like a beast in the bowels of the earth. No-oh! oh, no-oh!"

"Aaah, shut yure snivelling pus, yu bible-thumping bastard," Nicky snapped angrily. "No, it's food an' water Ah'm worried aboot. 'Specially watter."

Already the pavement water was swilling icily about our ankles, and I knew that the slow seepage would continue. I pointed word-lessly to our feet.

"Oh!, fer Christ's sake dinna drink thon," Nicky cried in a shocked voice. "It's fu' o' acid, an' millions o' years old tae. That'd rot yure guts oot, man; look at what it does tae yure boots."

"Here!," he suddenly shouted, "where's yure water bottle, ole turnip heid. Yu'd bring it up the face wi' yu, did yu no?"

"I laid everything between the pack and the conveyors," Davy wailed.

Nicky crawled over the conveyors and scrabbled furiously among the loose rubble in the narrow space. He emerged waving triumph-antly a tattered, old jacket. In one pocket of the ragged garment was a tin snack-box and, in the other, an army-type water bottle, three-quarters full. Now, with over half a pint of water and three

171

small sandwiches we were rich with hope. Nicky issued a mouthful of water per man at once, and then laying the articles lovingly in the conveyors, covered them carefully with the folded coat. The small drink refreshed us all and seemed to calm Davy Swordfish. He was sitting up now and blinking the round, ugly orbs of fear and humility that served him for eyes.

"I hope there's something good in that box, yu ole twister," Nicky said in an aggressive tone. "Yu used tae hae braw snacks in the old days." He settled his sinewy back against the conveyors and broke into a flood of half-humorous reminiscence. Now and again— under cover of guarded hands—I glanced covertly at my watch. Nicky's profanely-pawky voice dug into memory's pathetic earth and raised up before us a mountain of remembered joys and sorrows and ridiculous occasions, especially the latter.

The childish pranks that were played on one another by these grave-eyed, hard-bodied men, so that I was again reminded of the boy-like qualities that I had myself often glimpsed beneath the grim face and taciturn smile which nature uses to mask the collier's true features.

It was midnight on Tuesday when we were buried—happed up is the correct description of such a happening, for the collier does not use the word buried in ordinary conversation. And for that first dreadful, twenty-four hours, Nicky was our rod and our staff and our comforter. His pawky voice droned on, rising and falling, shrilling or deepening, as the nature of his tale required.

In one story he mentioned a collier nicknamed the 'Beetle.' Strangely so, I thought, for the man's real name was Adams. And Adams usually becomes "Fanny" without further ado.

When the story was finished Nicky said, "There's a man sittin' there could tell yu aboot the 'Beetle,' by Christ, he could. If ever a man suffered wi' the 'Beetle' it wis ole fatguts there. He's deid noo——aye, this ten year or more. But Ah'll bet Davy there hasnae fergot him."

"Ever scheming some new wickedness," Davy said in mournful tones.

"Aye, he wis a boy, wis the 'Beetle,' " Nicky affirmed. "Always up tae some mischief. Oooh, he wis a boy. Ah tell yu, he'd a' started a riot in a graveyard, the 'Beetle.' What a man he was fer a laff; an

172

aye after Davy there. Davy couldnae get peace frae him no way."

"I have prayed for his soul every single day since he died," said Davy Swordfish, and his several chins wabbled as he spoke.

"Ah wunner he doesnae come back an' haunt ye," Nicky grinned. "Ah bet that's the hardest part o' hell fer the 'Beetle.' He canna get at Davy nae mair. Christ, Ah mind yince, it wis the deid o' winter tae. Did he no shove Davy oota the baths an' bolt the bliddy door. Davy had tae go up the steps an' along the Main Road an' in the other door. He wis blue when he got back. It's a guid job it wis a black, dark winter's morning wi' a foot o' snow on the grun'. 'Cos if anyone 'd seen him runnin' alang the Main Road in his birthday suit he's a' got the jail.

"An' rats! Davy there wis aye feared at the rats. Christ, the 'Beetle' used tae hae him aboot aff his bliddy heid, Ah can tell yu.

"One section we were warkin' in there wis an' ole rat used tae come oot an' hang aboot while we were eatin'. Whiles o' cos someone would fling it a bit bread an' it wis gettin' as tame as a pit rat is ever likely tae get. Well, one day Davy wis late an' the 'Beetle' has a bit fur he'd been carryin' aboot ready. He chases the rat an' puts the bit fur in Davy's pocket where his grub box wis.

"When Davy comes aff the face the 'Beetle' says, 'See an' watch, Davy, the ole rat's no turned up the day, he's mebbe in amang oor claes.'

"Well, Davy puts his hand in his pocket fer his snack-piece an' what does his fingers touch but the fur. Christ! what a carryon. He flings his jacket doon on the pavement an' jumps on it—an' dances on it—an' batters at it wi' a wooden prop. Ooh! yu never see the like o' this. An' o' cos by the time he's finished wallopin' at it his tin box is smashed flat an' his snack is ruined. Then, when he sits doon wi'oot a bite tae eat, who's sittin' lookin' at him but the ole rat; he musta come back tae see what a' the racket wis.

"Another time when Davy wis last, the 'Beetle' only had dry toast, so he opens Davy's box. An' here, be Christ, does Davy no hae boiled ham atween his bread. 'That'll no tak' a trick,' says the 'Beetle.' 'They Christians is supposed tae give a' they hath tae the pair.' So he takes Davy's ham an' puts some bits o' ole rotten sackin' that wis lyin' aboot atween Davy's bread. An' here be jings, Davy wis in that o' a sweat o' hurry that he ate it an' never noticed."

173

Nicky turned to the 'Christian' and asked curiously, "Did he ever tell yu what yu eat that day?"

"Yes," he told me. "I was sick for a week over it."

Nicky said, "What happened the time he put the deid rat in yure empty box, just afore lousin'? Nane o' us dared tae ask yu aboot it at the time."

"It was terrible," Davy said. "My wife fainted at the kitchen sink, and the people next door had to come in and help us. I wasn't able to do anything after I heard her scream and saw the rat. That was a dreadful thing to do. I had a long struggle with my conscience before I was able to forgive the 'Beetle' in my heart, really forgive him, I mean."

"D'yu mind o' the bus, Davy?," Nicky asked with a salacious grin.

"Mind the bus?" Davy said with a quaver in his voice. "Yes I remember what happened in the bus. I'll never forget it. I've never been so ashamed in my life. A devil must have got into the 'Beetle' that day to make him do such a dreadful thing. I sometimes wondered if I would ever be allowed to forget it, it was the talk of the village."

"What happened," I wanted to know. I had found a dry perch on a long slab of rock, and stretched full length, was listening with close attention.

"We wis a' in the bus," Nicky started, "goin' hame aff the night-shift. It'd be aboot seven o'clock an' a braw summer's mornin'. Tae let yu unnerstan, at that time Davy didnae carry his snackbox in his hand or pocket like the rest o' us. Oh, no, he has tae hae a wee leather case tae carry it in. By the heavens he's never used a 'tachy case since that day, Ah'll betcha. By Christ, he hasnae. He carries it in his hand where everyone can see what he's carryin'. An' he dresses the same as us these days tae. At that time he wore a collar an' tie to an' from the pit. Oh, he wis a dressy fella in they days, wis oor Davy.

"Well, as yu ken, some o' they conductress lassies are just wee battle-axes who can gie as guid as they get offa anybody. But the one that wis on the bus that day wis a stern-faced, wee lassie; an' awfy quiet an' respectable. She wis a braw wee soul but, by jings, she wisnae goin' tae stan' nae nonsense of us colliers, no in her bus.

The 'Beetle' musta been relyin' on this, becos he gets up front wi' Davy an' starts a bliddy riot. Arguein' an' swearin' at Davy, an' carryin' on generally. An' o' cos Davy just sits there like a bliddy eedjit and didnae ken what tae do.

"Awa' goes the conductress doon the bus wi skirts fleein' an ticket-punch rattlin'. Ah, but she doesnae pick on Davy, like the 'Beetle' had planned. Na, na, she wis nae fool thon lassie. 'Ah'm no haein' this commotion in ma bus,' she sayd tae the 'Beetle.' 'For twa pins Ah'd put yu aff.'

" 'It's no me,' the Beetle tells her, 'It's him,' an' he points at Davy, sittin' a' red-faced wi' shame, wi' his collar an' tie an' his leather case on his knees. 'He shouldnae be in this bus, onyway,' says the 'Beetle.' 'It's a disgrace, the likes o' him ridin' in the same bus as decent warkin' men.'

" 'This is a Miner's Bus,' says the lassie, 'an' he's as much richt init as yu.'

" 'He's no a miner,' roars the 'Beetle.' 'Christ, ma lassie, look at him; did yu ever see a collier wi' a collar an' tie on? No,' says the 'Beetle.' 'But we ken what he is, the dirty beast,' an' he acts as if he's affronted.

" 'What is he then?,' asks the lassie, a' mystified.

" 'A traveller,' says the 'Beetle,' as quick as a whip. 'What d'yu think is in thon case o' his? He's a traveller in——' an' he leans forward an' whispers in the lassie's ear. Well, Ah sees the lassie's cheeks go red an' then, by Christ, the fun begins, Ah can tell yu. She opens the wee windy an' says somethin' tae the driver, an' the next thing is we're awa' full belt.

"It wis like bein' in one o' they Roosian Rockets. Fleein' past a' the stops, along the Main Road, doon the Brae, roon' the corner an' Bob's yure Uncle, we're at the Polis Station. Oot nips the lassie an' in a flash she's back again wi' twa big Polis an' gies pair Davy in charge fer breach o' the peace in a public conveenience.

"Laff, by Christ, Ah'll tell yu, Ah've never laffed like Ah laffed thon day. No—neither afore nor since. By jings Ah havenae."

"And what was the result of it all?," I asked. "What did the 'Beetle' say was in the case, anyway?"

"Och," said Nicky, "what d'yu think. He telt the lassie that Davy wis a traveller in contraceptives. Ah'll mind thon lassie's expression

175

till ma deein' day. Davy gotta lecture aff the Beak an' got fined twa pund. 'Cos, us that wis in the bus had a whip roon' an' paid the fine. An' by hokey it wis worth it, Ah can tell yu."

"Yes," muttered Davy, his face glimmering faintly in the light. "But I had to bear the disgrace. That girl is a married woman now with children, but she still turns her head when she passes me in the street."

"An' yu never complained," Nicky put in wonderingly. "By Christ, Davy, Ah'll gie yu that. Yu've loads o' patience. Fer all that's been done tae yu, an' yu've had some tricks played on ye over the years, nobody kens that better na me, Ah've never heard yu swear, an' Ah've never heard yu complain or greet tae a gaffer, no, not at the dirtiest trick. Aye, Ah'll gie yu that, Davy, yu've an awfy patience. Christ, Ah'd a' murdered the 'Beetle' if he'd a' done a quarter tae me o' what he done tae yu. Aye murdered him, Ah can tell yu——"

So it went on, story after story after story, and we lay back and listened gratefully while the terror-laden hours rode past on the slipping saddle of the small man's effervescent personality. And eventually the time came, as we had known it must come—it was the evening of the second day—when even Nicky's gallant soul lost all support and his brave voice was still.

The air had become sluggish and thick, debilitating, dulling the edge of our senses and chilling our spirits. The sandwiches were gone and only a sip of water remained for each. The last lamp was a sickly-pale, reddish shine, in which our eyes glowed evilly like the eyes of ophidians in the hibernacle of an ancient tomb.

We existed in an almost immaterial world of half-lights and fearful creeping shadows, the dusty images of terror dancing ever before our forlorn faces. A mind world of dreams of death, and the real world of the decaying gloom of our stifling, clammily-dripping coffin.

As the morning of the second day grew older we weakened steadily, our unbidden imaginings accumulating under our growing burden of fear. So that, while still living, we died a thousand times beneath the tyrannical persecutions of our own most secret emotions.

At some time I fell asleep, and slept until Nicky's wandering voice found and woke me. The lamps were all finished now but the dial of my watch was luminous and I saw it was three o'clock. I had to reflect and my dozing mind grumbled at the effort thus forced upon it. It was the morning of the third day and I knew with sudden, awful clarity that this was our last day. Tonight we would die and, knowing this, I lay back in the icy water and cringed in the livid face of regret for a thousand things undone that I might have done; a thousand things seen that I might have known and come to love had I not wasted my seeing on less valuable things that I knew could never be known and which it was impossible to love.

Nicky's words crawled thinly about the small place of our confinement, cracked words, quavering, and half-mad with barely-suppressed terror.

Davy sat up and then knelt. I don't know how I knew that, perhaps one can sense a movement—but I knew—as surely as though I had seen him do it. I put my hand on Nicky's side. Breathing heavily, he was stretched beside me and my fingers lay on his narrow, gasping ribs.

Davy Swordfish said to Nicky, "Yes, I can pray, Nicky. I have never ceased to pray. Do you wish me to pray aloud?"

And his voice flew about our small tomb like an eagle ranging an eternal sky. His voice came out of the darkness like the warm, steadying arm of an old and trusted friend. Calm and beautiful was the voice of Davy Swordfish, calm and beautiful and strong, so that my weary heart lifted to its soaring flight and I felt Nicky stir uneasily beside me.

"Pray, Davy——," he whispered huskily. "Pray fer us—oot loud—Davy man," and each word was a strangled sob from far back in his throat.

And Davy Swordfish prayed. And the words of his praying swirled about us, and the waves of his praying rolled over us, and we were comforted. And the great eagle of his voice flew about the world and when—ten hours later—a probing, careful pick came through the wall of rubble, he was still praying, and it was his great voice that had borne us up and bade us live.

Swiftly then, scrabbling hands followed the pick and there was the questioning, grimy face of a fellow man. And there was light, blessed, blessed light that blinded us with its kindness to tired eyes, and the last words of Davy's prayer rang out in a glory of praise and thanksgiving.

Then quickly came more men and a doctor who examined us. Then we were helped over to the small mouth of escape that framed a smile of welcome.

*　*　*　*　*　*　*　*

"Come on, fer Christ's sake," screamed Nicky, shoving madly at the huge buttocks that swayed before him. "Yure like a bull at a bliddy christening!" Davy hurriedly scrambled another yard and stood up.

"What the muckin' hell did yu stop there for?" demanded Nicky, after he had made sure that I, too, was out of the tunnel. Davy, his eyes revolting in their meekness, flinched away.

"The bastard," snarled Nicky ferociously. "Gets oot hissel an' then stops tae hae a wee bit squint roon' aboot an' us stuck in that bliddy hole ahint him, gasping tae get oot. . . .Sticks there waggin' his backend under me snitch an' admirin' the muckin' view." He took a deep gulp from one of many proffered water-bottles and in his rage and relief nearly choked.

I leant against a girder and the cold, dew-damp steel was grateful to my burning skin. Chest heaving weakly, I waved off a thousand anxious hands. I knew that for a moment I had to be still. Maybe it was what they call the moment of truth. I don't know. But I did know that I should never be the same person again.

I had become another man; perhaps he had always lain, unsuspected, in my being, an inner self. Now he had arisen and demands to live and I am tranquil and happy, for he will be a better man than I have ever been.

Ah! with what heady rapture we grasp again that slender thread of life, we, from whom it has been so nearly snatched away. And so, flooded with an unspeakable joy and relief, I leaned against the cold girder and was quietly aware, with a greater, more subtle awareness than I had ever thought possible. Calm now and full of a sweet ease of spirit, I listened to Nicky's continued tirade. And my new sensibility told me that he was a brave little man for whom things had become too much, as indeed, they sometimes become too much for the bravest. And the only way he could regain his self-respect was by shouting and cursing and humiliating. And I saw, too, with my

178

newly-awakened clarity of vision, that Davy Swordfish also had his place, though it was but to be the target for the jibes of others.

In the darkness I had found the light of understanding and I now knew that no single life is ever wasted or without purpose, no matter how obscure and pathetic that life may seem to be.

" 'An' if you went up to the lunatic asylum an' asked yin o' they loonies tae come doon here an' dae whit we're daein'—d'ye ken whit he'd say——?' There was an impressive pause to give added emphasis. 'He'd say—d'ye think Ah'm daft'. And the two of them nodded their heads wisely over this inescapable conclusion."

CHAPTER FOURTEEN

LIKE A SHOT FROM A GUN

IT was piecetime and we were sitting in the Heading when Bomber Brown, our Section deputy, arrived. He puffed heavily over a dirty notebook. "Ah'm needin' men for Sunday," he said sadly. "It's a double shift, ye ken."

"Include me oot," said Nicky McFish, the leading cutterman. "It's aye Monday afore Ah get sobered up."

"Aye," said the Bomber offensively—"The followin' Monday, fine we ken."

"Put me doon," said Heelplates McSobb, the propdrawer, as the rest of us shook our heads.

"What's up?," asked Nicky. "Do you no see enough o' this den through the week?"

"Ah'll suffer it for once," said Heelplates. "Ah've promised the bairn a bike for her birthday."

"By jings," Nicky murmured reminiscently, "Ah mind o' gettin' ma fust bike. Whit Ah suffered for thon machine."

I settled my back more comfortably against a girder. "Tell us about it," I suggested.

"Och," Nicky began, "we wis just laddies at the time an' on the drawin'. Ye ken, bringin' empty tubs up tae the fellas at the 'face' an' shovin' awa the fu' yins. Well, the Bonhoose Section, where we wis warkin', closed—so that wis that. The next day me an' the Bomber comes doon the pit wunnerin' if we'd get wark someplace or if we'd get sent hame. Ah wis worrit but Ah dinna think the Bomber wis botherin' ower muckle aboot it. He wis a' bunged up wi love at the time, an' floatin' aboot wi' a dreamy look on his pus an' his heid in the cloods like a flat-footed fairy. Ah tell you, it wis pitifu' tae watch. He fa's ower props an' that noo, but in them days he'da tripped ower a spent match.

181

"Well onyway, the gaffer sends us intae the Twenty Foot tae draw tae Beestie McGrief, 'cos his last twa laddies had flung their haun's in an' gone fer sodgers. An mak' nae wunner. After a week drawin' tae Beestie Ah wis haein' a struggle passin' the recruitin' office masel'.

"By jings, he wis some boy this Ah'll tell you. Wark! . . . that's a' thon maniac lived for. He wis a wee, fat fella an' as bald as a neap; whit you ca' an eggshell blond. 'The Toothless Terror' the laddies ca'ed him 'cos he wis naethin' but gums. But his richt name wis Beestie, wi' him bein' a beest for wark, ye see. Well, he mebbe wisnae nae oil paintin', but his dochter . . . Ooch!, whit a smasher.

"She'd big googly een an' a wee, roon mooth like a bunch o' cherries. She lookit as if she wis just made tae be cuddled. Her hair wis the colour o' lager beer. Ye ken, thon warm, chestnut colour wi' the licht shinin' through it. Ooh, she wis a braw bit stuff, Ah'll admit that, but tae hear the Bomber ravin' aboot her you'da thocht she had gold-plated een an' tartan hair. By jings, he wis in some state, Ah'll tell you, an' a' eaten up wi jealousy. The lassie likit the dancin' ye see an' the best dancer in the village wis a sleekit wee cuss ca'ed Beeswings McGlubb. The Bomber hadnae got a look in there; he dances like a coo wi' a blistered heel. He used tae come ravin' tae me aboot her an' whit he'd like tae dae tae pair wee Beeswings.

"Well, at the time, as Ah've telt you, Ah wis desprit for a bike. Ah couldnae afford a new one and Ah wis savin' up tae buy one offa Beeswings secondhand, so the Bomber didnae get muckle sympathy frae me wi' his romantics. Ah wisnae wantin' Beeswings offended.

"But, however, we goes scavanglin' intae the Twenty Foot this day, an' Ah'll tell you one thing an' that's no twa, Ah wisnae lookin' forward tae it, not one bit. Ah could see us gettin' killed aff in oor prime wi' thon Beestie. Not only that, we'd aye been used tae hand-drawin' an' rope haulage, an' in the Twenty Foot it wis ponies. Ah tell you, Ah wis a' knockit aff ma ways o' daein' thon day. But it's true enough whit they say. Laff an' the warld laffs wi' you, but greet, an by jings you'll get leave tae greet alane. The Bomber, the eedjit, wis fair awa wi' hissel' 'cos he wis goin' tae wark wi' the lassie's paw.

182

" 'If we can keep pace wi' him in tubs,' he says, 'it's boond tae mak' a good impression on Hectorina 'cos he's never kept laddies lang afore. They just canna keep up wi. him. An' Hectorina's like her Paw; she admires a warker, an' thon Beeswings'll neither wark nor want.'

"Ah tell you, if the Bomber's brains wis gelignite there wouldnae be enough tae blow his bunnet aff. A' Ah could see wis us gettin' murdered wi' overwark. 'Would it no be easier if you learnt tae dance?,' Ah says. 'It's nae use warkin' your way intae her Paw's hairt just for her tae shed taers ower oor youthfu' graves.'

" 'Dinna be daft,' says the Bomber. 'Hard wark never hurt nae-buddy.' Well, o' cos, the only ones that could'a argued wi' him aboot that is a' lyin' in the Kirkland Cemeterry, so Ah let it go. 'An' onyway,' he says, 'think o' ma romance. Ah will invite you tae the weddin'.'

"Ah wis goin' tae point oot tae him that we wis mair likely tae qualify for a funeral than a weddin', but by that time we're in at the foot o' the Brae an' there's Beestie stripped tae the waste waitin' for us. An' alangside him a feerocious lookin' quadruped that cairtainly made up for Beestie's deeficiencies in the way o' teeth. There didnae seem tae be naethin' else tae thon pony but teeth an' the muscles tae scrunch 'em wi'.

" 'Tak' your claes aff, laddies,' says Beestie. 'We'll manage tae keep warm wi'oot claes in here.' Then he sees me starin' at the double row o' steel stakes in thon animal's mooth.

" 'That's Impatience,' he says. 'He kens his wark. He hauls oot fower fu' tubs an' brings us back fower empty yins. We ca' him Impatience 'cos he doesnae like tae be kept waitin', so we aye has tae hae fower fu' tubs ready for him.' Ah listens tae this an' Ah could feel the blisters risin' on me haun's at the thocht o' whit wis in front o' me. 'You'll notice,' Beestie goes prattlin' on, 'he's got a chain on ahint him wi' a hook on the end. Well, just unhook that from the empty tubs an' hook it on the fu' yins, an' awa he goes. Then you slew the tubs across they steel plates on the pavement here and hook 'em on the end o' that rope.

" 'Then you run up the Brae'—by noo Ah'm sweatin' freely—'an' gie me a haun tae fill the tubs. We hooks on the fower fu' tubs at the top o' the Brae an' knocks oot the catch. It's whit you ca' an

Airyplane Brae ye see. When the power fu' tubs runs doon the Brae they hauls up the fower empty tubs that you hooked ontae the ither end o' the rope. Meanwhile you laddies run doon the Brae'—Ah sat doon tae listen tae the rest 'cos Ah wis tired a'ready—'an' swing the fu' tubs ower the plates tae the rails, an' hook 'em on the pony, who by noo will be back again an' foamin' at the mooth tae be aff, then you run up the Brae——'

"He'll no be the only one that's foamin' at the mooth," Ah says. "You're goin' tae see we dinna get fat onyway."

" 'Aye,' he says. 'Ha-ha,' an' he rubs his bare belly. 'Thats no' fat,' he says. 'That's ma bump o' good nature. Ah'll keep ye fit, ha-ha! Noo see an' mind, there's twa things you've aye tae watch when you're warkin' wi' ponies.'

"Aye," Ah says, "the hind feet."

" 'No—no,' he says. 'Don't be reediculous. First, don't overload 'em; they ken as well as you hoo many tubs they're s'posed tae pu', an' if you overload 'em they'll no move ava.' Second, watch them teeth.'

"Well, that wis that, an' we gets torn in aboot it. Wark!, by jings Ah never warkit like thon in a' ma days. It wis like an ice rink, wrastlin' them tubs over the plates, slippin' and slidin' aboot in oor ain sweat, an' then fleein' up an' doon thon Brae an' shovellin' coal. Ah tell you, we didnae ken if we wis comin' or goin'. Ah could see me gettin' worn doon tae a skellingten wi'oot the strength tae pedal a bike afore Ah'd saved up the money tae buy it. An' Ah couldnae see nae road oota ma troubles 'cos that eedjit the Bomber wis lappin' it up.

"O' cos ole Beestie wis gie'in the Bomber a big build-up noo wi' thon Hectorina. You shoulda' seen 'em at the dancin', talk aboot Mutt an' Jeff. The Bomber goin' roon the flair wi' his een a' glazed an' a glaikit sorta smirk on his pus, an' the wee soul tryin' tae keep frae unnerneath the Bomber's big beetlesquashers. But Ah think she had a wee bit notion for him for a' his big feet an' a that. Beeswings thocht so tae an' he keeps greetin' tae me aboot it.

"One day we're sittin' at oor pieces when in comes Impatience an' the fust thing he sees is the Bomber haudin' up his haun wi' a big piece in it. Well, there wis just one gulp an' that piece wis awa. Ah thocht the Bomber wis goin' tae hae a fit, Ah tell you; he near bruk his hairt. We needed oor grub on thon job, Ah can tell you. We couldnae afford tae be gie'in' it awa tae nae pony.

" 'You micht as well shift the hook,' says Beestie, 'seein' you've feenished your piece.'

"Well, Ah think the Bomber musta been half mesmerised still at loosin' his dinner, 'cos he got in the road an' Impatience steps on his tae. Oooh!, whit a carryon. He draws back an kicks the pony in the ribs.

"Well, o' cos, the Bomber's got feet like armoured cruisers an' Ah don't think thon pony kent where it wis for a meenit. It just stood there wi' its legs a' spraggled oot an' the wind whustlin' oota it like a busted barrage balloon. Then a' o' a sudden it got its breath back an'—clunch! The twa sets o' steel traps comes thegither an' when the Bomber gets awa he's minus half a yard o' moleskin an' half a pun' o' steak. Well it's no hard tae mak' him loss the heid at ony time an' he grabs a wooden prop an' belts Impatience ower the lollipop.

"By jings, that wis worth the watchin', Ah'll tell you. Thon pony's een wis goin' roon like pitheid wheels, each one in a different direction, an' the look it gied the Bomber . . . well, Ah'll tell you this, Ah woundnae care tae be warkin' doon nae coalpit wi' an animal that lookit at me the way Impatience lookit at the Bomber.

" 'That's an awfy way tae carry on,' says Beestie. 'Ma dochter telt me you wis a nice-natured laddie, but Ah doot she's never seen ye strikin' pair dumb animals what canna defend theirsel's.'

"The Bomber looks doon at his torn breeks an' opens his mooth an' Ah waits for the fiery blast tae come. Ahh, but he never says a word. After a', ye canna flee wi' the crows an' roost wi' the doos, an' love wis ower strang for him. But Ah'd seen a wee road oota ma preedicament, an' at the next dance Ah has a bit word wi' Beeswings. 'Bust up thon romance,' he says, 'an' Ah'll gie you ma bike.'

"Well time goes on, an' me an' the Bomber is gettin' worn doon tae shaddys, fleein' up an' doon thon Brae wi' tubs for thon maniac at the 'face.' The Bomber wisnae greetin' o' cos. He's a big strang fella an' by noo he's beginnin' tae regard Beestie as his future paw-in-law. It wis me that wis sufferin'. A' Ah stood tae collect wis a wooden overcoat.

"Ah ken Ah've gotta dee o' somethin' but Ah wisnae wantin' it tae be wark. An' there wis nae hope wi' Impatience 'cos him an' the Bomber wis a' lovey-dovey again. The Bomber fetched doon a big piece an' lettuce for thon beast every day an' used tae feed it fust. Ah tell you, it would'a' made ye eat your young watchin' this. Well, Ah wis desprit for thon bike an' yin day Ah gets a brainwave.

"Ah tak's doon a jar o' mustard an' laagers it a' ower Impatience's piece an' lettuce while the ithers wis awa. Then at piecetime Ah gets roon the back o' thon pony so Ah wis oota range o' the teeth while the Bomber gies him his tit-bit.

"Oooh!, whit a carryon; he wisnae whit you'd ca' a dainty feeder, thon pony. Wi' him it wis one gulp an' awa. By jings he musta thocht he'd swallowed an atom bomb. He lets oot one Hee-Haw an' mak's a dive at Beestie an' the Bomber.

"By jings, it wis a good job they wis in trainin', Ah'll tell you. But mind thon pony could go . . . he should'a' been a racehorse. Every few yards he'd get near enough tae get them pearly gates o' his clashin' a coupla times, then they'd put on a spurt an' draw awa oota range again. You never see nothin' like this in a' your days. By the time they reached the pit-bottom they hadnae enough claes atween 'em as woulda' made a fingerstall for a flee.

"The Manager comes tearin' oota his office as they goes screitchin' past an' here—does the hook at the back o' Impatience no catch in his breeks, an' the next thing is the Manager goin' doon the Bottom at fu' speed in a sittin' poseetion, stottin' frae sleeper tae sleeper an' ca'in' doon black burnin' murder on a' aboot him . . . whit a day!"

"What happened?," asked Heelplates.

"We a' got fined twa pund apiece for the Hospital an' Beestie flung me an' the Bomber aff the job. Tried tae mak' oot we'd pisened his pony."

"Well," I said, "that would suit you. You'd have plenty of time to ride that bike you'd won."

"Ride a bike!," Nicky said disgustedly. "It wis six months afore Ah could sit doon in comfort."

"What do you mean?," I demanded. "You said you kept well clear of his teeth."

186

"Aye," Nicky grunted, "but Ah forgot the twa things aboot a pit-pony that you aye has tae watch. An Airyplane Brae—huh, it wis me that wis the airyplane. Ah went forty yards up that Brae withoot touchin' the grund after he got me wi' his twa hind feet. Talk aboot gettin' shot oota' a gun . . .!"

"In the gloomy galleries far below the earth men go on their knees and tremble to every sound; hot air and blinding dust oppress the spirit and the world is constricted by the darkness to the ring of a feeble lamp beam."

CHAPTER FIFTEEN

THE NATURE OF THE MAN

IT was early afternoon on a wet Saturday in April when I called at Red Rab Balcaskie's house in the Miner's Row to deliver a parcel of dahlia corms. My visit was the result of a conversation in the village pub on the previous evening when Rab, having overheard a comment that it was time for planting out, had eagerly begged some corms.

While not wildly keen, for he was a man of short-lived enthusiasms and I knew what would be their eventual fate, I had agreed. Rab, I knew, liked to feel himself a participant in everything that was afoot: his very nickname stemmed from a brief flirtation, while still a young man, with left-wing political ideals; that had been during the nineteen twenty-six strike and, though his ardour had quickly cooled, the nickname stuck.

He was not at home when I knocked and I should have been well pleased to leave the parcel and escape, but Rab's white-haired old wife persuaded me to wait and, so sweet was her smile and so gracious her manner, I could not well refuse. She brought me tea and so put me at my ease that I was soon well enough content to sit by the fire and listen to her chatter.

She appeared older than her fifty-eight years and, remembering that Rab looked less than his age, I wondered if there was a connection and if the marriage was a happy one. I knew that there were two children, a son and a daughter; both grown now and married themselves and living away and I recollected hearing that they usually visited their mother when their father was absent. Rab was unemployed; when one local pit was shut and production curtailed at another, he was among the first to be paid off. I wondered if this was the cause of marital discontent; for the Scotswoman who is

189

collier bred has little time for a man that'll 'no work,' and Sarah Balcaskie had told me that she was off mining stock.

Thus I mused, and listened to her gentle voice telling me of the old times until there was a rattle at the door and she said in a voice that had suddenly dulled, "That's him now, I expect."

It was, and so full was Rab of what he had just seen that my presence went unnoticed.

"Hey!" He drew his wife to the window. "Hey, Sairy, come and see this—your secret passion half-way down a drainhole."

"My what . . ." She glanced at me and coloured.

"Ah, come off it," he asserted, "you've aye had a soft spot for Gus Oliphant; don't tell me you haven't. Well, there he is now; all laggered up with mud and on his knees in the gutter. Oh hello, Dave," he saw me, "come and get a look at this; it's a sight that'll interest you—a pit union delegate." I joined him at the window and he gripped my shoulder with one hand and rapped the glass with the knuckles of the other.

"Take a look at that: Area General Manager of the National Coal Board crawling about in the gutter with the four-year-old bairn of a collier."

"Yes," Sarah confirmed in a voice of amazement; "that's wee Andrew Condie, Magnus Condie's laddie. . . ."

"And the tall chap?" I asked, for I hardly knew whether to believe Red Rab.

"Yes," Sarah nodded; "that's Angus Oliphant right enough: why, that's an awfy thing; that suit he has on must have cost all of forty guineas and look at it—it's ruined: and look at the mess he has that overcoat in, and it silk lined too; the good Lord alone knows what that'll have cost. And what is he supposed to be doing—the man must be mad. Oh, I never saw the like of this: Angus Oliphant I'd never have believed it of you."

She rounded on her husband, "What in the name of heaven is he supposed to be doing?," she demanded: "you were out there; did you no ask?"

Rab grinned: a grin that was half a sneer. "Oh, I asked," he said. "I was there for quite a wee while watching the antics of the two of them; but I wanted you to enjoy the show, too, so I came in to tell you about it."

190

"And what is he supposed to be doing—imagine messing about in the road after the week of rain we've just had—and what has wee Andrew to do with it?"

"It's Andra's thruppny," sniggered Rab; and his wife shrilled, "What thruppny?"

"Wee Andra got a thruppny off his dad," Rab explained; "to buy sweeties, and did he no let it fall down the drain on his way to the shop. Well, as you know, Gus visits his old mother in her cottage at the end of the Rows every Saturday afternoon. He came along today as usual and saw the bairn greeting and stopped to ask what was the trouble. . . ."

"Aye," Sarah said softly, "he's always had an awfy fondness for bairns. . . ."

". . . and that's him there, yet," continued Rab, "trying to fish that thruppny out of the drain: I thought I'd seen all there was to see, but that's the best ever—and mind," he turned his bleary eyes on me, "he knows whose bairn it is, 'cos the first thing Gus did was to ask wee Andra his name."

"What has that to do with it—the name, I mean?"

"Big Andra Condie has an awfy hatred of Gus Oliphant," Rab replied.

"Condie asked for all he got," Sarah put in quickly; "and I bet Angus never gave it another thought, once the case was over: he's not the sort to bear malice, and well you know it."

"I dunno," Rab grunted doubtfully, "he got an awfy doing off Condie and his pals—he's supposed to have never really recovered from the internal injuries he got." He turned to me. "It was long ago, Dave," he explained: "long afore you came into this district. In those days Gus was Section Oversman at the old Mary Pit; he and the Under Manager found Condie asleep underground: they reported him and . . . well, you know the Coal Mines Act: Condie was prosecuted and sacked. . . ."

"If Angus had been alone when he found Condie," defended Sarah, "he'd have let him off with a warning."

"Mebbe," said Rab, "Gus was a canny enough fella up aben but he was damned strict down below, especially when it came to interpreting the Safety Regulations . . . aye, mebbe he'd 've let him off . . ."

191

"What do you mean, mebbe: he caught you asleep in the same pit when he was alone; and he let you off with a warning because there was bad air and it was easy for a man to doze off. . . ."

"Allright, allright," Rab said frantically. "Well, anyway, Condie was a hard nut in those days and in with a bad crowd."

"Angus Oliphant was no chicken," put in Sarah, "and he was no boozy windbag."

"Oh, he'd have been a match for Condie alone," Rab agreed, "but when they jumped him it was Condie and two of his pals and they gave him an awfy kicking once they had him down."

"And what happened?" I asked.

"Oh, Condie and co. got eighteen months apiece, and Gus was off work for almost a year and that was the end of it."

"And that's Condie's laddie out there now?"

"Na," Rab grimaced: "that's his grandson. Big Andra—him that did for Gus—'ll be sixty now and carries the mark yet that Gus put on him: they didna just get him down that easy. That's his son's laddie—Andra's grandson—that's lost the thruppny. . . ."

I looked curiously through the window at Angus Oliphant for, though he was a man of whom one heard a great deal in mining circles, this was the first time I had seen him. He was tall and well built though lean of frame; his hair was a silvery grey and his features were finely cut and well proportioned; he had an air of distinction about him and was very much what people used to call "a fine figure of a man." I remembered things I had heard about him; his fierce intolerance of any lack of skill underground; his hatred of laziness; and most of all, the resolute integrity that had, in negotiation, won the complete trust of union officials. Now, as I watched, he hooked a thin length of wire and, after consulting gravely with the urchin, bent once more over the square open hole of the drain: the cover, I noticed, had been removed and put carefully to one side.

Rab turned away in disgust. "He's off his head; imagine getting in a state like that for thruppence: he'd 've got a sack of thruppnies for the cost of the clothes he's ruined." He sat by the fire and stretched out his legs. "He's off his head," he repeated oracularly.

192

I said—I was still at the window—"I can't understand how a man in his position could bother with such a thing: is that his car parked down the street?"

"Aye," said Rab; "a beaut, eh!"

"Yes," I agreed, "if it was mine I wouldn't be fishing in a drain; I'd be over the hills and far away. . . ."

Sarah said softly, "Angus Oliphant could never resist a problem. Anything that seems the least bit different or difficult intrigues him—he's always been like that; that's how he's got on so well."

"He was lucky," Rab interrupted her, "that was all there was to it: he's aye been lucky."

Sarah shook her head stubbornly. "No, it wasn't luck," she insisted, "though, mind, I'm not saying he's all that brainy either; but he has an insatiable curiosity and no matter what the odds, he's always game to have a go: there's just nothing Angus won't tackle. My father was a colliery deputy and he always maintained that mining is largely a matter of controlling and exploiting the unpredictable. I'm an old woman now, but I've often thought about those words of my daddy and I can see how a man like Angus would get on in mining."

"You've known him a long time, then," I said.

"Oh, yes," she smiled at the memory; "since we were bairns, though there's been long spells when we saw little of him: he was abroad for many years. But so long as he was in this country he always visited his mother every Saturday, here in the 'Rows.' She's over eighty and Angus would have liked fine to see her in a better place; but she's a determined nature—like him—and she still bides in the wee house she was born in."

"We were all laddies the gither at the schule," Rab intervened, "Gus and Andra Condie and me, and Gus was never no different to the rest of us; I was the better scholar, in fact. And when we left the schule we all started work in the pit the gither: Gus was just another collier laddie same as the rest of us. Then the twenty-six strike came and it was like a madness; marches and meetings and the soup kitchens and we all sorta lost touch with ordinary things . . . when the pits opened up again Gus started going to nightschule in the evenings. . . ."

Sarah made to say something, but he waved her into silence. "I know what you're going to say," he declared, "but it's no true: Gus wasn't the only one to realise that it was safer on the other side of the dyke; there was plenty other lads saw the light, too, after the troubles. Some, like me, took to politics and tried to fight the coalmasters; others, like Gus, studied for tickets and became the coalmaster's lackeys. . . ."

"Angus Oliphant was never no lackey," snapped Sarah.

"Depends how you look at it," Rab retorted, and I wondered at his resentment—so unusual in a miner—of another man's achievement and I decided that it must arise from the reserve of his one-time playmate rather than from any worldly success. The collier admires "the lad o' pairts" who has got on. I think what aroused hostility, veiled as it was, in Rab was the fact that unlike the rest of those who had been boys together, Oliphant held always back a certain inviolable part of himself.

Rab found it difficult to comprehend what was, in effect, a double aspect of a single personality. It mystified him that a friend and neighbour could suddenly turn into a martinet; or become that detached, and detested arbiter of a mining village's destiny—the Manager—and then as suddenly, the moment over, drop back into the old easy friendliness. It was not his schoolmate's success that Rab resented, but his "difference"; the unconscious aloofness that set Oliphant always apart and kept him from becoming one of the herd.

"Anyway," Rab resumed his tale, "Gus got his deputy's ticket, like a lot more afore him, and that was the end of it. In those days someone had to die afore you got a deputy's job, and even then your face had to fit. . . ."

"At least he was trying," Sarah observed, "but you were out drinking with the Comrades."

"Aye, and wenching you," Rab reminder her maliciously.

She said flatly, "We were not wenching! I'd go out with you an odd time, and you'd mebbe take me home from the dancing now and again—he was a fine looking chap in those days," she assured me "—but we never started to wench seriously until after Angus Oliphant went to West Africa. . . ."

"As I said," Rab resumed command of the narration, "someone had to die and did the deputy in Gus's section no do just that. Aye; dropped down dead on the coalface right at the start of the shift. Well, with Gus having a ticket and being on the spot, the Gaffer told him to take over for the rest of that day to give them time to arrange about another deputy; there were men who'd been on the waiting list for a deputy's job long before Gus Oliphant. Ah, but when Gus got the lamp and made his inspection, he discovered a pocket of gas and ordered all the men out of the section: till that moment such a thing had never been heard of.

"You see, there'd always been gas in that part of the pit, it seeped in from old workings—our lamps wouldn't even burn properly because of it—but no one had ever complained, so no one had bothered. Well, you know what it was like in the Twenties: supposing we'd all been gassed to death, it wasn't supposed to stop production. The Section Oversman ordered Gus to get the men back on the 'face' and Gus refused, so the gaffer sent for the Under Manager who was in the next section. What would have happened then was that the section gaffer and the Under Manager would have made an inspection and declared the place safe; the men would have gone back, and Gus would have been got rid of—then or later. But he was dead lucky, was Gus.

"At that very moment the Manager was on his way inbye with an Inspector of Mines who'd turned up out of the blue and decided to inspect the section beyond ours. It was some dump, even for those days, and the Manager knew that if the Inspector got one squint at it, he—the Manager—'d probably get the jail. Thanks to Gus he never got there.

"When he arrived at our bit he stopped to investigate the pocket of gas and him and the Manager and Gus went into a huddle about how to permanently seal it off. He came back the following day for the other section; but by then it had been pumped out and propped up and was in reasonable condition. When the Inspector left he told the Manager he had been most impressed by the high standards being maintained by the deputies and this made Gus the Manager's blue-eyed boy; but the 'High Heid Yins' weren't too happy about a young deputy who was ready to put safety before production. They couldn't sack him in case the Mines Inspector got to hear about it;

195

so they found him a special job where he could be as safe as he liked without being able to hinder coal coming up the shaft: they put him in charge of the Escape Road for the whole pit.

"This was a five-mile tunnel that had been kept open when old workings were allowed to collapse: it ran out under the sea to link up with the disused Main Level of another old pit—the Lady Sophia which had closed down half a century before; but the shaft of the Sophia had been kept open and this was the Emergency Egress for the pit where we worked. Well, as the road was the only bit left standing in a vast area that had all been worked out, you can imagine the pressures it was subjected to, and the state it was in; over the years it had been so neglected that it was about ready to collapse completely and had become little more than a rat route. But the law required that it be patrolled every twenty-four hours by a qualified colliery deputy.

"That's where they stuck Gus. He was put nightshift, and it took him the whole shift to crawl and twist and drag himself the five miles and back. And that was that: the coalmasters were happy because a man with a mind of his own had been prevented from holding up production; and Gus was happy because he'd once more got a problem.

"At the end of his first shift he reported that the road was unfit for use and was told, 'You're in charge of it: you sort it.'

"And that's what he did. I heard tales of him dragging lumps of fallen roof-rock for miles to a wide bit where he could get 'em stowed at the side; and every night he'd start his shift by pinching props from the tubs of materials waiting to be hauled into the production sections; and he'd stagger off with a load of them to his old forgotten road. It was said that after a year of his maintenance work—mostly done with his bare hands—you could have driven a tramcar along that old level to the Lady Sophia. I could well believe it, mind, because he was a grafter: even as Manager and inspecting a 'face' during the production shift, it was nothing for Gus to grab a shovel or pick and muck in with some young stripper who was making heavy going of getting his coal away. . . ."

"Aye," Sarah murmured, "the men liked him for that; and they knew it wasn't for show: he'd help anyone who was trying: what he could never bear was laziness. . . ."

Above: Pit-head workings of an old-style colliery scar the rural landscape

Below: A modern show pit complete with car parks. Bilston Glen Colliery, near Edinburgh

"As I was saying," Rab glared at his wife, "Gus sorting the Escape Road was all right for the coalowners, but it left him with nothing to do and that didn't suit him. The next thing we knew he was back at evening classes and studying for his Manager's Ticket. He used to take his books down the pit with him and, now that he could do his inspection in an hour or two due to the improved conditions, he was able to spend every night studying. When he sat the Exams in nineteen and thirty-seven there was only one pass from his part of the country—that was his.

"It didn't do him much good, of course: in those days the usual routine was, first an oversman's job, then undermanager at another pit; but the boys at the top had never forgotten his behaviour over the gas, and oversmen and undermanagers are mainly concerned with production. I think there was a grudging respect for him, and I'm pretty sure they knew his worth. The men trusted him, you see, and at any given moment he could have proved a valuable man to have in the pit. So Gus was sent back to 'the lonesome road' as we called it, and all the years of studying—it's five years for a First Class Mining Engineer's Certificate—went for nothing. . . ."

"You're a fine one to criticise," snapped Sarah.

"Ach," Rab shrugged his shoulders carelessly; "I did have a bit notion to better myself in those days; but I was a strong, husky fella and, so long as I took out my coal, I could make more than a deputy."

"Yes," Sarah complained, "and if you'd gone to evening classes you wouldn't have been able to sit in the pub at night discussing how to put the world to rights. . . ."

"It wasn't that at all," Rab told her; "but what was the point in getting a deputy's ticket when I could make more money without one."

"Only as long as your strength lasted," his wife reminded him; "but, there, you never could see farther than the next lamp-post: the easiest way was always the best way for our Rab. They made Angus a Section Oversman in the end, didn't they?"

"Aye," Rab admitted doubtfully. "Least, it wasn't quite like that: you make it sound as if they'd promoted him or something; what they really did was to take advantage of his stupidity. . . ."

"His keenness. . . ."

197

"I said stupidity," Rab growled and turned to me with an expression of disgust on his face. I had left the window, the little scene was over, and was again sitting by the fire. "The Section they gave him had broken the hairt of every gaffer in the pit. No one, it seemed, could make it pay; and we all swore there was a hoodoo on the place, Not only that, all the malcontents were sent there in the hope of getting rid of them, so there weren't even steady men to work the place: it was half under water most of the time and the roof conditions were so bad that the coal that came out hardly paid for the cost of props to secure it—not that it was ever very secure. Well, it seems that there'd been a conference of the heid yins and they'd about decided to withdraw the coalcutter and write the seam off; but the same manager was still at the pit and he persuaded them to let Gus have a go. . . ."

"And he made it pay," Sarah's face, eyes shining, popped round the scullery door and disappeared again.

"Huh." Rab coughed heavily and spat into the fire. "Aye, he made it pay; but it cussed near killed him. At the finish he was near living down the pit; it was nothing but laddies coming to his mother's door at all the hours for a 'bite of bread and a flask of tea for the gaffer, please, and he says you've to go away to your bed and no wait up for him.' "

"But he made it pay," Sarah's voice resounded triumphantly above the clatter of dishes.

"Oh, for Pete's sake," Rab spread his hands in mute appeal, "a fella can make a go of any job if he's prepared to live on the top of it. Gus never had a minute to himself: you should know that better than anyone; you aye had an eye open for Gus in those days. Mebbe if he hadna been in love with that Section, he'd 've . . . ."

She said sharply, appearing before him, hands on hips, "He wasn't in love with the section: it was just that he couldn't resist a challenge. He never knew when he was beat; and a man like that canna be beat."

"He can be made a monkey of, though," said Rab, "and get his hairt bruk: aye, and that's what they did to Gus. He slaved to get that section going and then, a few months after it had started to pay its way, the whole pit was shut down and we all got flung on the dole."

I said, "It reminds me of the saying that a doctor buries his failures: it would seem that a mining engineer sees his successes buried as well."

"Aye." Rab sighed gustily. "They were haird times for us all, but Gus had got the biggest sickener of the lot- it nearly finished him. . . ."

"It did nothing of the sort," Sarah joined us. "Him," she nodded to her husband, "and the rest acted as though it was the end of the world and settled down on the dole hoping to get a start at another pit sometime; but Angus packed his bag and went off to the gold mines in West Africa. . . ."

"I couldn't have gone to West Africa," Rab defended himself; "the minimum qualification for those jobs was a deputy's ticket. . . ."

"What was to stop you from getting one?," she asked him; "it only took six months at night school, three evenings a week; and you were eighteen months on the dole. I wanted him to go to school," she assured me; "we were wenching steady then."

"Aye," Rab sucked moodily at his pipe. "I never took a tumble at the time but it was queer the way you suddenly started going steady with me after Gus had cleared off to Africa. Anyway," he declared, "supposing I had got a deputy's ticket—that was no guarantee that I'd 've got a job in Africa."

"You'd have got a job all right," she told him. "Those gold mines were always needing men because of the high sickness rate and the bad climate."

"The climate sorted Gus out in the end," he reminded her.

"Only because he stayed too long; if he'd taken regular home leaves when he should have done . . . but the war was on then, and he was asked to extend his tour of duty and, of course, Angus agreed—it was just like him."

"He's paid for it since," Rab informed me. "He picked up some bug that gives him jip every wee while."

"Aye," Sarah confirmed in a voice of ready sympathy: "his mother tells me he suffers something awfy with it."

"It canna be all that bad," Rab muttered; "it doesna keep him away from his work."

"A thousand bugs couldn't do that," Sarah asserted; "and well you know it."

199

"Bug or no bug, going to Africa was a stroke of luck for him in the end; but, there, he's aye been lucky. If he fell in the dock he'd come up with a box of kippers," continued Rab with an air of resignation. "Anyway, the war was over when Gus finally got home. The pits were being nationalised, and it was nothing but new methods and modern machinery. Gus was familiar with these techniques because the gold mines had always kept up to date; so you see, once again he fell on his feet. Instead of having to start again from scratch like anyone else who'd been away for years would have had to do, Gus walked right into the Manager's job at the new pit that'd been sunk along the coast.

"Well, in the days after nationalisation a pit manager couldn't go wrong; his main problem, labour troubles, had been solved because the miners were tied hand and foot. For the first time in history the collier had his own party in power and the ball at his feet—but he wasn't allowed to kick it. Every time there was a dispute or a strike, all you could hear was our union shouting: 'don't rock the boat—get back to work—the pits are yours now—submit and all will be well.' Talk about a let-down.

"The miners voted Labour to get free of those they considered their oppressors—the coalowners; but they had never been chained as tightly as they were after Labour got in. But they were great days for the officials, even those eedjits who only had a job because they had married a coalowner's niece; and when it came to real practical mining men like Gus Oliphant . . . well, he was bound to get promoted. . . ."

"But they broke his hairt," Sarah said sadly. "They broke his hairt."

Rab nodded agreement. "Aye," he grunted. "You see, Gus was out to get the industry back on its feet and into production as soon as possible but he was up against a brick wall; you know what things were like?" Rab looked questioningly at me, and I nodded. I had seen what things were like and had been forced to a grudging sympathy for the managers in the predicament in which they found themselves. Heaven may be promised from the hustings, but never can a coalpit be more than a hole in the ground.

The mining engineers were expected, and were daily exhorted, to produce coal during a world scarcity of the vital materials without

200

which no pit can survive; with an unskilled, hastily recruited, and largely hostile—for the men had been promised Utopia and now saw that it could never be—labour force; subject to everchanging governmental whims and the "advice" of those who knew coal only as something that one removed with tongs from a scuttle by the fireside; and from pits so long neglected that they were little more than subterranean scrapyards. Only now, when most of those semi-delerict pits have been closed, and when two-thirds of the labour has been replaced by machines, is coal at last being produced abundantly and competitively.

"Yes," I answered Rab's question: "yes, I know what it was like, and I can understand the anxieties that a man like Oliphant would have at such a period."

"It wouldn't have been just so bad if there was anything now to show for his labours; but they shut down the white elephant that he'd given his best years to." Sarah shook her head in wonder at such heartlessness.

"Aye," Rab took up the theme. "It's a funny thing, that; oh, not that Gus broke himself trying to turn that underground nightmare into a going concern; but that he—of all people—must have known from the start that it was hopeless. . . ."

"What are you saying?," Sarah cried. "Angus Oliphant never thought anything hopeless. There was nothing he wouldn't try; and the harder and more impossible it seemed, the more he would work to make it a success."

"All right, all right," but, though Rab's words were impatient, his voice was strangely gentle. "I'm not saying that Gus gave in. He fought that pit for fifteen years: from when the Coal Board was dreaming public dreams about it, and the highest in the land were trailing through it's galleries on conducted tours, right down to the last stage when the Coal Board was trying to forget it existed and there was nothing but abuse for them that were still wrestling with its difficulties.

"Aye, Gus fought that pit to the bitter end and to the best of his abilities—but that pit should never have been sunk in the first place; we all knew that, all us old colliers about here." He turned to his wife. "We know the run of the strata underground, Sairy, and we all knew that a pit sunk where that one was sunk was bound to hit

201

water; a bottled-up underground sea of it that all the pumps in creation couldn't have kept under control. And you can bet your boots that if the likes of us common five-eights knew it . . . then Gus Oliphant knew it a thousand times better."

He paused and then continued with an air of mystification. "It fascinates me, you know—the mentality of a man like Gus. A bunch of public-placating civil servants had provided him with a dirty black hole in the ground which he knew only too well led to useless rock and dangerous water; yet he battled on without a word of complaint—and not for a few weeks, mind. But for fifteen long weary years. . . ."

"And if they hadn't shut the thing down," Sarah snapped, "he'd be battling yet. No matter what others thought, Angus must have believed he could make it produce. . . ."

"Na." Rab shook his head stubbornly. "He never 'thought' nothing: he 'knew'; and what he knew was that he was holding a brick instead of a baby. Take it from me," Rab leaned forward and wagged his head wisely, "where coal's concerned, Gus's head doesn't button up the back. He knew from the start that he'd never get anything up the shaft of that pit but rock, and two kinds of liquid—underground water and tears. So why, knowing that, did he struggle on all those years? All he had to do was to join the chorus that everyone else was singing, you know, 'nationalisation will never work in Britain.' " He sank back in his chair and was silent.

"Probably just the nature of the man," I suggested. "Like a dog with a dry bone; he couldn't help from worrying it: it was habit."

"Na," Rab shook his head. "Gus knew what he was doing, coal-wise, anyway. If he went on flogging a dead hoss it could only have been because, although he knew the hoss was dead, flogging its carcase was the only thing that made sense. I know his nature and I'll admit that given a problem to tackle, Gus 'll never give up; but there was no problem about the New Pit—not after the first five years. By then, every heading they'd driven and every bore they'd sunk, had confirmed what Gus must have known from the start. They say there's nothing a man canna do if he's daft enough and anxious enough; but Gus must have known that no matter what he did, he'd never get coal up that shaft."

Sarah, her eyes bright, said softly, "I've often thought that it was mebbe a voiceless gesture: you know, everyone else was whining that nationalisation would never work; maybe Angus thought it should be given a try and judged on its merits. He isn't the sort to go about preaching; he's a mining engineer, not a politician, and he knew that his first duty was to the industry and to the men who had been placed in his care. Perhaps he thought that by doing his best with what he had been given, he could set an example to management and men alike. I bet that's it," she cried and chuckled delightedly.

"It could be," Rab grudgingly admitted . . . "but I'd never have thought him as noble as all that. . . . All right . . . All right." He lifted a hand in mock defence; "we know you canna see the sky for Angus Oliphant."

"What happened when the New Pit was closed?," I asked.

"Gus had been made District Manager by then," Rab told me, "and a young chap had taken over the 'pumping station' as we called it. Gus had overall responsibility for seven pits; but six of them could run themselves—he spent most of his time supporting the young manager of the 'waterhole.' At last it was shut down by the gov'ment and a wee while afterwards Gus was promoted Area General Manager.

"He's secreterry now, and a big Coal Board house and his own office; but he'll no stay in his office. That's why there's such a high output per manshift in this area—they never know where he'll turn up next: he's forever away down this pit or that one. He was always the same; he could never bide still when there was work afoot. We don't see a lot of him now—just once a week as he goes past to see his old mother. . . ."

"And he aye gives us a wee toot on the horn as he passes the door," Sarah informed me, and Rab added sarcastically, "And you're aye out on the step in a clean pinny to give him a wee wave."

"Why not?" she demanded. "We were all bairns together once. His position's never made no difference to him: he's just the same Angus Oliphant, cept that . . . that." She paused, and then slowly spoke out her thoughts. "He's quieter now, and to me he seems a wee bit lost and sad, as if he was bewildered by things; all the changes there's been; and how easy and valueless things are today compared to when he was struggling to make his way in the world.

He's got on, of course; he's got a fine position, but he's had a haird life and success 'll be like everything else in this world—it'll have had to be paid for in blood and bone and tears. I often wonder if he isn't maybe a little lonely," she turned away from Rab and dabbed impatiently at her eyes.

"He's had a haird life, has Angus; a haird, solitary life and now he's little more than a husk: a great gaunt shell-that's all that's left of the braw lad that went away to Africa so long ago. But the inner flame burns yet. Aye, the inner flame; and the enduring heart and the unquenchable spirit." Her voice died away but her eyes were full of expression; a maternal, solicitious expression that was yet possessive and full of pride.

"Not endurance," Rab mocked her, "curiosity and obstinacy; and that's what got him into the gutter today in his fine clothes. What's wrong he couldn't just put his hand in his pouch and give the bairn another thruppny—he's money enough. But, oh no! Not Gus. First he was curious to see if he could fish that thruppny out; and when he found he couldn't, he was too obstinate to admit it and give up. That's not a sign of character; that's a sign of stupidity, that's what tha . . ."

"But he did get the coin," I told them: "he got it at the end."

"He did!" Sarah's face crinkled with pleasure.

"Yes," I told her. "He fished and howked for long enough with that piece of wire, but he'd no luck. I think the wee chap thought it was a hopeless case, too, because after a while he toddled away up the road crying. But Oliphant persisted for quite some time before he threw the wire away. He took off his coat then and laid it along the kerb, rolled up one sleeve, lay down on the coat and plunged his arm into the drain.

"Two seconds and he had the thruppny. He got to his feet, replaced the drain cover, and was putting on his coat when he noticed that the bairn was missing. He seemed surprised at first, but he shrugged then wiped the coin on his handkerchief and laid it carefully on the kerb where the child would see it if he came back. Then he got into his car and drove away."

Rab said in a dull, flat voice, "I still can't see why he couldn't have just put his hand in his pouch and given the bairn another thruppny. Surely," he appealed to me, "that would have been the easy way. . . ."

There was silence and, after further rumination, Rab said positively, "That's what I'd have done!"

"Fine we know that," snapped his old wife: "fine we know that's what you'd have done." And bristling with indignation she bustled out of the room.

"Their faces were bristly-grey and expressionless, and their garments, though of orthodox mining pattern, had the ancient greeny glow that one associates with great antiquity. They loped along in single file, looking neither to right nor left, and disappeared, with a furtive little flurry of dust from each pair of heels, in the dark shadows of the six-foot level."

CHAPTER SIXTEEN

NICKY THE STRIKE-BREAKER

It had been what the collier calls a "canny shift." Nothing untoward had occurred, the work had gone according to plan and now, finished early, we were sitting in the Heading waiting until it would be time to go down for the bogies.

Bomber Brown, our section deputy, crawled past us to make his final inspection of the "face" and even his mournful features wore something approaching a smile . . . as near anyway as the Bomber was ever likely to get to such a thing.

"O-o-o-h," Heelplates McSobb, the prop drawer, sighed as he eased off his boots and shook out a shower of small coal. "Whit a relief. Ye ken," he stared sorrowfully at his large feet, "they used tae be a pair o' socks wi' holes in 'em. Noo they're holes wi' bits o' sock roon 'em. Ah'll hae tae invest in anither pair o' socks."

"Och, Ah wouldnae dae that," said Nicky McFish, the leading cutterman. "Gie your feet a good wash. You'll mebbe fund an ole pair!"

"You're boond tae hae plenty o' money onyway," put in Beetle McSair, the other prop drawer. "Goin' aboot in rags."

"Aye," said Heelplates sarcastically. "An' Ah also tak' in stairs tae wash. Ah'm steamin' wi' money. It's time we had a strike, so Ah can get spendin' it."

"You're steamin' a' richt," Nicky grunted. "But it's no wi' money. For Pete's sake put your boots on, an' dinna talk tae me aboot strikes. Ah got a sickener wi' strikes yince that Ah'll no forget in a hurry, Ah'll betcha. An' that mournful lookin' eedjit the Bomber wis the cause o' it tae. Ye hear 'em talkin' aboot the sufferin' proletairiat. Well, here wis one o' the proletairiat that suffered onyway. As wis cussed near teetotal afore it feenished."

207

"Come on," I said, scenting another chapter in the lifelong feud between Nicky McFish and Bomber Brown. "Let's have it."

"Ooh," said Nicky. "It happened a few year ago, afore the Bomber got on for deputy. In September it wis, an' man, whit braw weather. Just like summer; comin' doon here on the backshift when the sun's shinin' thon way woulda bruck your hairt. Not only that, ah wisnae needin' tae wark. Ole Maggie an' the dochter wis at the tattie-gatherin'.

"Six pund a week each they had, that wis twal' pund a week comin' intae the hoose, an' me trailin' doon this hole in the grund every day an' knockin' ma soulcase oot. It wis reedeeculous, but ah kent better 'n tae say onything tae oor Maggie. If there's yin word sends her aff her heid in connection wi' me it's the word HOLIDAY. Ah'da' been crooned wi' a kale pat afore Ah got the second seelabul oot!

"But somethin' had tae be done, 'cos nobuddy in their richt mind is goin' tae come doon a coal-pit when they've got money. That's whit you come doon here tae get; there's nae sense comin' doon if you've got it. So there's only one thing for it—a strike. If there wis a strike at the pit then ole Maggie couldnae say nothin' tae me for supportin' ma fella workers. That's one time when you're aye on safe grund wi' a collier's wife; they mebbe greet a bit, but they'd never dream o' chasin' you back tae your wark. The trouble wis that at that parti'kler time there wis nae disputes in the pit. Ah dinna ken hoo it come aboot but they wis nothin' but harmony a' over the place, it woulda made you sick.

"Well, onyway, we comes doon this day on the backshift an' it wis an awfy struggle, Ah can tell you, wi' thon sun blazin' doon an' me kennin' ole Maggie wis wallopin' up an' doon the rows o' tatties."

"Man," said Heelplates dreamily. "Ah love a tattie."

"Aye," said Nicky. "They're braw things, an' handy for keepin' ole Maggie oota the hoose an' lettin' me get a wee kick at thon toyteeshell cat o' hers. However, we comes doon the pit this day an' yin o' the dayshift fellas sees us in the pitbottom an' he tells us that oor Section wis closed an' we wouldnae be able tae get in there that day. The hale length o' face had shut tight.

"Well, o' cos we kent whit that meant. We wis spare men an' we'd just get handed ower tae ony gaffer that needed men for his section.

Ah tell you, it's like a slave market. Well, we wis sittin' in the tubs prayin' we didnae get sent tae the Barncrick Section 'cos it's an awfy hairy place; the fellows that warked in there regular wis a' clappit-jawed wi' fright.

"An mak' nae wunner, thon place woulda put grey hairs on a tombstane; an' not only wis it dangerous tae wark in, but Paunchy McPinch wis the gaffer. An' gettin' bluid oota stane is a piece o' cake compared tae gettin' money oota thon character. Ah, but whit does we see comin' alang the line o' tubs lookin' for us but McPinch an' oor ain dep'ty. An' whenever Ah sees 'em Ah has a notion that Ah can mebbe get somethin' stairted wi'oot bein' too mixed up in it masel'.

"Ah wis sittin' in the tub o' cos but Ah'm that wee ma heid wis below the top an' they couldnae see me. A coalpit's no what you'd ca' a brightly illumeenated place at ony time. Not only that, but the Bomber wis stannin' in front o' me. He's that langleggit an' akward he used tae tak' cramp in the tubs an' he never got in till they wis ready tae move aff. Well, as you ken, the Bomber's a wee bit hard o' hearin' an' he's no whit you'd ca quick on the uptake, an' that's whit Ah'm relyin' on.

" 'Here's some mair o' them,' says oor dep'ty when they stops in front o' the Bomber. 'Mister McPinch is picking men for his section,' says the dep'ty. So Ah says quietly from behind the Bomber—'He couldnae pick his nose.'

" 'Ah'll pick a nice job for you onyway,' says McPinch tae the Bomber. An' if looks coulda killed, the Bomber wis buzzard-bait there an' then. 'See an' mind,' says McPinch, 'It's me that assesses whit you're tae be peyed.'

"You couldnae assess a fish supper," Ah says from behind the Bomber.

"Ooooh! whit a look. McPinch's een comes oot, smacked the Bomber on the pus, an' went back intae their sockets. By this time the Bomber wakes up, an' even he can sense that the atmosphere isnae very friendly.

" 'Is that you growin' a moostash?,' he says, tryin' tae be sociable. He's a plausible customer the Bomber, mind. 'Aye,' says Paunchy, fair awa wi' hissel. 'D'ye think it suits me?'

" 'Ah thocht you had a rat in your mooth,' Ah says, afore the Bomber could speak.

" 'You'd be better gie'in' your heid a bit bang on a girder,' says McPinch, sorta frigid-like. 'It'll mebbe tak' the glaze aff your een.' Then he turns tae the dep'ty. 'Ah'm no wantin' that eedjit,' he says. 'He doesnae hae enough brains tae grease a haulage clip.'

"O' cos, by noo the Bomber's beginnin' tae loss the heid. 'Who are you ca'in' an eedjit,' he says, an' Ah backs him up. That's a' Ah'd been waitin' for.

" 'Comrades,' Ah roars, jumpin' up in the tub. 'Brithers, fella workers, mates. Are we doon here tae be spit upon an' insulted by these Capeetalist Lairds an' Gaffers o' the Coal Board?'

"Ah'd heard the Union Delegate use that one, an' it would aye fetch 'em oota their seats. Not only that, Ah wisnae the only one that had noticed that the sun wis shinin'. The Bomber wis stannin' gogglin' at me as if his een wis goin' tae pop oot. He'd never thocht he'd live tae see the day when Ah'd stick up for him, Ah'll betcha. Then Ah starts again, 'cos ole McPinch kent noo who had been doin' the talkin' an' things wis gettin' desp'rate.

" 'Is ma honest, hard warkin' neighbours here tae be insulted by thon wattery-heided welt McPinch?,' Ah asks 'em at the tap o' ma voice.

" 'No,' they roars, an' they a' stairts clammerin' oota the tubs. An' McPinch stops tryin' tae reach roon the Bomber an' get at me, an' beats it. It wis a cussed good job tae, Ah'll tell you. If he'da' got grip o' me ma troubles wis over—in this warld onyway.

"Well, o' cos, we a' marches doon the pit bottom an' Ah'm congratulatin' masel on as nice a piece o' hanky-panky as has ever been warked an' prayin' it hadnae stairted tae rain. But na, when we gets up the pit the sun wis shinin' harder an' ever, but there wis a big fly in the ointment waitin' in the pityaird . . . the Union Delegate wi' his secryterry.

"Whenever Ah see him Ah thocht that wis the ba' bust for sure. If there wis yin character that could mesmerise 'em an' talk 'em back doon the pit again, that wis him. Thon Delegate o' oors coulda' selt ice cream tae an Eskimoe. An' when Ah sees him puttin' his teeth in his pooch an' lickin' his lips ready for action, it nearly bruck ma hairt. Ma only hope wis that he'd talk that lang we'd hae

210

tae extend the strike tae hear him oot. But na, na, he's determined tae get us back doon that pit. Ah aye thocht them Union boys wis on oor side. They're wuss than the gaffers.

" 'Nonsense,' says the Delegate. 'Rubbish! Imagine you men comin' up the pit for a thing like that. Ah will tak' this man'—an' he grabs aholt o' the Bomber—'tae the Manager at once, and Ah have every confidence that the Manager will instruct McPinch tae apologise. Never in the History o' British Minin' has men gone on strike over such an easily settled matter.' Ah tell you ma hairt wis doon in ma boots.

" 'It is a stonewall case,' he says. 'It is impossible tae loss it. Wait here,' an' aff he goes wi' the Bomber, an' Ah strolls over tae the pub, 'cos whenever Ah heard them words Ah kent we wis richt enough.

"It's a funny thing," Nicky said, his eyes glinting wickedly, "but the only cases that Union Delegates ever loss is the stonewallers. He wis back in thirty seconds wi' a flee in his ear that the Manager had put there, an' roarin' for us tae picket the pit and send a delegation

211

tae London or somewhere. He coulda sent a delegation tae Siam, but thon Manager wouldnae even discuss the case till we wis doon the pit again, so that wis that.

"Ah has a coupla pints an' put awa a coupla bets an' aboot three o'clock Ah decides tae tak' a stroll hame an' settle yin or twa scores wi' thon savage toyteeshell cat o' Maggie's afore she come hame frae her wark. It's nothin' but a miracle Ah didnae tak' a hairt failure thon day. Wha's sittin' by the fire quite jocko but the Breid Winner o' the Family. An' thon feerocious, man-eatin' cat sittin' in her lap lookin' at me as if tae say, 'Touch me if you dare.'

"Pardon me bustin' in on you like this," Ah says, "but would you mind tellin' whit you're doin' sittin' here at this time o' day, as if there wis nae tatties grown in Scotland?"

" 'We're on strike,' she says. 'They've lengthened oor bits.'

"By jings, Ah had tae reach up tae ma heid an' mak' sure that ma ears wis fixed on richt, Ah'll tell you.

" 'They've lengthened your bits?,' Ah says, a' amazed. 'They musta been ower short then. The farmer fella wis quite richt tae lengthen 'em. You're needin' slimmed doon.' By jings, Ah wis mad. As usual Ah hardly dare open ma mooth in the hoose but Ah wis that mad, Ah wis feared at nothin'.

" 'That'll no tak' a trick,' Ah telt her. 'By the hokey, me aff ma wark due tae a sudden wussenin' in the field o' Labour Relations, an' you come waltzin' in here like Lady Muck frae Stoury Castle an' tell me you're on strike. D'ye ken that Ah'm dependent on you for a bit bite o' breid an' a moothfu' a beer? Can it be, wumman, that you are withoot either shame or a sense o' responsibility? Na, na,' Ah tells her, 'That'll no tak' a trick, ma lady. Ah'm no harbourin' nae agitators in ma wee hoose. You'll be at your wark the morn, an' Ah'll be there tae see you go, s'posin' Ah've tae carry you.'

"Ah rampaged roon the hoose thon day, Ah'll betcha." Nicky's eyes shone at the memory. 'Goin' on strike?,' Ah says. 'You're needin' your heids looked. Ah've never heard such nonsense in a' ma days. Tee Vee's tae pey up,' Ah says, 'an' great ravenous-hungry toyteeshell cats tae be fed. By jings, it's somethin',' Ah says . . . 'An' where am Ah tae get money for beer? Ah need mair when Ah'm aff tae keep ma spirits up. Thon cat'll hae tae go,' Ah says. 'We canna afford tae maintain nae meenagieries o' wild beasts if you're no goin' tae bide at your wark an' dae whit you're telt.'

"Ah opens the door an' puts the cat oot an' she never says a word. Ah wouldnae a' heard her onyway, the noise thon cat made when Ah just lifted it wi' ma foot.

"Well, o' cos, the next day Ah had tae be up at the crack o' dawn tae get 'em awa tae their wark an' see that there wis nae mair o' the agitatin' nonsense. An', o' cos, Ah hadnae slept ower muckle through the nicht 'cos Ah kept thinkin' o' new things tae say tae ole Maggie, an' Ah had tae get 'em aff ma chest whilst Ah had her on the run.

"Ah tell you when Ah went back tae ma bed at seven o'clock Ah wis exhausted. Ah wisnae lang drappin' aff tae sleep, Ah can tell you, when here by jings is there no an awfy bangin' at the door at eight o'clock, an' when Ah gets up an' opens it, wha's stannin' there but ole Maggie an' the lassie.

" 'Whit are ye doin' back here?' Ah says. 'Don't you have the audicity tae tell me that you're on strike again.'

" 'No,' she says, 'we've lost our places. The Bomber 'n his wife wis oot yesterday afternoon. They've got oor bits noo!' "

"*The Scots collier calls his workmate 'neighbour' or, as is more usual, the affectionate diminutive 'Neeb.' Unless indeed he truly loves that neighbour as himself; unless they are joined together in a mutually trusting union, then the relationship becomes void, and work underground is impossible.*"

CHAPTER SEVENTEEN

THE FATAL MISTAKE

M Y supervisor and neighbour during the last stages of my "face" training was Nicky McFish, the crop-haired, blue-scarred, little humorist who had been in the pits since he was twelve. Unlike most miners he had read a great deal and during wartime had travelled extensively as a soldier. In consequence, he added to his own professional caution a puckish cynicism for his fellow men and the Capitalist Muckheap, as he described Western Europe.

When I questioned him about his political views he would say, "All colliers are Communists at heart, though the maist of them dinna realise it. Ah'm merely one that's tumbled tae the fact. Christ, it's no much more than a hundred years since we got the wooden collars aff oor necks.

"The last two groups o' slaves tae be freed in this world were the Russian serfs an' the Scottish colliers. There'd be something bliddy wrang if we didnae hae the same kinda notions aboot things—would there no?"

Well, at the end of one night's shift Nicky and I were waiting in the icy, air blast of the pit bottom. With several hundred others we squatted on our hunkers, talking quietly amongst ourselves. As we shivered, a man stumbled past us to the head of the queue. The rags about his body were sodden and filthy and an evil smell lingered in his wake.

I knew a sudden feeling of nausea. Underground, smoking is forbidden and as a result one's sense of smell is more acute. Nicky, however, had recovered, glanced at my agonised expression, and laughed aloud. "That wis Willie McGlaikit, the Sumper," he said with a grimace; then I understood.

Underneath the wide, concrete-paved pit bottom with its multiple **tracks of glistening** rails and rows of gleaming lights was the huge tomb-like sump. There all the acid-rich waters of the pit collected, and from there were forced by powerful pumps to the surface, from whence they were pumped over the short stretch of beach to the sea. A man was employed to prevent the fouling of the pump roses.

Down there in that vast cesspit toiled the sumper, chest deep in evil-smelling fluid and half-gassed by dreadful fumes. A miner's job in the very nature of things can never be a pleasant thing, but compared to the sumper, the ordinary collier was in heaven.

"You canna expect Willie tae smell very sweet," said Nicky. "There's mair than twa thoosan' men come doon this pit every twenty-four hoors, everyone here fer eight hoors an' there's nae lavatories doon here. This isnae one o' they factories wi' music while ye wark an' a' conveniences laid on. Ye ken it's a bliddy wunner we dinna a' get cholera or typhus or somethin'."

It was true, I reflected; men urinated and defecated wherever the impulse took them; what else could they do? And because in a pit water is continually seeping, dripping and running, so eventually everything collects at the lowest point, the sump.

I said in horror, "What a bloody awful job. Why does he tolerate it—isn't he fit for other work?"

"He's fit all-richt," Nicky said. "He's a brainy one him. Got a deputy's ticket an' a'. But fer Willie it's the sump or nothin', an' a married man canna live on the dole."

I scented a story. "What did he do," I asked, "to be condemned to that?"

"It's what he didnae do," Nicky grunted. "Ah keep tellin' yu, always check for yersel'. Mebbe the last shift says the roof's a'richt, but never accept second-hand information. Always check for yersel'. Willie didnae check, that's where he slipped up."

Nicky took his lamp off the front of his safety helmet, slipped the battery off his belt and slowly, with scarred, stubby fingers, began to wind the cable round the heavy battery.

"Willie," he began thoughtfully, "wis in the pits afore the war. He wis just a laddie then, runnin' aboot the roads an' pushin' tubs o' coal. When the war started he beat it tae the Air Force an' he finished up in bombers—navigator or somethin'."

"Navigator——," I exclaimed.

216

"Aye," said Nicky. "Och aye, Ah telt yu he had a head on him. Well as ye ken, after the war the pits wis nationalised. That was Willie's fust mistake; having once escaped he shoulda stayed away. There wis plenty o' jobs going elsewhere at that time an' he wis a young, single man wi' nae ties.

"But no, Willie come back and we wis in the same section. Ah wis on the machine an' Willie had a job on the propdrawin'. He had all his worries too, Ah can tell yu. It wis a helluva bad roof, the Seven West. Drawing props in there woulda' put grey hairs on a tombstone. Willie began to realise that the only future in his job was, at the wust, a wooden overcoat an', at the best, a broken back. But he wis convinced he could get on; those Coal Board adverts had really got him goin'. He telt me one night in September that he had enrolled fer the deputy's course at the night school in Bencrick. 'If Ah get ma ticket,' he says, 'Ah'll be put on the list in the check office, and when a vacancy crops up Ah'll get a job on the shotfiring. That's me on the ladder then. Ah'll no longer be just another collier but a member o' the staff an' ma future'll be assured.'

"Well, o' cos, he got his ticket. Ah telt yu he had a heid on him, did Willie. When he told me aboot passin' his exam Ah says, 'Yu've just one mair thing tae do now, Willie—join the Buffs.'

"He laffs at that. 'Because the Manager's a Buff?' he asks. 'Na, na, Nicky, them days is past. Since nationalisation a man is promoted on his merits.'

" 'Don't yu believe it,' Ah says. 'This is a coal pit, nothin's changed here. The same ole gang's still runnin' the show. It's not what yu know but who yu know that counts, same as it always did.' He laughed again, but after six months he wis still on the prop-drawing an' others had been promoted over his head.

"Well, as Ah've told yu, he wis nae fool an' he wis real ambitious. The third man in my team wis a Buff, an' Willie starts tae get awfy palsy-walsy wi' him. Then one day he tells me that he's joined the Buffs and within a month he wis promoted shotfirer and sent awa tae a section on the other side of the pit, the four-foot seam doon the Mark Dook.

"It was aboot this time that Willie got married, an' several months later in the baths, he comes over one day fer me tae wash his back. 'Well, Willie,' Ah says, 'hoo's the warld treatin' yu these days?'

217

" 'Fine, Nicky,' he says, 'fine, yu'll mebbe be seein' mair o' me in a wee while.'

" 'Hoo's that?' Ah says. 'We don't need shotfirers on the coal-cutting shift.'

" 'No,' he says, 'but yu need deputy's on every shift.' 'Oh, Ho,' says I. 'Yure fleein' high noo.'

" 'Why not?' says he. 'Ah've the ticket an' the experience, an' there'll be a vacancy at the New Year when Accy McIlly retires.'

" 'Aye,' Ah says tae him, 'but yure only a Buff an' this new Manager who's just come is high up in the Masons. Ah'll tell yu this, there'll be mair than one vacancy fer deputies in a wee while. What aboot Mucky O'Hara an' Batsy McFoochan—they're both Cath'lics. Hoo lang dae yu think they'll last wi' this Masonic character runnin' the Pit?'

He smiles a sly smile. " 'Don't worry, Nicky,' he says. 'Yu give me good advice once an' yu'll no need tae repeat it. Ah learn awfy quick,' he says. 'Ah havenae been wastin' ma time, Nicky.' An' here he has a wee grin tae hissel.

" 'Ah'm goin' through ma Third Degree next Thursday evening. By eight o'clock Ah'll be a Master Mason, an' what's mair . . . the Manager'll be there tae seeit.'

" 'Boond tae be an expensive business this gettin' on in the warld,' Ah says.

" 'What's a fiver when yure future's at stake,' says he. But Ah could see it had hurt him tae part wi' the money. He wis a tight lad wis Willie. As tight as a duck's ass, an' that's watertight.

" 'Mind, Nicky,' he says. 'Mum's the word.'

"Ah just nodded an awa' he goes tae dry hissel', as pleased as a whippet wi' a rabbit, an' his bare ass waggin' like a dog's hintend." Nicky sighed and eased a probing finger round the sweat band of a lifted helmet.

"Did it work?" I asked.

"Did it wark!" he sniffed derisively. "When didn't it wark? Aye it warked, as it always has warked, ever since pits wis pits. Whether it wis a' cos the Manager had taken part in Willie's Initiation or no, Ah dinna ken. But Willie become his special pet. He could dae nothin' wrang.

218

A man-riding train taking miners from the shaft-bottom to the outer
reaches of the pit—sometimes a journey of several miles

"He come intae oor section again as a deputy an' fer a while he wis content. But not fer lang. As Ah said, the weird, new policies o' the National Coal Board wis noo bearing fruit. Whether it wis a case o' jobs fer the boys or what, Ah dunno ken, but it begun tae get so you could hardly move fer offeecials. In the ole days one gaffer an' one deputy would be responsible fer mebbe twa or three sections, an' the deputy would do the shotfiring. But noo . . .?; every little section has tae have its ain gaffer an' its ain deputy, an' o' cos the deputy's too busy tae fire shots, so there has tae be a shotfirer tae. The newspapers are aye greetin' that since nationalisation the pits havenae made a profit. It'd be a muckin' miracle if they hadda made a profit, when ah think o' a' the jobs that've been manufactured by the N.C.B. Aboot the only person it's hard tae find in a coalpit these days is a collier.

"They've Explosives Officers and Safety Officers, an' they's Air Inspection Officers an' Roof Control Officers. An', o' cos, there has tae be Officers tae inspect and control the Officers. Ah'm buggered if Ah know hoo we manage tae pay 'em a', cos they've a' got good wages, an' them wages has a' tae come aff the point o' the pick.

"Well, onyway, Willie decides—an' who's tae blame him in oor 'muck you Jack, Ah'm a'right' society—that there's nae reason why he shouldn't be a Gaffer tae.

"O' cos, a Gaffer is concerned wi' production an' a deputy wi' safety. Two things that don't go well the gither. So fer Willie tae try fer a Gaffer's job involved a certain sacrifice o' principles. But Willie wasn't goin' tae let a detail like that stop him. Safety wis forgotten an' production become his one aim. He wis a real slave-driver tae, Ah can tell yu. He crawled up an' doon that face like a rat on a hot-plate. The stretcher wis never oota the Level an' the ambulance wis never awa' frae the pithead. It wis mair like a battle-field than a coalface. Ah think that's when Ah fust come tae really hate the bastard.

"Then, in May that year, the Manager wis promoted tae some staff job in Edinburgh an' wi gets anither. This one come frae the West o' Scotland so there wisnae muckle chance o' checking up on him. An' he wis one o' they dour bastards that gie nothin' awa'. The gaffers an' deputys wis a' killin' 'emselves wi' fricht. They didnae ken which way tae turn tae please him. An' of them a', the maist sair troubled wis Willie.

"Willie hunted like a trapped cat fer a safe line o' conduct. He even eased up a little on the slave-driving in case the new Manager considered a miner's life mair important than an extra tub o' coal. However, it soon become known that the present Manager wasn't one o' them. It wis coal he wanted, an' he wasn't very particular aboot the means that wis used tae get it. Willie got worse than ever. Wark wis a' he thocht aboot. Coal!!—an' mair Coal! He hardly ever carried oot an inspection o' the section, an' as fer gas testin', fer weeks at a time he didnae even carry his gas testing lamp. Something had tae be done an' Ah wis determined tae do it. Ah'd developed an awfy hatred fer the broon-nosed, snivellin' sod. But what tae dae?—that wis the problem. An' so the weary days drags on into June.

"One mornin' aboot half past six Ah'm goin' hame aff the night-shift an' Rab McStottie was goin' up the road wi' me. As we're passin' the Catholic Church at the top o' the brae we sees a lotta folk goin' in and cars stannin' at the gate.

" 'The're queer folk, them Papes,' Ah says. 'Imagine goin' tae church through the week.'

"O' cos, Rab's a dyed-in-the-wool Orangeman, an' tae his sort a' the trouble in the warld is caused by the Pope o' Rome an' the Cath'lics. Suddenly Ah stopped. 'Christ,' Ah says. 'Is that no the new Manager's car?'

"Rab stares across the road. We couldnae see the number plates becos' of cars in front and ahint. But the car certainly looked like the one owned by the new Manager. Rab seemed a' shaken at the thocht o' it. It wis horrible the way he swore.

" 'The Manager, a Pape!' he says. 'By Christ, that's a good un. The Manager o' oor Pit a Pape? Noo, Ah'll tell yu somethin' . . .'

"And he did. Yu never heard such language in yure life as he come awa' wi. Ah tell yu, by the time he left me at the crossroads Ah wis sick o' the Pope an' King William o' Orange tae. It woulda made yu sick tae listen tae such drivel. As if the result o' the Battle o' the bliddy Boyne wis likely tae mak' ony difference tae oor standard o' livin' today. As Ah've said, fanatics like Rab are so busy hatin' ither workers o' a different complexion that they tolerate the bliddy system, which is the real enemy o' every worker."

I could see that Nicky was getting carried away so I gently drew him back to the main subject. "About Willie," I asked. "Did he become a Catholic?"

Nicky looked at me seriously. "He did," he said. "Least he started; Ah dunno if he ever finished. That night at the pit Ah telt him what Ah'd seen that morning. He went white. 'Oh Christ, not a Pape, Nicky?' 'Well,' Ah says, 'there wis his car, so you can draw yure ain conclusions.'

"Aboot a week later he gets me alone in the top road. Ah went oot fer sharp picks fer the machine an' he wis sittin' there, deep in thocht. 'Nicky,' he says, 'did yu ever mention aboot me bein' a Mason?'

" 'No me,' Ah says. 'It's nae business o' mine what yu do in yure spare time. 'Well,' he says, 'yu can go on keepin' quiet aboot it cos Ah've given it up.'

" 'But', I said, 'Ah've heard, once a Mason, always a Mason.' 'Don't yu believe it', he says. 'Not me onyway.'

"Ah stared at him good an' hard. 'By Christ,' says I, 'yu'll stop at nothin,' willya?' He wis a bit on the defensive then but as determined as ever. 'It's no ma fault,' he says. 'It's the system. Ah thocht it woulda a' changed when the Labour Party took over.'

"He was that miserable I almost felt sorry fer him, but na, he'd sunk too bliddy low, him. He shines his lamp roon aboot, but we were alone an' he moves a bit closer.

" 'Ah wis up tae see the Priest last night,' he says.

" 'So you're noo a Cath'lic,' Ah says, an' Ah dunno hoo Ah kept the disgust oota ma voice.

" 'No,' he tells me. 'It's no just sae easy as that. Seems that fer some weeks Ah've tae go once a week fer instruction. Ye ken,' he goes on, 'them Catholic Priests are awfy innocent. Yon one Ah seen woulda believed onything.'

" 'That's the idea,' Ah tells him. 'Men o' God are supposed tae be innocent, same as Christ wis.' But Ah could see that what Ah wis sayin' wis wasted on him.

"He goes on. 'The Priest said Ah must make a point o' going tae Mass, an' Grace would come tae me—whatever he meant by that.

Ah wouldn't unnerstan' it at fust. It's a' in Latin ye ken. But that it wouldn't do me ony harm tae go.'

"He grins again. 'Ah'm bliddy sure it'll no do me ony harm,' he says. 'In fact it's gonna do me an awfu' lot a' good, an' Ah don't mean goin' tae heaven.'

"Ah says, 'Yu'll need tae fund oot which service the Manager goes tae an' mak' a point o' bein' where he'll see yu.' 'Don't worry,' he says. 'Ah'm goin' tae a' the services. Ah'll be cussed near living in that Church frae noo on.' 'Yure some boy,' Ah says, an' picks up ma bag o' picks.

" 'Wait,' an' he grabs me arm. 'Look,' he says, 'if yure talking tae the ither men yu can let it be known that Ah'm a staunch Cath'lic. Ye ken what Ah mean, spread the glad tidings aboot the pit. It'll mebbe come tae the Manager's ears.'

"But Ah didn't need tae spread no glad tidings. He did that hissel'. Whatever else he wis, he wis thorough that schemer—he'd a' made bricks oota Margarine, him.

"Within a week the hale pit wis ringin' wi' the news o' his conversion. The Cath'lics in the Section wis in clover. He favoured them every way he could. The non-religious ones like me just got ignored. He musta thocht we wis beyond hope. But the Orangemen!—by Christ did he chase Rab McStottie an' the rest. Ah tell yu, they couldnae get time tae breathe.

"Well, things went on like this until the Twelfth o' July. That night, after Ah'd read the evening paper, Ah folded it up an' took it doon the pit wi' me. When we went oot tae the top road at snacktime, Willie follows an' sits doon tae watch us. That wis one o' his tricks; tae mak' sure that we didnae hae mair than the regulation twenty minutes. Ohh, he wis a tight bastard, Ah'll tell yu.

"While Ah'm eatin', Ah pretends tae read the evening paper. When Ah got tae the picture page in the middle Ah lets oot a gasp.

" 'Somethin' interesting, Nicky?' asks Willie. An' the big-headed sod holds oot a haun' fer ma paper as if he had a richt tae it.

" 'Aye,' Ah says, an' gie's him the paper. After a second or twa Ah hears his breath go in wi' a whistle, an' when Ah looks up . . . Christ! Ah thocht his eyeballs wis comin' oot on stalks. It wis pitifu' tae watch. When Ah couldna stan' it nae langer Ah flung ma bread tae the rats, an' crawled awa' back tae the face.''

"Well," I demanded impatiently. "What was in the paper?"

" A big picture o' that day's Orange Walk," said Nicky unemotionally. "An' at the head o' the procession wis oor Pit Manager"!

When I could control my laughter I turned again to Nicky. We were on our feet now and moving steadily down the pit bottom. "But, Nicky," I said. "How could you make such a mistake? Surely, if the Manager was such an important official of the Orange Lodge, Rab McStottie would have known and told you that morning."

Nicky grinned with great simplicity. "He did know" he chuckled. "And Rab did tell me that morning. In fact he wis that far up in the air at ma suggestion that it was the Manager's car ootside a Cath'lic Church, that Ah thocht he'd never come doon again. Na, na, Ah made nae mistake. It wis Willie that made the mistake—he didnae check what Ah telt him."

I stood staring into Nicky's wise, eternally-lauging, little eyes. "Come on," snapped the onsetter, his finger trembling on the signal bell. "Are yu dreamy bastards wantin' up the pit, or no?"

We hurried into the cage, the greasy bars dropping with a clang behind us. A bell rang and we were whirling swiftly, happily upwards through the clammy air, into the golden light of a summer's morning, the darkness and the tomb forgotten.

"What a wonderful people they are; these stern-faced, hard-bodied men with hearts of giants and a pawky humour which, though almost child-like in its simplicity, is their one sure shield against the underworld."

CHAPTER EIGHTEEN

THE BOMBER'S SAIR THUMB

COMING out on the nightshift that night we had found a huge heap of coal lying in front of the coalcutter, and we were instructed by our section deputy, the Bomber, to "fill it awa." We were shovelling away merrily when the conveyors stopped with an awful jerk and the Bomber hurriedly switched off the power. The chain was caught in the first tray and the Bomber crawled into the conveyors to attempt to free the jammed link.

"Go to the button, Nicky," he shouted to my 'neighbour' the leading cutterman. "An' gie 'em a wee touch in reverse, but be ready, an' when Ah shout, run 'em the richt way."

Whether Nicky misconstrued the orders, or whether the mishap was due to the fact that he was not familiar with the working of the conveyors, I don't know. But he did as he had been instructed, and as a result of two convulsive jolts in opposite directions the Bomber lost his balance and fell over backwards and, kicking and screaming helplessly, was carried away down the "face" by the endless, rapidly moving chain.

I crawled hastily round to the control button to find Nicky lying on top of it, helpless with laughter, and the Bomber must have travelled at least a hundred yards before Nicky was in a condition to get the conveyors stopped. He sat in a heap of small coal and wiped his eyes. "By jings," he grinned. "Ah bet that's the fust time Bomber Broon's gone doon this 'run' feet fust an' horizontal."

"I hope he's not dead," I said. "I wonder if he went over the shute at the loading point?"

"If he's deid," Nicky said, "he's a cussed lively corpse. Listen tae him."

From far away in the darkness we could faintly hear the Bomber's outraged howls of vituperation, mingled with dreadful threats of what he would do to "that glaikit, turnip-headed eedjit on the button."

"By the holy," snarled the Bomber when he was once more within range. "If they piled a' your brains in a heap there'd be a big hole."

"Aye," Nicky said, "an' you'd trip over it!"

"You micht hae killed me," growled the Bomber, rubbing his bruises. "Ah never did like they scrapers, death traps, that's what they are."

Nicky's eyes, luminous and livid in the shifting shadows, were like the eyes of a demon of the underground. Alight with wicked glints and aglow with a pawky sheen.

"You liked 'em well enough in Newcastle," he bristled. "Tell me," he asked politely, "wis that you singin' doon there?"

The Bomber glared at his small tormentor, opened his mouth for a devastating reply, and then, as though realising the hopelessness of waging a battle of words with Nicky McFish, he stalked huffily down the Heading. There was a tremendous crash and a string of muffled curses. "Ah knew it," snickered Nicky. "Ah warned ye aboot that big hole sticking up there where you buried ma brains," he shouted into the darkness of the Heading, but this time the Bomber was not to be drawn.

"He got a fright," I said, when I could stop laughing. "He was white."

"Aye," Nicky smiled impishly. "But it wis wi' me mentionin' singin'. It wisnae the trip over the scrapers that scared him—it wis him mindin' the trip tae Newcastle."

"What trip was that?" I asked. "A football game?"

"Na," said Nicky. "It wis when they fust installed them scraper-conveyors in this pit. They wis gettin' advertised a' over the place at that time, an' wis a' the rage. There wis a demonstrator come wi' 'em to show us hoo they warked an' that. Well, the fella has just finished explainin' that they wis foolproof, an' even a child couldnae get hurt wi' 'em, an' he signals tae stairt 'em up.

"The next thing we sees is the Bomber goin' doon the run screit-chin' his heid aff wi' his thumb caught in the chain. Holy smoke, whit a carryon! Well, Ah dunno if it wis part o' the advertisin' o' the scrapers, or if it wis tae cover up whit had happened tae the Bomber's thumb, but a' the fellas in the section, aboot twenty o' us, gets invited tae Newcastle for the weekend. By jings, it wis a braw thumb the Bomber had. It swelled up as big as a swede neap.

"It wis a smashin' weekend tae, a' expenses paid an' a special bus laid on for us. On the Saturday we got showed roon the factory an' got oor tea, an' then they tak's us back tae a posh hotel where we wis tae stay. We put oor bags in oor rooms an' then we could dae as we liked till the bus left at Sunday midday.

"Well, we has a braw Saturday nicht oot in Newcastle. The Bomber even forgot his sair thumb. Once he got a coupla nips he wis as happy as a whippet wi' a rabbit. It wis after midnight when we got back tae the hotel. You'da laffed. It wis a posh place ye ken, an' we wis a' rollin'. Heelplates McSobb fund oot hoo tae wark the lift an' we rid up an' doon in it for an hoor haein' a singsong. The Bomber's a braw voice, ye ken."

"I've never heard him," I said.

"Na," Nicky grinned mysteriously, "he's given up the singing. At the end o' oor corridor there wis a notice board wi' the room numbers an' the times the folk wanted up. One fella had got written, 'Five a.m. Urgent.' 'That's too early for that pair sowl to get up on the Sabbath,' says Heelplates. An' he changes it tae two p.m. Then he changes a' the others. Laff!

"Ye ken whit it's like in they posh hotels. They a' puts their shoes ootside their doors for cleanin'. 'Lotta lazy devils,' says Heelplates, an' he changes 'em a' roon. Laff. Ah tell you, they wis a' aff their heids in that hotel the next mornin', whit a carry on.

"Well, we wis a' ready for oor beds when Heelplates suggests a game o' pitch an' toss, so we a' goes oot intae the passage in oor shirt-tails. But we didnae hae nothin' tae play wi', so Ah nips intae Bomber Broon's room and gets his bonnet. He wis lyin' sleepin', wi' his sair thumb stickin' oota the bedclaes like a size five fitba'.

"We plays for hap'nies at fust but it wisnae lang afore that got too tame, so we plays for halfcroons. Ah . . . but the Bomber hadnae been asleep at a'. He musta been lyin' listenin', an' when the bunnet wis fu' o' half croons oot dashes the Bomber—scatters us—grabs the bunnet—an' awa back an' locks his door. Whit a carryon! We nearly bust the door doon tryin' tae get in. He's a fly yin, the Bomber. 'Awa an' get your ain bunnets,' he shouts. "

I said thoughtfully, "He's never struck me as fly. I've always thought him a wee bit simple."

"Don't you believe it," grinned Nicky. "He's fly enough, is Bomber Broon. Ah thocht Ah wis fly, but he taught me a trick or twa.

"The very next day," he continued, "on the Sunday we left Newcastle aboot one o'clock o' the day, an' after a while the bus stops at a hotel so we could get a refreshment. Efter the Saturday nicht oor tongues wis hangin' oot, Ah can tell you. The Bomber goes up for the fust roon for us twa, an' when he come back tae the table he wisnae very pleased. They'd charged him nine bob for twa pints an' twa nips. When Ah goes up for ma turn Ah queries the price, but the Boss says if we didnae like it we kent whit we could dae. So that wis that, we wis too thirsty tae argue.

"Where we wis sittin' there wis twa o' them brass ashtrays on the table. They wis braw things, a' carved. Afore we left the Bomber puts one in his pocket an' gies me the ither tae even things up. Well, Ah doot someone else has the same idea, cos when we're sittin' in the bus waitin' tae move aff oot come the Manager wi' a coupla Polis . . . an' the word goes roon that they's a fountain pen missin' from the Reception Desk, an' they're goin' tae search us a'. Holy smoke! Me an' the Bomber nearly took aff. But as the Polis wis gettin' intae the bus someone discovers the pen, an' aff we goes.

" 'By jings,' says the Bomber. 'That wis a narrer shave. I wis nearly climbin' up the wa' when Ah see them Polis.'

" 'Aye,' Ah says. 'So wis Ah, but Ah wis fly enough tae drop ma ashtray intae Big McSair's pocket in the hullabaloo.'

" 'You werenae fly enough,' says the Bomber. 'You've lost your ashtray. But Ah've still got mine,' an' he reaches intae ma coat pocket an' lifts it oot. By jings, Ah wis white for an hoor just thinkin' aboot it. Ah michta been pinched.

"But anyway, that wis us on the road hame so we gets a singsong goin' an' a lotta us had got bottles o' beer. Ye ken, there's a lotta bus conductresses . . . well, you can get awa wi' anything, but by jings, no wi' the one we had. She wis a bonnie wee lassie mind, wi' an awfy serious face wi' red cheeks an' muckle-big, blue een. Her face wis near a' een. You'd a thocht that when she wis born she'd grabbed a coupla chunks o' sky as she come through. But strict, by

228

the holy! she wis strict. An' once we crosses the border intae Scotland she stops a' the carryonski.

" 'This is the Sabbath Day,' she says. 'An' noo we're oota that Heathen Land there'll be nae nonsense in ma bus, or Ah'll put you aff.'

"Well, o' cos, it's mebbe richt enough talkin' like thon tae ordinary folks, but no tae colliers oot for the day. We wisnae drunk ye ken, but we'd had a drink, an' fust yin an' then anither would bust oot singin'. Each time it happened the lassie 'd go tearin' doon the bus wi' fleein' skirts an' red cheeks gettin' redder. An' a' the time wee chips like blue ice is beginnin' tae flee aff her een. She wis a richt Christian, Ah'll tell you.

"Well, ye ken yersel' whit colliers are; them that was nae tryin' tae sing wis argueing aboot fitba', or goin' tae murder each ither ower the speed o' some whippet that couldnae run across the road, an' o' cos the lassie wis beginnin' tae loss the heid.

" 'We're no Christians,' someone says tae her. 'We're colliers.'

" 'Ah'm no carin' whit you are,' she says. 'We're in a respekable country noo, an' this is a respekable bus, an' Ah'm no haein' a' this carryonski.'

"Then by jings, when things is at their wust, does the Bomber no get cramp in his legs and Ah tells him tae stick 'em oot straight, an' o' cos the lassie fa's ower his big feet. Ah tell you, it wisnae canny ava' the way she lookit at the pair Bomber after we'd picked her up an' dusted her aff. The blue icicles wis stottin' aff his ugly mug like bullets aff a dyke. Laff, Ah tell you, by the time we got hame thon lassie wis aboot aff her heid. Well the bus shoulda drapped us at the pit gate, but she says something tae the driver, an' he tak's it along tae the top of the Brae where twa big Polis is stannin'.

"Well, the lassie nips oot fust, an' by jings it wisnae canny whit she cried us tae them Polis. She didn't half go her length, Ah'll betcha.

" 'Ah've had an awfy time wi' 'em,' she says. 'They're a' drunk!' Well, o' cos, the Polis could see that the maist o' us wisnae drunk. An' it wis obvious that they kent the lassie had gone ower the score a bit. Folks is aye runnin' doon the Polis, but they'll no pinch you if you havenae done nothin'. Well, me an' the Bomber wis the last twa oota the bus an' Ah wisnae feelin' like singin', Ah can tell you.

Ah wis still medeetatin' on the narra shave Ah'd had wi' the ash tray, an' the Bomber wis quiet enough.

"Ah! but whit a shame," said Nicky, with an innocent smirk. "Here did Ah no accidentally slam the bus door on the Bomber's sair thumb."

"What did he do?" I asked.

"Gie such a display on the pavement that they pinched him there an' then. Ah mak' nae wunner. It wis somethin' awfy, the language he wis usin'. The lassie's ears near drappit aff. He'd calmed doon, o' cos, by Monday when he comes up afore the Beak but he got fined twa pund for singin' and dancin' on the Public Highway, an' creatin' a disturbance on the Sabbath Day."

"Is that right?"

"Aye," Nicky said with a grin. "He's never sung a note since."

230

"*Certainly I have seen deeds of Christian charity far below the tumbling waters of the Forth that could never have had the same impact in the sunlit pleasant world that lies above, the towns and cities near its shores. It may be that only, as in the pit, when man has been shorn of his vanities and the trappings of conventional life; only then can the true nobility of the spirit shine through as our Creator meant.*"

CHAPTER NINETEEN

AT THE END OF THE DAY

H E sat contentedly on the public seat near the flower beds, across the road from the pub. Around him, framing the lofty pithead gear with its eternally-spinning wheels, clustered the grey-stoned, red-tiled, miners' "rows."

Beyond the pub the brae swept steeply down to where, far below him, the sunlight waters lapped lazily about the rusty hulls of two, anchored, tide-awaiting ships. He sighed and leaning back in the seat, rubbed his scarred, hard hands gently up and down the tops of his thighs. He was happy again now, really completely happy, for the first time in thirty years.

He closed his eyes and gratefully let the summer sun feel warmingly over his tortoise-like, old eyelids. He could remember when, where he sat, had been all fields. It was in 1904, he remembered, when they had completed the sinking of the new shaft and the building of the first "rows" of red-tiled, two-roomed houses, set one above another in back-to-back blocks of eight.

His father had been one of the first colliers to be brought by the Laird to the new pit. He chuckled heavily in his chest as he recollected the day they had moved into the new, and to them, palace-like house. He had been fourteen and the youngest of three sons. They had come up the pit in the afternoon to find the hired cart waiting for them. When the furniture was loaded they had set off up the brae for the "new hoose." They had thought that they were turning their backs for ever on the low-roofed, dripping, lightless hovel down on the foreshore. But on arrival they had discovered in the big living-room-cum-kitchen of the new place only a black gaping hole in the plastered wall. The Laird did not provide stoves for colliers.

232

He remembered his mother's tears . . . a collier's "hoose" without a fire . . . it was unthinkable.

So, tired as they were, three sons went back down the brae and along the foreshore in the wind-whipped darkness for their old stove. The cart had been returned to its owner and when they had torn the heavy, iron contraption from its place they had had to man-handle it over the grey, foot-stealing beach and up the moon-slashed brae, while over their heads the storm clouds scudded madly and the wind lashed at them in a salty frenzy.

The stove installed, the whole family sat down to a supper of kale broth. After this, tired by the day's exertions, they fell heavily asleep. During the night the men's pit clothes, strewn round the huge fire to dry, had caught alight and the next morning they had had to go down the pit in their best suits, ruining them for ever. What a hoosewarming that had been!

The old man opened his eyes at the rumble of an approaching bus. He incuriously watched the blue monster bumble past and nodded gently.

They said today that the miner's rows were insanitary; that the back-to-back houses were anti-social and should be torn down; that for a whole family to live, eat and sleep in one narrow-windowed, bed-recessed room was not hygenic; that the warren of close-packed hovels afforded no privacy. But he had loved the "hoose" . . . loved the animal, hairy warmth of his brothers' bodies beneath the blankets; the movements of his father's heavy frame in the other bed and his mother's whispers; loved above all the huge fire and the leaping, dream-laden shadows that painted surrealist fragments on the grey walls.

Then his father and oldest brother had been killed together in the pit. Soon after, Muir, his second brother, had gone to America. So that when, at twenty, he had brought home his bride there had been only his mother to welcome the swarthy-skinned, dark-eyed collier lassie.

In the early twenties the Council began building houses a mile or two inland from the pit on the shoreline. In vain had his young wife begged him to apply for one. Only when the third child arrived did he give in.

It was 1928 when they had moved away from the "rows" and it was as though a chapter of his life had closed. He was leaving not just a "hoose" but a place of memories. It was the place to which the broken bodies of his father and brother had been brought. The place in which his old mother had gasped out the last of her brave life, in the grey dawn of a winter's morning. It was the place in which his children had been born.

He had never felt settled in his home in the new housing estate, with its tiled bathroom and huge windows. The narrow, fashionable grate never seemed to give a proper heat, and it was impossible to build a real collier's fire. There was a big garden which the Council under its byelaws insisted should be tended, a task for which few miners have left the necessary physical strength.

Like most of the older colliers he had always been at the pithead at four-thirty in the morning, an hour before the first cage descended. Now he had to wait for a bus which was often late. Home from the pit and fed, the collier's true relaxation was denied him; he would never have dared to squat on the pavement on hunkers, spitting into the almost antisceptically clean road. And who could he have "blathered" to? His cronies were still in the old rows.

Perhaps most of all he had missed not being able to stand and watch the black smoke belching and pouring from the pit "lum." The regular bouts coughed out by the sky-scratching chimney was a sign that all was well below. He hated being so far away. If a disaster occurred it would be an hour before he heard and got down to the pit . . . mebbe too late to help.

But it was not his nature to complain and the slow years passed away. His two daughters went to London to train and then abroad to work as nurses. After the news that his son's bomber had gone down in flames, he became quieter, more indrawn, but that was all.

In 1955 when he retired he felt completely cut off from the only life he had ever known. When his old wife died he had known what he must do. A young, married collier occupied his old house and was willing, nay eager, to exchange.

That had been six months ago, but there had been no hasty decision. He had gone about the thing in his quiet, methodical way. But eventually the formalities were completed and on the previous day he had moved back into his old home.

Last night, happily sleepless, he had lain in bed watching warm memories leap and clamber about the shadowy walls. That morning the first thing he had done was to go the door and assure himself that the bouts of black smoke regularly belched from the "lum."

Now he gently stretched out his legs and drew them slowly back. His old, wrinkled eyes, ignoring the flower beds at his feet, watched the big wheels madly spin, stop—and then spin as madly in the reverse direction. He looked carefully at his watch. It was twelve noon.

"Should be a thousand tubs off the bank by noo," he said softly to himself.

"Ah'll just walk across and see . . . then Ah'd better awa hame an' put some mair coal on that ole fire o' mine."

THE WORLD UNDERGROUND

The circle of a single shift,
Embraces all that life has ever meant.
Awakening.   The tender dawn of hazel eyes.
Sorrows, softly, sadly worn.   Farewell.
The earthy, sanguine dark descent,
Where ancient rocks, our bones despise.